WOMEN

of the

SILK

WOMEN

of the

SILK

GAIL TSUKIYAMA

ST. MARTIN'S PRESS

New York

Design by Susan Hood

Library of Congress Cataloging-in-Publication Data

Tsukiyama, Gail.
    Women of the silk / Gail Tsukiyama.
        p. cm.
    ISBN 0-312-06465-9
    I. Title
    PS3570.S84W6   1991
    813'.54—dc20   91-21006
                                                      CIP

3   5   7   9   10   8   6   4   2

TO MY MOTHER,

who taught me to embrace the past

Wind, light and time ever revolve;
Let us then enjoy life as best we can.

—Tu Fu, "The Winding River"

WOMEN

of the

SILK

Chapter One

1919

Pei

Her first memory of pain was an image of her mother. Pei was three or four the first time, and the same thing that had happened then was happening now. Her mother's moans almost woke her from this daydream, but she squeezed her eyes shut, and could see her mother's silk painting with the five white birds on it. Three of them were perched upon branches of white blossoms, the other two in flight. It was the only beautiful thing in their house, and Pei could see it even in her darkness. When she asked too many questions about it, or about anything else, Pei's parents became angry. Her father made a clicking sound with his tongue, and her mother would say her mind wandered too far from home. So Pei tried hard to keep very quiet like her sister, Li.

Her mother's moans grew louder. When Pei opened her eyes she could see, in the light of the flickering candle, her father sitting by the door. His long legs were spread out, one crossed over the other, as he stroked the thin hairs on his upper lip. She glanced at Li, who sat quietly in the corner mending some tattered clothing, as she always did in the evenings.

Pei's mother was in the next room, separated from them by a heavy, dark curtain she had had up for as long as Pei could remember. The midwife, Ching, was with her. The moaning and heavy breathing continued, as Ching whispered words of encouragement. The last time this had happened, her mother had become thin again, and they had a new baby sister.

That little sister cried and cried. No matter what Pei's mother did, the baby would not take her milk. For days her mother cradled the baby in her arms, walking from one end of the room to the other, until she formed a narrow path in their dirt floor. Her father bought herbs for a broth from an old woman in the village. It smelled of burning leaves as it boiled, but the baby refused to take it down. Soon Little Sister lost all strength to cry and simply lay stonelike in her mother's arms. Not long after that, Pei's father took Baby Sister out of the house, and when he returned looking sad, like a defeated animal, it was without her.

"Where is Baby Sister?" Pei asked.

"She has died of sickness like the other one," her father answered. "It would have been different if they had been sons."

Pei's mother stood swaying slightly back and forth. Her clothes were unkempt and her hair strangely out of place. There was something cruel about the fine lines that moved from her lips as she pressed them tightly together. Never once did her mother cry, but Pei knew something was wrong, that she was in great pain, even when her mother nodded her head in agreement with her father.

Her mother's moans grew more desperate. Pei knew that that meant another baby would soon come. It was only a few steps from the table to the curtain, and Pei moved quietly so she wouldn't disturb her father. When the last baby sister came, they were not allowed to enter her mother's room for a month. This was so they would not anger the gods. But she couldn't see the gods being angry at her for taking a small peek.

Pei lifted the curtain. Candles shone from each side of her mother's bed. The tiny space seemed suffocating with the smell of sweat and burning wax. There were candles close by Ching, who bent over, telling her mother to push. "Push now, Yu-sung, push, yes, yes and now breathe." Her mother was on the bed, a large wooden board covered with a thin mat, half-lying, half-sitting against the wall, her knees pushed up, her legs spread open. Underneath her legs was a large piece of brown paper, which Ching constantly straightened as her mother pushed against it. Her mother moaned louder and let out a small cry when she pushed down as Ching instructed her. When she let her head drop back down, she breathed in rapid pants as Pei had heard dogs do when they were thirsty for water. She wondered if her mother might want some water, but even as Pei tried to speak, no voice would come from her opened mouth. Pei was frightened by her pain. Her mother looked so tired and sick, her fingers tearing at the cotton netting which hung down to keep the mosquitoes away. Then once more her mother raised herself, and pushed with a renewed strength. She let out a small cry and pushed again.

"Yes, Yu-sung," said Ching. "There is the head, the baby comes, the baby comes!"

And there between her mother's legs Pei could see the baby's head emerge. It was a dark, wet, ugly thing, sliding out so slowly with each push. She wanted to step forward and see more, but her legs felt weak. When Pei turned around to share this with Li, she saw that Li had her eyes closed tight, even as her hands continued mending the cotton trousers.

"The baby comes face up," Ching said, in a worried whisper.

In the next moment the baby's entire head appeared, with tiny dark lines for its eyes and mouth, and a flat, small nose. Ching cupped the back of its head, and with another push, the rest of the baby's body quickly followed, along with a lot of blood and water.

"It is a girl, Yu-sung," Ching said softly, examining the baby.

The new baby sister let out a loud, clear cry. Ching clipped the cord attached to the baby with a small, sharp knife, and tied it. "She appears well." Ching wiped the baby and placed her in Pei's mother's arms. Her mother looked exhausted, and so sad, but she accepted her fifth daughter with a tired smile.

Then before she could move, Pei felt the strong grip of her father's hand, taking her arm and pushing her to the side. At first she was terrified that he would punish her for looking, but then Pei saw that he really didn't even notice her. With him, he brought the heavy scent of smoke and sweat into the thick heat of the small room.

"Is it a son?" he demanded.

No one answered. Pei turned to Li, who was looking down at the dirt floor. Ching busied herself with cleaning up the remains of the birth, wrapping it all in the brown paper to be buried in the earth as Pei had seen her do before.

"Why?" she had asked Ching the last time.

"Because it is dirty," Ching answered, placing the bundle gently into the hole she had dug.

"Why is it dirty?"

"Because it is," Ching said. "And we must spare the gods the sight of it. Someday you will understand."

When her father looked down at the baby and saw that it was healthy, he removed the blanket she was wrapped in. But when he saw that the baby hadn't the requirements of a son, he made that clicking sound he always made when he was displeased, and left the room. Pei quickly moved to one side so he wouldn't see her.

Her mother rewrapped the baby and kissed her lightly on the cheek.

"The next one will be a son, Yu-sung, you just wait and see," said Ching.

"There will not be a next time," her mother answered.

Yu - sung

For a month after giving birth, Yu-sung stayed with the baby in the confines of their house. During this unclean period she did not bathe or wash her hair. This was done to spare the highest god, T'ien Kung, the sight of them. From the village herbalist, Ching bought herbs for soup, and Yu-sung ingested an array of strengthening tonics.

As always, her third daughter, Pei, asked too many questions. All during the month Pei wondered why Yu-sung could not go outside anymore, and what would happen if she did. It was always Pei, with all her curious ways, whom Yu-sung worried about most.

"But why would the gods not want to see a baby?" Pei asked.

"Because we are unclean," she answered.

"And you will be clean after a month?"

"Yes."

"Was I unclean as a baby?"

"Yes.

"But why is everything dirty?" Pei insisted.

"Because everything to do with the birth is unclean, even for the month afterwards. Now go!" she said, pointing toward the door so Pei would go outside. "And you must help Ba Ba during this time and not ask so many questions!" Yu-sung reminded Pei again and again, as Pei lingered at the table, her finger tracing small circles on its surface.

The month Yu-sung spent in the house felt very long. After the births of her other daughters, she was always occupied with their dispositions. Even the two who had since gone on to the other world had kept her busy. But this girl child they named Yu-ling spent so much of the time sleeping.

After the first week, Yu-sung scrubbed everything from top to bottom. Then she grew restless and disturbed that she could not be outside helping her husband, Pao, pick the mulberry leaves, then pack them in the baskets for him to take to the market. She knew how difficult it was for him, even if he said nothing. On a sheet of paper she made crosses to count the days. There were only two days remaining, and then she would be released from the confinement.

Other things never changed. Every morning Yu-sung rose while the rest of the house slept. The first thing she did was start the fire to make jook, the rice porridge that would carry them through the day until their evening meal. Then she boiled the water for their tea. With the soft murmur of the water boiling, and the steam filling the cold spaces, it was the time Yu-sung heard her thoughts most clearly.

Sometimes she was reminded of having once been very pretty. It struck her at the oddest times—when she was stirring the jook or stripping the leaves from the mulberry trees. It was always when she was working. Yu-sung was still startled by the thought of once being pretty. It seemed so long ago. Unlike her husband, she was fair-skinned, with delicate features that had hardened over the years from working, both inside and out. She had a small frame, which made childbearing very difficult. The last child had been no easier than the first, though Yu-sung prayed to the gods that it would be.

In the far corner of the room slept her daughters, Li and Pei, huddled together on a makeshift bed her husband had put together for them. It was a strange thing, the way they had always taken care of each other, even with all their differences. She and Pao were partly the cause, since they were as silent with the girls as with one another. Pao hardly took notice of his daughters, and she had given them little affection in the last few years. To show them anything more would just make things more difficult when the time came for them to leave. With Li, there were fewer problems. She was quiet and kept to herself. But with Pei, who touched and hugged, and who always sought answers to the questions she asked, it was less simple. Yu-sung had to quiet her spirit with scoldings, so that life would be easier for her later. It was hard enough to find a husband of worth, because a girl with such spirit was not wanted by most families. How often Yu-sung had wished one of them were a boy, something Pao could be proud of, something of value.

Yu-sung looked up when the curtain stirred. Pao stepped out from behind it. He had had a restless night, lying awake, while she pretended to be asleep. Neither of them said a word as her tall, weatherbeaten husband came toward her and sat down at the table. In all the years they had been married, they'd spoken only when it was necessary. Pao never had any need for more.

Pao Chung and Yu-sung had been promised to one another by their families. They were still children, brought together by a fortune-teller because of the date and year of their births. Yu-sung came to Pao and his family when she was barely sixteen. She left the warmth of her family near Nan-hai, not far from Pao's family in Kwangtung province, expecting to find the same kind of warmth and happiness. She did not know then that her new home might as well have been a million miles away. No longer was she to have those evening meals filled with laughter and voices. From the moment Yu-sung married into Pao's family, she was no longer a member of her own.

Pao was the tallest man she had ever seen, standing at least a head taller than her own father. He was much taller than most of the fishermen in their village. He had told Yu-sung it was because they were descendents of the Hakkas, the guest people, who migrated from the north. Pao's grandfather had migrated south, with the last migration of the Hakkas at the end of the Taiping rising. Pao had heard many stories growing up, and told some of them to Yu-sung in those early days of their marriage. His grandfather had been a born fighter; he lost two fingers on his left hand, chopped off by a disgruntled villager who did not like Hakkas. With blood pouring from the open wounds, his grandfather beat the man to a bloody mess. He then picked up his two fingers and walked calmly away. One of the private things Pao revealed to her was that his grandfather kept the two shriveled fingers in a pouch around his neck, forever proud of his Hakka strength. The Hakkas were different from those of the south. They were taller, with bigger bones and wider, flatter features. And they did not speak the same language as in the south. Her husband was very Hakka, though his mother was a Cantonese. Her daughters, Lin and Pei, were taller than most of the other children they knew. At eight years old, Pei was already as tall as Li, who was two years older.

His family had been so different from hers. They were without even the most natural comforts of life. Her family was no wealthier than Pao's family, but she had been accustomed to certain luxuries. Yu-sung still remembered how smooth the silk comforter felt against her skin when she was a child, and the wonderful vivid colors of red and green on the paintings that graced the walls of her parents' modest house. Unlike other girls, Yu-sung was also taught to read and write the simplest characters by her mother, as her mother's mother did. But nothing could have prepared her for the sight of Pao's own house. At first she thought it such a luxury to be living apart from his family. It was a rarity—and a blessing, since she could not understand his father's Hakka dialect. His mother had died shortly before she came, so Yu-sung did not have a mother-in-law to guide her.

At first Yu-sung thought the reason for Pao's unkempt appearance was that there was no female to wash and clean. But what she was to encounter was the most unbearable filth she could have ever imagined. Pao lived like an animal, the stench almost unbearable when she walked through the door. Night soil was left in clay pots by the bed, and spider webs grew thick with dirt in every possible crevice. Yu-sung could hardly keep down her vomit when she saw the rotting food, thick with growth, scattered on a table. On his bed was a dirty, coarse blanket, which was all he slept with. Pao showed all this to her without the least bit of shame, only the same measured-out words he was always to use. Pao had grown to manhood surviving on the barest necessities, while everything was given to the mulberry groves and fish ponds, and what they produced. It did not take Yu-sung long to realize that stripping the mulberry trees of their flat green leaves and packing them into straw baskets would be her life's work. These groves, along with the fish Pao cultivated in the ponds, would always be of greatest importance.

Little changed after their marriage, except that gradually, the filth and stench disappeared. Even then, Pao never said a word, nor did he seem to notice the difference. For the first few months life was unbearable. Yu-sung cleaned endlessly during the day and submitted to her husband's desires after dark. And how it had hurt. The pain of his entering her terrified her so much, she could not even cry out. But Yu-sung could never refuse her husband; it would have angered the gods and brought shame to her family. There was nothing more she could do but to tire herself out completely during the day and hope that Pao had done the same. She did this with such efficiency that even the bedbugs sucking on her legs, and the bugs' foul odor, ceased to bother her. Only when Yu-sung was with child, and during the month after, did Pao leave her alone. Now there would be no more children; her body had delivered its last child. Yu-sung was certain. She could feel the emptiness.

Over the years, she had grown as silent as her husband. She had learned to keep all her thoughts to herself. Yu-sung had let go of the spontaneity of her girlhood. The years of gathering the mulberry leaves and inhaling the stale, dank earth of the fish ponds had squeezed her life dry. All that was left of Yu-sung's other life was stored away in her wooden chest at the foot of their bed. Sometimes, when she was alone, she opened the chest, releasing the strong smell of camphor. Below the layers of white paper Yu-sung had carefully folded the red silk dress her mother had made for her, and the lace handkerchief given to her by her grandmother. It was then that she felt most alone. Yu-sung could see her lost joy in Pei, even if Pei most resembled her father. It was Yu-sung's past life Pei carried in her. And in Pei, she could see her greatest pleasures and her worst fears.

Pao sat across from Yu-sung, sipping hot tea. He looked across the room at their two daughters sleeping in the corner, and then turned back to her. She knew there was something bothering him, but she kept silent.

"This baby sleeps easy," Pao said quietly.

"Yes, she is very easy," Yu-sung answered, remembering the disturbances the other babies caused. "But you have not slept well?"

"No. It has been a bad harvest; we will have problems when Hung comes to collect."

Her husband's face was stern as he said this, his dark eyes looking past her. She got up quickly and dished some jook into a clay bowl.

"In a day or two I will be able to help again," Yu-sung finally said.

"There is nothing to help with, it's done."

"I could mend or clean for others."

"Who would have you? You have just given birth and cannot be away from the child. Besides, it is just as bad for the others."

She remained silent.

"When the month is over, we will go to the village to see the fortune-teller," said Pao, looking down at the table.

They had spoken of this only once before. Never would she have dreamed that the gods could be so cruel, that the fate of their daughters would end up in the hands of a blind old man. Yu-sung nodded her head in agreement.

The Fortune-teller

Pei loved going to the village. Her mother was clean again, and finally able to leave the house. Her usually silent father said they would go to the village in celebration. Even Li, who was always quiet, moved through the house excitedly the morning they were to go. Neither of them could sit still without moving while their mother braided their hair.

"Keep still or you are not going anywhere!" their mother said, threatening them into silence.

Pei's father borrowed an ox and cart for her mother and the baby to ride in. She and Li would take turns sitting next to her. The baby, Yu-ling, was strapped tightly to her mother's chest with an old gray blanket. They brought rice and vegetables to eat along the way, and their father had promised each of them a sugar candy if they were good.

Pei longed to see the village, though it was no more than a cluster of makeshift buildings, situated along a much-traveled road. At the far end of the village was a larger, more ornately decorated ancestral hall. Pei had been inside just once. Her mother had told her people went there to honor their dead by lighting long thin sticks of incense, which smelled like something sweet burning.

When the village finally came into view, Pei jumped down from the moving cart and ran ahead. At the edge of the village she stopped to wait for her family. There was an old woman sitting in front of a small shack, spinning thread from one end to the other of a strange wooden contraption.

"Ba Ba, what is that woman doing?" Pei asked when her father came.

"She is spinning silk," her father answered. "Now come along before we leave you!"

Pei caught the hard edge of her father's words, but it never frightened her as it did Li, even when he became so angry he took a stick to her. After the beatings, her father would go out to the groves, and her mother would always calm her tears by reminding her to keep her words to herself. "It is a lesson," her mother would say, though Pei never really understood what the lesson was. Eventually she did learn when to stop questioning her father.

Pei skipped alongside the cart as they moved deeper into the village. They were soon surrounded by throngs of people moving toward the marketplace. Stray dogs and cats were left to fend for themselves among the bamboo cages, stacked high and filled with chickens. The dogs yelped and snapped at the ruffled chickens, whose feathers floated in slow motion through the hot air.

The marketplace provided a source of pure delight for Pei. She loved the crowds and the noise. She watched the men and women behind their makeshift stalls, selling whatever they could.

Voices beckoned to them.

"Come this way, I will certainly give you the best deal!"

"The finest flutes in all of Kwangtung!" another voice rang out.

"Missy! Step up here! I will read your face for a pittance!"

They were all there, from the letter writers and herbalists to the marriage brokers and spiritualists. Pei marveled at their persistence, as Li clung to her arm. Farther on, the stalls contained fruits and vegetables and served hot dumplings in soup. Pei looked around, stumbling after her parents, hoping to find the sugar-coated candy she and Li wished for. Everywhere around them was the tantalizing aroma of food.

Her father slowed down and finally stopped. Behind two wooden crates sat a man her father called the fortune-teller. He was the oldest man Pei had ever seen, with a long white beard that hung in ragged strands down to his chest. In his long, crooked fingers he held a brush, with which he wrote in black ink on a piece of paper in front of him. He stopped and tilted his head toward her father, though he couldn't have seen a thing, for his eyes were sewn shut. Pei watched as the fortune-teller smiled kindly and lifted his brush in greeting. Her father spoke, as Li's hand closed tighter around hers.

"This is my eldest daughter," her father said, pushing Li forward.

"Come, child, do not be afraid," the fortune-teller said. "I only want to see what life will bring to you."

Li obeyed and sat down on the stool across from him. Her father moved closer and gave the fortune-teller the time, date, and year of Li's birth. The fortune-teller listened, and with a slight nod lifted his large, crooked fingers in front of Li's face, moving them in small circles, closer and closer until his fingers rested on her face. His fingers moved gently from her forehead down to her chin, and then away from her. He remained silent for a few moments, mumbling inaudible words to himself.

"This daughter will marry and bear two sons," the fortune-teller finally said. He looked up at them through his darkness. "There may be illness, but she will survive."

Then it was Pei's turn. Her father pushed her roughly forward. He gave the necessary dates, and the fortune-teller, who looked asleep with his head tilted downward, began the same ritual he had just done with Li. When his fingers touched her face, Pei felt a tingling sensation, which left when his fingers did. When the fortune-teller was finished, Pei looked up at her

father. He stood back, watching the fortune-teller with the same
intensity as he watched his groves and ponds.

"Can we go soon, Ba Ba?" Pei whispered.

"Quiet, girl," he snapped. Her mother and Li stood quietly
behind him.

"She is a curious one," the fortune-teller then said. He
straightened his back and tugged at the strands of his beard. "I
see many numbers in her life, perhaps miles."

Pei's father glanced down at her. "Will she marry?" he asked.

The fortune-teller turned his head from side to side, stroked
another strand of his beard, and slowly said, "This I cannot see
clearly."

"Is she of the nonmarrying fate?" her father pressed on.

"She will be loved," the fortune-teller continued, in a slow,
even voice. "By more than one, but there will be difficulties."

"I see," her father answered in a tone of agreement.

Pei thought of nothing but the sugar candy. She watched her
father take out two silver coins from a small leather pouch and
place them in the fortune-teller's hand.

When they returned from the village, Pao said very little and
went immediately to check on his ponds. Yu-sung and his
daughters hurried into the house to prepare their evening meal,
their voices drifting slowly away. Pao looked down to the immense floodland below. The burnt-orange earth, crisscrossed by
the numerous canals, looked like a web. His grandfather had
liked being near water; the delta provided the waterways and the
wet, sandy soil, which was suitable for fish breeding and the
cultivation of mulberry groves. The fish and leaves were packed
in baskets and boated along the canals to market. They were
then sold for the highest price to the silkworm owners. This
ritual had gone on for hundreds of years, though the floods of the
past few years had left very little to bring to market.

Pao loved the rich, fertile land. He worked for it as hard as his father and grandfather had. As a boy, Pao had been told over and over how his grandfather had taken one look at the land where he stood, then dropped to his knees to rebury his ancestors' bones. It was the land Pao had hoped to pass down to his own son, but with the birth of his fifth daughter, he could see that this day might never be.

The sky was darkening; a faint shimmer of light from the moon reflected off the empty ponds. Along with the bad harvest, the Warlords had begun placing taxes on everything from rice and candles to windows and chairs. Pao could only be grateful that there were no glass windows in his house.

Pao wrinkled his brow and sighed. A decision must be made. There was nothing he could do but wait for the harvest to improve again, even if it meant the sacrifice of one of his daughters. He could at least count himself lucky that daughters were of some use. The fortune-teller had as much as predicted that Pei was of a nonmarrying fate. Then what would she do? An unmarried woman had little in this world without a husband and his family to care for her.

Pao had heard, from other men along the canal, of steam-driven machinery used in the big villages for silk work. These silk factories accepted unattached girls to work in them for very good wages. There were many girls left to this unmarrying fate in the silk villages, earning money for themselves as well as for their families.

Pao turned and walked back toward the house, looking hard to see his land in the darkness. He had no other choice. It was not an easy decision to make, since Pei, with all her spirit and imagination, might be the closest thing he would ever have to a son. And it seemed his Hakka blood flowed most prominently in her. He gave one last look towards the shadows and made his decision. Pei would be sent to the silk village.

* * *

Yu-sung put the baby down to sleep. She moved quietly back into the other room, careful not to wake Pao, who slept soundly for the first time in many nights. The shadows cast by the single flame she carried flickered and danced when she placed it on the table. Her two daughters slept in the corner of the room, where the light barely touched.

In the dull and serious light, Yu-sung poured herself a cup of tea. She sat down, weary from their trip to the village. Now that she could be outside among the mulberry groves again, she was certain that things would be better. It was with this same certainty that she knew her husband had made his decision to send Pei away.

Yu-sung sipped her tea and closed her eyes. There would never be any mystery for her daughters to decipher. From the moment they came into this world, their fates had been sealed. If Yu-sung pitied them, then she would have to give herself that same pity. And it would not change anything. There was also the chance that Pei would be happier where she was going, make a better life for herself.

Still, Yu-sung could not help thinking that perhaps everything might be different if she had given her husband a son, a continuance of himself. More than once she had told her husband to take a concubine, another woman who might give him a son, as many other men had done. But always he remained silent.

Yu-sung stood up. Without taking the candle, she moved toward her daughters in the murky light. As usual, they slept huddled together under a single blanket. It was always Pei who had her arms wrapped around Li, with her knees brought up to her chest and her head resting on Li's shoulder. Li slept straight and with little movement. Their dark hair carried the small waves of the undone braids, spreading out in a tangled web. Yu-sung could hardly tell one head of hair from the other. Even if she did try to straighten Pei out, she would simply return to the same position by morning. Yu-sung pulled their blanket up, and moved their hair away from their faces. It was all she could bring herself to do.

The next morning Pei ran down the slope ahead of Li and then stopped to wait for her. Li had always been a slower runner. During the summer they always played down by the ponds when their father took the boat to market and was not around to scold them. He had left the house very early that morning, while Pei lay in bed pretending to be asleep. As usual, her parents spoke a few words in whisper, and then said nothing at all.

Sometimes, her father would do something to let them know he thought more of them than just being a female nuisance. Yesterday in the village, after they saw the old fortune-teller, her father bought her and Li not one, but two pieces of sugar candy. Pei placed one immediately into her mouth and began sucking the sweetness out of it. The second piece she let sit on her tongue, sucking little by little as they made their way home, hoping to make the candy last as long as possible.

It was only that morning that Pei found out Li had not eaten either piece of her candy. Li had saved them, tightly wrapped in a piece of paper in her pocket. Li slowed down even more when she saw Pei waiting for her.

"Please give me a small piece?" Pei asked.

Li walked right past her toward the pond, knowing how Pei could keep on and on until she got what she wanted.

"You have your own," Li answered.

"I have eaten them," she said, skipping after Li. "Just a little, please?"

Li shook her head no.

Pei stuck her tongue out at Li and ran down to the pond. The pond with its muddy contents had always been her favorite place. She slowed down and squatted closer to the water, trying to catch a glimpse of the fish who used to make it their home. When nothing stirred, Pei became impatient for some movement and threw in a rock, then picked up a stick to stir things around. Before the floods, she would have seen hundreds of dark shadows gliding back and forth in the water, sending white foamy bubbles to the dark surface, but now, the pond was always still.

Li squatted down beside Pei as she dropped another large rock into the pond. Her reflection rippled alongside Li's as they watched one circle grow out of another. They looked so alike in the dark water, with their pigtails and their matching blue cotton shirts. Both of them had dark, round eyes, though Li's rose up slightly at the corners. Pei had always loved Li's eyes.

But as much as they looked alike, they were different in every other way. Next to her, she could hear Li's even breathing and feel her calmness. Li's hands rested quietly on her knees, while Pei's felt the ground beside them for anything that would make the water splash. She didn't dare glance at Li now to see the serious look on her face.

Pei let another rock drop into the pond, her hand plunging in after it, wetting her entire sleeve. "I wonder what they think of us?" she asked.

"Who?"

"The fish."

Li looked down into the pond, but there was no movement. "I don't think they think at all, they just swim around waiting to be caught."

"We must look like big foreign devils staring down at them," Pei said, rolling over onto her back. "I bet they really do think about things."

"About what?" Li asked, though she knew Pei was just playing with her.

"About their families, and what they are going to eat."

"You're just being silly," Li then said, getting up and walking along the edge of the pond. "We better go before Ba Ba gets back."

"He won't be back so soon."

"Do what you want, then," Li said, in a tone that let Pei know she was still the oldest.

Pei heard her mother calling for them when she was almost back up the hill. Not far ahead of her, she could see Li scrambling to get up. She called for Li to wait for her, pulling at her clothes and using her sleeve to wipe the dirt away from her face.

Together they walked toward their unsmiling mother. She immediately snapped at Pei, "Look at you, your clothes are a mess. Why can't you stay clean like your sister? Now I'm going to have to wash your clothes as well as give you your lessons!"

Pei said nothing. They walked past their mother's angry stare into the house. Pei took off her summer clothes, which her mother scrubbed and hung out to dry. For the rest of the day, she did her chores, then sat down for their reading and writing lessons, wearing her thick, uncomfortable winter clothing.

Her mother taught them to read and write in the quiet moments of the evening, or when her father was busy down at the ponds. Once, her father came in while they were having their lessons. He watched them for a moment, saying nothing. Her mother didn't look up and continued teaching. Only when he quietly left the house again did her mother pause, and let out a small breath before continuing.

"Sit still," her mother said, as they sat across the wooden table from her, fidgeting.

Pei loved to watch as her mother took great care to write the difficult strokes on the precious pieces of paper she bought in the village. Her hand moved up and down in small waves. Sometimes, Pei wanted to reach out and touch her mother's traveling fingers, but she didn't dare.

Her mother taught them only what was necessary. She told them over and over again, "Too much knowledge will only lead to heartaches for a female. Especially for one as curious as you!" she said, turning towards Pei.

That evening, when her father returned, he whispered a few words to her mother before leaving them and closing the curtain to their room. For the first time Pei could see tiny lines from the corner of his eyes, and his shoulders seemed heavy with some invisible load.

"Is Ba Ba all right?" she asked, looking up at her mother.

"He is tired. He has traveled a long way today."

"Where did he go?" Pei persisted.

"Far away," her mother snapped, turning abruptly around and putting an end to her questions.

Pei was relieved when they were finally lying quietly in their bed. Her mother's anger would, she hoped, be put to rest with the beginning of another day. Pei lay still and listened to Li's quiet breathing. Sometimes, she wondered what it would be like to be more like Li, to move through each day with so little trouble. When Pei turned towards Li, she could only see the shadowy outlines of her sister's face, a face so similar to hers. And even as Pei began to drift off to sleep, she couldn't help but smile about the piece of sugar candy Li had finally given to her.

Chapter Two

1919

Pei

Pei felt herself being awakened by a tapping on her arm. She opened her eyes to the murky light a single candle gave off, barely able to make out the dark figure of her father standing over her. With the back of her hand Pei rubbed her eyes and looked again. Her unsmiling father was still there. When he bent closer to her, Pei could smell his salty scent, of work and the ponds.

"You must get up now," he whispered, trying not to awaken Li.

"Why?" Pei asked, before her father put his finger to her lips. She moved quickly and quietly into the chill of the morning air.

"You and I must go on a journey," her father then answered.

Behind him Pei could see her mother sitting as still as stone at the wooden table. Pei put on her summer clothes, whose last bit of dampness sent a shiver through her. She watched as her father said something to her mother and then went outside. When Pei was dressed and sat down at the wooden table, her mother quickly put a bowl of jook in front of her.

"Where are we going?" Pei asked.

There was a long pause before her mother answered. "You will see soon enough. Now you must eat."

Pei looked down at her bowl of jook and took a large swallow of the thick porridge. Her mother stood behind her, combing out her hair just as she did every morning. Then with quick and able fingers she divided the hair into two parts and braided two even pigtails.

"Are you going?" Pei asked.

"No."

"And not Li either?"

"No."

"Why not?"

"Because your Ba Ba has decided that you are to go."

Pei turned to look at her mother, whose hands rested gently on her shoulders. But before Pei could catch sight of the dark, sad eyes she knew so well, her mother turned away and was back standing by the fire.

The dirt road was a dull orange as Pei and her father began their journey on foot. Her father walked in silence, his quick pace easily leaving Pei behind. As the sun rose, its light spread across the open fields, revealing a beautiful puzzle of land and water, which seemed to come together in one silent breath of air. Pei lingered, picking up rocks and pulling out wildflowers for Li and her mother. Every once in a while, she waited to see if her father would turn back to make sure she was still following, but he never did.

At first the daylight opened her eyes to all that was around her. Pei watched the small birds in the trees, fluttering from branch to branch. It was almost as if they were watching her, too, their wings spread open before folding neatly back to their sides. In the far distance there was the lonesome sight of a farmer working in his field, following his dark, strong oxen. But soon the sun felt very hot on the open road. Pei's legs ached from trying to keep up with the long strides of her father. More than once Pei tried to capture his attention by clearing her throat, but her father walked on with no regard for her until she ran after him and was forced to tug at his sleeve. By noon Pei had traveled farther than she had ever gone before.

"Ba Ba, is it much farther?"

Her father cleared his throat. "A little farther and we will stop."

Pei watched as he shifted the cloth sack he carried from one shoulder to the other, then followed him obediently. Gradually the land changed to a flatter, more populated area, with ponds and whitewashed brick houses sitting closer to the road.

They finally stopped under a thick cluster of trees that shaded the road. From the cloth sack her father brought out two Jong, and handed her one of the fist-sized balls of sticky rice. Pei loved eating Jong. They were stuffed with salted pork, nuts, and an egg yolk, all completely wrapped in lotus leaves like a small gift. Usually, her mother made them only once a year, on the day of the Dragon Boat Festival. Then her mother would repeat the story of Ch'u Yuan, a high official who had drowned himself in the river Mih Lo when he could not fulfill his duties to the emperor. Each year after, on the very day of his drowning, the officials and village people would throw these Jong into the river so that he would not go hungry. Pei thought of the story and relished every mouthful. When her father finished eating, he stood up, glanced toward her, and began walking again.

The afternoon sun beat down so heavily on the dusty road that Pei felt as if her feet were swollen. Nothing could distract her from the heat and tiredness that filled her entire body. But as they followed the turn in the road, Pei saw that just beyond them was a river, and beyond that, the tallest buildings she had ever seen. When they came to the edge of the very large river, her father put the cloth sack down and said, "We will wait here."

Pei sat down and watched, fascinated with all the river life that moved around her. The river smelled different from the ponds. There was a lingering heaviness in the air that was both fishy and something else, something like night soil left in its jar too long. Pei wrinkled her nose, but was quickly distracted by the men and women traveling across the river in small, half-covered boats her father called sampans. She watched as they balanced themselves on the edges, maneuvering their boats away from the others with long, thin poles of bamboo. On the larger sampans anchored to the side of the river, Pei saw entire families moving within their cluttered bounds as if they were on dry land. Their voices sounded strangely familiar, yet unlike anything she had ever known. The boats moved rhythmically from side to side, pulling away from one another, then coming back and touching with a dull thud.

Across the river sat more of these floating houses, a dark outline of boats among the tall sturdy buildings behind them. Pei had never seen buildings like these before. Each one seemed ten times the size of the buildings in their small village back home.

"Where is that, Ba Ba?" Pei asked, pointing across the river.

"That is the village of Yung Kee. Would you like to go there?" her father asked.

"Oh, yes!" Pei answered. She saw her father smile for the first time in a very long while.

The buildings across the river were of all shapes and sizes. From some of the larger buildings, thick, gray smoke billowed out of long pipes protruding from the roofs.

"Why is there smoke coming out of those buildings?" asked Pei.

"Those are the factories that breathe life into China," her father answered. "You will see soon enough what they are about."

Pei looked on in quiet amazement.

The boat that arrived to take them across the river was a larger sampan. It hovered at the edge of the river, allowing the people to disembark before Pei and her father could board. The sampan creaked and swayed and was badly in need of paint, but

Pei thought it was the loveliest boat she had ever seen. Hanging on to the edge as it slowly glided across the water, Pei no longer felt the heat or the tiredness that accompanied it. Instead, she tried hard to remember every small detail of her journey to bring home to Li and her mother.

The streets of Yung Kee were hot and dusty. More people than Pei had ever seen before were gathered at storefronts, bargaining in high, experienced voices. "Too much, too much, I will give you half that!" an old woman said. "Do you think I was born yesterday?" another voice cried out. Pei watched shirtless young and old men pull carts and sedan chairs down the wide street, skillfully avoiding the throng of people moving toward them. She and her father walked past rows and rows of tall gray buildings, divided by narrow passageways that led in and out of other streets. She held on to her father's sleeve as they walked deeper into the maze of streets and people.

From one passageway they emerged onto a wide dirt road shaded by trees. Pei's father looked down at her and said, "It isn't far now."

"Where are we going, Ba Ba? Did you come here yesterday?" Pei asked. Her throat was dry and scratchy from the heat.

"It isn't far," her father repeated, suddenly quickening his step.

When they finally did stop, it was at a large wooden gate with a surrounding stone wall that made whatever lay behind it difficult for Pei to see. Her father pulled the string dangling on the side of the gate and immediately a small bell began chiming with each tug he gave.

"Who's there?" a high singsong voice asked from the other side of the gate.

Her father cleared his throat and said, "Pao Chung and daughter Pei."

There was little hesitation before the heavy wooden gate swung open. Behind it stood a short, heavyset woman who smiled widely, exposing a set of crooked, discolored teeth.

"We have been waiting for you," she said, opening the door wider so Pei and her father could enter. "It must have been a very long and hot journey!" She smiled at Pei.

"Yes," her father answered.

Inside the gate was a large courtyard with a table and several ornately decorated stools around it.

"I'm Auntie Yee," the smiling woman said to Pei. "Please sit."

The house itself was a two-story red-brick building tucked securely away from the street. It was the biggest, most beautiful house Pei had ever seen. She stood gazing at the one floor built on top of another, with flat, wide steps you climbed just to reach the front door. She'd never seen anything like it before. Pei could have gone on staring at the house in a daydream, if she had not seen another woman peering out from behind the opened door.

"Moi!" Auntie Yee called out in her singsong voice.

In the next moment Pei saw the woman disappear back into the house, only to return again carrying three cups of tea. Pei was then introduced to Moi, who was Auntie Yee's cook and housekeeper. Moi was younger and thinner than Auntie Yee, and she had a bad foot, which dragged slightly behind her as she walked.

The warm tea soothed Pei's parched throat. She looked over at her father, who sipped his tea slowly and avoided her questioning looks. Pei wondered who these women were and what they were doing here, but she knew it was not her place to ask such questions. Instead, she watched in silence. Auntie Yee appeared nice enough, with her crooked teeth and her round, smooth face that glowed with a perpetual smile on her lips. Pei wanted to laugh at the tight knot of jet-black hair on the top of her head.

"Would you like to see the house?" Auntie Yee asked.

Pei looked to her father. He hesitated a moment and stood up awkwardly, then nodded his approval. "My daughter would be very pleased to see the house."

"Very good." Auntie Yee smiled.

Pei watched her father move from one foot to the other. He watched them with an uncomfortable look in his eyes, a look Pei sometimes saw when she asked him a question he couldn't answer.

"You be good with Auntie Yee," her father said.

"You aren't coming?"

"No," he said looking down. "You be good."

"I will, Ba Ba," said Pei.

"I'm certain Pei will be a very good girl," Auntie Yee said. She took Pei's hand and led her up the steps to the house. At the top of the steps Pei turned around. Her father still stood by the table watching them.

The house was large and cool inside. A sharp smell Auntie Yee called ammonia filled Pei's head. Downstairs were four large rooms, one of which was the dining room, with an enormous round table. Beyond that was the kitchen, larger than their entire farmhouse; in the corner was a stained screen, and behind it a bed where Moi slept.

"This is the reading room," Auntie Yee said proudly. She swung open the doors to a large, airy room with shiny wooden tables and cushioned chairs. Along the walls were rows and rows of books. "The girls have reading lessons in here. It's also our gathering place to talk or to read and write letters, or for when family and friends come to visit."

Pei nodded her head and followed Auntie Yee up a flight of wooden stairs.

"This is where the younger girls sleep. The older girls share the room across the hall," said Auntie Yee, stepping into a long, open room. Against the wall was a row of narrow beds with a small basket beside each one. And like the rest of the house, the room was spare and clean.

"Do you like it?" asked Auntie Yee.

"Yes, it's very nice," Pei answered, remembering to be on her best behavior. "How many daughters do you have?"

Auntie Yee laughed. She put her arm around Pei gently. "I think you will like it here." She walked down to the bed at the farther end of the room. Patting the gray blanket that was fitted tight and smooth over it, she said, "This will be your bed, then."

Pei stood still, saying nothing. For a moment she thought she had heard wrong. Surely there must be some mistake, because her father was waiting for her downstairs and they would soon be going home.

"I don't understand," Pei finally said.

"You will be staying with us now, child. It won't be bad, I promise," said Auntie Yee, stepping toward her.

"It can't be, it's a mistake! My father wouldn't leave me!"

Pei turned around and in the next moment was stumbling down the stairs towards her father. "Ba Ba! Ba Ba!" Pei screamed as she swung open the front door and looked out to the empty courtyard. Panic and fear twisted in the hollow of her stomach as she ran down the steps and through the courtyard to the gate. Once again she was out on the hot, dusty street, but her father was nowhere in sight.

The Girls' House

If it had been a dream Pei would have awakened huddled beside Li as the thick warm smell of boiling jook filled the room. But when she opened her eyes, all she could see was a plain brick wall in front of her. The sharp smell of ammonia made her feel sick to her stomach. It was hard to tell how long she had been asleep, but light still filtered in from the window and the beds beside her remained empty. Pei tried to move, but her legs ached and her head throbbed with a pain she had never felt before. But it did not compare to the ache she felt at being left alone at this house with strangers.

She thought of everything she had done to deserve such a fate. She tried not to cry, but the tears came anyway, hot and burning. When she closed her eyes she saw her mother hovering over her, as clearly and painfully there as her mother had been for so many mornings. Once the tears came, she couldn't stop crying for her mother and for Li. Everything else seemed too hard to imagine.

Pei cried until there were no more tears, only the dry heaving that made her entire body shake. And then, before she knew it, she fell asleep again. When she awoke some time later the room was dark and cool. She tried to lift herself from the bed, but her head felt light and dizzy. No sooner did she rise than she let the weight of her body fall back down again. A thin dull light now came from underneath the door. Her body shivered when she heard voices and movement coming from downstairs.

There were three quick knocks on the door that sent her heart racing. The door opened slowly and a bright glow of light and shadow entered the room, followed by someone other than Auntie Yee or Moi. Pei tried to sit up straight. When her eyes grew accustomed to the light, she could see that the person who approached, carrying a lamp, was a girl, slender like herself, but older.

"Are you feeling better?" the girl asked. Her calm, steady voice was very pleasant.

"Yes," Pei quickly answered, though her head was still spinning.

When the girl held the light up closer to her, Pei could see that she was wearing white cotton clothing and her hair was cut

straight across her forehead, with one thick braid that swung to
the side when she turned to put the lamp down. The girl's gentle
smile met her frightened gaze, clear dark eyes staring with
kindness out of a pale, slender face. Pei had never seen a face so
smooth and delicate before. The girl's face was so different from
the large features that she and Li shared. It was the most beautiful face she had ever seen.

"My name is Lin," the girl told her. "Auntie Yee asked me to
bring you down to meet the others if you are well enough."

She nodded and immediately tried to get up, but the room
began to spin again.

"Do you feel faint again?"

"Did I faint?" Pei asked.

"Yes, Auntie Yee and Moi found you on the street and
brought you back up here."

Pei looked away from Lin, ashamed of her weakness.

"Many of us have a difficult time when we first come here, but
it passes." Lin smiled.

"Where am I?" Pei asked.

"You're at Auntie Yee's girls' house."

"What if I don't want to be here?"

"I'm afraid it's not your choice to make right now," Lin said
gently.

Pei swallowed hard and raised herself to a sitting position. For
a few moments she felt frozen in that position. She tried to move,
but she seemed to ache all over. Then, without saying another
word, Lin took hold of her arm and helped her gently to her feet.
Standing next to Lin, Pei felt terrible, her clothes soiled from
travel.

"Would you like to wash your face?" asked Lin.

"Yes, please."

Lin left her sitting on the bed and returned moments later
with a basin of water and a towel.

"There, that's much better," Lin said, gently wiping her face and dropping the dirt-stained towel into the basin. "We'd better hurry now. Everyone is waiting for us."

Downstairs the loud hum of voices stopped when they entered the dining room. The girls sitting around the large dining table turned their curious stares toward Pei. They all looked so alike, each one wearing the same white clothing, their hair cut short in front with a long braid hanging down in back. When Auntie Yee told Pei their names, it was as if she were talking to someone else. Pei sat so still she could hear her own heart beating. She tried hard not to cry, and thought of dashing toward the door and out—but how would she get home in the dark? Relief finally came when Moi carried in the food, one dish at a time. The girls began to eat and took no more notice of her. Pei sat in a daze, sipped her tea, and ate very little of the food placed in her bowl.

In the morning Pei remembered little of the night before. Her mind began to clear enough so she could take in the large, new room she slept in. Along with the fear and shame of being left behind with strangers, she couldn't help being curious at all that was happening around her. The girls who slept in the beds next to hers rose and went about their business as if she were not there. But with the help of a round-faced girl named Mei-li, Pei acquired a basin of water to wash her face and a clay jar for night-soil purposes.

Mei-li was friendly and talkative, leading her from one thing to the next. "Did you sleep well?" she asked when Pei was done.

"Yes." Pei was almost ashamed at how well she had slept.

"That's good, because you have a full day to look forward to. Now come, or we'll be late!"

She followed Mei-li downstairs to their morning meal of jook and another roomful of curious stares.

When the meal was finished, Pei watched the girls rise from their seats in unison. With the confusion of voices and the clatter of their wooden sandals against the floor, they collected their tin lunch pails and moved in a large group out the door. She remained seated, and much to her relief, so did Lin. Seeing her anxiety, Lin smiled at Pei with her beautiful dark eyes.

"Where are they all going?" Pei finally asked.

"To work at the silk factory. That's what we all do here, and what you'll soon learn to do." Lin said, rising from her seat.

"Are you going?"

Lin smiled and took her hand. "Today I am going to show you your new duties, but first come along and I'll get you some fresh clothes."

Pei looked down at the dirty clothes that she had put back on, but she could only think of her sister Li, who so often turned away from her questions, while Lin listened and responded kindly. They were so different, but she could not look at Lin without thinking of Li. And even when Pei thought of fighting this new life she had fallen into, she knew it was her father's desire that she be here. She had nowhere else to go. All her other thoughts of rebellion were quickly put away by the calm, soothing voice of Lin, whose kindness was a comfort.

Pei was given a set of white cotton trousers, with a shirt that buttoned up to her neck and a pair of wooden sandals such as all the girls in the house wore. After changing into them, she sat down to have her hair combed out. Very carefully Lin undid the braids her mother had tightly bound the morning she left, which now seemed so long ago. Lin stood behind her just as her mother did every morning, brushing gently through the difficult knots until finally the brush flowed through her hair with ease, stroke after stroke. Pei could almost imagine she was still at home, but she turned around quickly to see for herself that it was Lin doing the brushing. And when Lin gathered her hair together in one large handful and let the brush work its way underneath and downwards, it was a gesture she knew her mother never had time for.

The heavy footsteps of Auntie Yee echoed throughout the house, and in the next moment she filled the room with her strong scent of soap and ammonia. When she smiled, her crooked teeth protruded from her shiny, well-scrubbed face. Auntie Yee ran her plump fingers through Pei's hair and said, "Ah, it's very lovely." Then from her pocket she took out a pair of scissors and with a sigh said, "I'll need to cut just a little."

Pei jerked forward and turned towards Lin, who nodded her head reassuringly.

"You won't feel a thing," Auntie Yee said. She took hold of the front strands of Pei's hair and quickly snipped, leaving the shortened hairs to fall straight across her forehead. Then Lin divided her hair into three equal parts, twisting them into a thick single braid.

"Now look," said Lin. She gave Pei a small silver mirror to see herself.

Pei looked into the mirror and saw her somber reflection, framed by the straight black bangs, just like every other girl at the girls' house.

Chapter Three

1919

Pei

Pei had never seen anything like it before. The building was of whitewashed brick, standing the height of three houses and the width of at least ten. To one side of it stood two other buildings of equal size and shape. She followed Lin and looked up at the big building which Lin told her was the Yung Kee Silk Factory.

Seeing her surprise, Lin took Pei's hand and led her into the large open room of the first building. The room was very hot, and Pei felt as if she were suffocating. From the wooden rafters above hung several greasy fans, which turned too slowly to generate any real relief. Girls stood behind several long tables covered with small mountains of white. When Pei's eyes grew accustomed to the darkness she could see the sharp stares and hear the loud whispers of the girls who were working there. Even though she was dressed like them, Pei still felt like a stranger in their world.

Lin leaned over to her and whispered, "Don't worry about them."

Pei tried to smile, then looked away. She felt tired and uncomfortable.

"Those are the cocoons," Lin said, pointing to a white-covered table. "They're the first step in spinning silk."

Pei's eyes scanned the crowded room. Everywhere were large

cloth bags filled three feet high with the white, peanut-shell-sized cocoons.

"This is where the girls sort the good from the bad cocoons," Lin explained.

Pei watched as the girls flattened the cocoons on the table. Their quick hands then tossed the darkened ones to the side like stones, while they put the good ones into small baskets. Then a girl carted the filled baskets into another room.

Pei reached out and gently picked up a cocoon from one of the opened bags. It felt light and fragile in her hand.

"May I have one?" she asked.

Lin nodded. "Take as many as you like."

The cocoon was about half the size of Pei's longest finger, and when she shook it, the dead seed Lin called the chrysalis bounced against its hollow walls. She ran her fingers across the outside. It was hard and slightly bumpy, with a thin, fuzzy layer of hair surrounding it. Pei held the cocoon in her hand like a new toy.

Next to the sorting room was a larger room filled with steam as thick as smoke. Pei wrinkled her nose and rubbed her eyes. The heavy steam smelled almost sweet. Through the vapor Pei could see two rows of wood and cement counters that ran down the length of the room. Sticking up from the counters were metal arms moving up and down. The steady spinning noise of the funny metal machines filled the room. At the far end of the room Pei could see a grim-looking man pacing up and down, holding a long wooden stick.

"That's one of the managers hired by the owner, Chung. For the most part, they're harmless. They know very little about the silk work; they're just here for show, to make sure we do all the work," said Lin, watching Pei. "Come this way," Lin then said, moving toward one of the counters. "This is where we unwind the cocoons. The threads are very delicate. Sometimes they're so fine you can scarcely see them when they wind themselves onto the bobbin."

Along one side of the counter, a row of older girls was seated before metal basins of steaming water, spinning the silk. Directly across from the spinners were the younger girls, no older than Pei, who stood in front of pot-sized bowls, holding their forked sticks as they soaked and turned the cocoons brought to them in baskets.

"The younger girls are soaking the cocoons in boiling water until the silk threads loosen. It's one of the most important jobs here. They have to find the main thread from which the entire web of silk is unraveled," Lin continued.

As each girl found the main thread, she lifted the steaming bundle, which looked like a wet animal, and placed it in the basin of the older girl across from her.

Pei moved closer to the basin, careful not to slip on the wet cement floor. She saw dozens of the white cocoons dancing on the surface of the water. The older girls gathered the main threads from each one and twisted them together into one single thread. Pei watched so closely her eyes began to water from the heat. She wanted to touch the thin, almost invisible line, but she could only watch in fascination as the quick fingers of the older girls connected the threads with another set of cocoons before the first threads ended.

Pei walked slowly down the aisle away from Lin, who had stopped to speak to one of the spinners. Pei could feel the girls watching her out of the corners of their eyes, even as they continued their work. She recognized several of the girls from the house, but kept her eyes lowered. The younger girls, some of whom could barely reach the basins in which their cocoons soaked, looked wilted in the heat.

Not until Pei saw the pleasant, round-faced Mei-li did she

stop. Mei-li nodded and smiled as she stirred the steaming cocoons.

"It isn't difficult once you get used to it," Mei-li said with a smile. "But you must be careful not to burn yourself."

"You're very good at it."

Mei-li laughed. "I'm one of the slow ones. There are others here who are very quick—you'll soon see for yourself!"

"Have you been here long?" she asked Mei-li, her finger lightly touching the edge of the basin.

"For almost two years." The steam rose as Mei-li stirred the new batch of cocoons.

"Do you like it here?"

"It's not bad, you'll get used to it all. At least my parents aren't here watching over my every move." Mei-li laughed, until the older girl sitting across from her sharply told her to return to work. "Don't mind her," Mei-li whispered. "She's always in a bad mood."

"I'm sorry," Pei said, quickly moving away.

In the steamy atmosphere, with all the girls dressed alike, it was hard to tell one from another, much less find Lin again. Moments later, Pei saw Lin and another girl emerge from the haze. From the distance, Pei could tell they were both about the same age, fourteen or fifteen, though the girl who was walking with Lin was short and thick, her heavy features appearing even coarser next to Lin's. As they came closer Pei could see the square line of her jaw and her dark piercing eyes, which were filled with a fire that made Pei want to turn and run away.

"This is Chen Ling," said Lin. "She's the one you should talk to if there are any problems here."

Pei nodded shyly, shifting her weight from one foot to the other.

"Welcome, Pei," Chen Ling said, in a low voice that carried over the noise of the machinery. "I hope you'll like it here."

Pei whispered, "Thank you."

Chen Ling paused for a moment. Pei could feel Chen Ling look hard into her eyes, sizing her up with an expression that seemed as if she were hiding what she really thought. "If you need anything, I'll be glad to help you," Chen Ling finally said.

Then, before Pei could say anything else, Chen Ling turned abruptly and walked away.

"Don't worry," said Lin. "That's Chen Ling's way. She's very different from Auntie Yee."

"Auntie Yee?"

"Chen Ling is Auntie Yee's daughter—the daughter from her husband and his concubine, but her daughter just the same."

"Auntie Yee has a husband?"

Lin laughed. "There's a lot you will have to learn, little one."

From this steam-filled room Lin led her into another one, where a huge metal pot boiled the water that filled the metal basins. The steam rose up like a thick cloud of smoke. Several girls leaned over the edge of the pot with large wooden spoons, scooping out the hot water into barrels, which were then transported into the basin room. Suddenly Pei was reminded of her mother and the way she took care not to spill any soup or jook. She felt a hollow feeling in her stomach and tried hard not to cry. When the girls stood straight again, their faces were flushed pink, their hair pressed wet against their foreheads.

They passed through into another smaller, enclosed room.

"This is where the silk is sorted into different qualities to be sold for the highest price. That's our best," Lin said, pointing across the room. On wooden poles slung from one side of the room to the other, the best silk hung like the thick blond hair of the white-devil missionaries Pei had once seen in their village.

"The poorer silk is also sold, or put aside and used in other ways, for lining in bedding or clothing. Nothing is ever wasted here," said Lin, with obvious pride.

Pei moved around the crowded room, where the baskets were piled high in clumsy stacks against the wall, so that if just one

of them were pushed, the rest would come tumbling down. Pei
looked over at Lin watching her and shifted uncomfortably, her
arms glued to her sides.

The street felt strangely deserted when they emerged from the
building. The glare of the bright sun made Pei close her eyes for
just a moment.

"Come this way," Lin said, taking Pei's arm. "I want to stop
at one more place."

They hadn't walked far before Lin slowed down and turned
into a small teahouse tucked away from the main road on a quiet
street. The men and women villagers in the teahouse glanced up
and stared rudely at them. Pei followed Lin to an empty table
in the back, away from all the curious stares they attracted.

"Why do they watch us like that?" Pei asked when they were
seated.

"They don't know any better," Lin answered. "They think
we're different because we work in the silk factories and make
our own way."

"Are they angry at us?"

Lin smiled and said gently, "They don't know what to make
of us."

Then, turning away from Pei, Lin ordered several plates of
food. One by one they came: white, plump buns filled with meat
that was sweet on Pei's tongue, tiny balls of orange-veined
shrimp wrapped in a thin rice-flour skin, and noodles fried
crispy on top, with an oyster sauce. Pei ate, with an appetite she
had not realized existed, until all the plates were empty. Never
had she tasted food so delicious.

"Would you like something else?" Lin asked.

Pei sat up straight and felt a hot rush of blood color her face.
"No, no, thank you."

Lin smiled. "I know it's all a great deal to take in at one time,
isn't it?"

Pei nodded, thinking how beautiful Lin was with her pale smooth skin and her dark, kind eyes.

"It was for me, also," Lin continued. "I was older than you are now when I first came to Auntie Yee, and the first days were very difficult. But it passes."

"How long?" Pei asked. She suddenly had to know when the ache inside of her would leave, when she would stop thinking of her parents and Li, and even of the baby sister whose face she had not yet totally memorized.

"Time works differently for each one of us," Lin said softly. "You'll see, it will soon get better."

"Is that how it was for you?"

"Yes."

"Why did my father leave me here?"

"He had no other choice," said Lin gently.

"But why?" Pei tried hard to hold back the tears that rose in her throat.

"Sometimes things don't work out as they're planned, and there have to be sacrifices in order to make things better again. The money you'll be earning at the silk factory will help your family a great deal."

Pei made a small sound, trying to comprehend everything Lin was telling her. But she could find little comfort in Lin's words, and the absence, like a small tear, grew wider. Pei couldn't help but feel in her heart that she had done something terribly wrong to make her mother and father hate her enough to leave her with strangers.

Then, in a sudden outburst, Pei said, "I would never leave my daughter!"

"I know," Lin said softly. "Just understand that you may think this is not a very good place, but it's not a bad place, either. It's just another place for you to be right now."

Pei looked up at Lin and slowly began to understand what she was saying. Pei tried to speak, but couldn't say anything because the words seemed stuck in her throat. The oily aroma of cooking filled her head and settled in her stomach. All at once the events of the last two days came back to her, stinging her memory like Auntie Yee's ammonia. Her hand searched her pocket for the dry shell of the cocoon. All around them were the low hum of voices and the clinking of bowls against plates.

Auntie Yee

Moi drove Auntie Yee crazy. At least once a week, she complained about the vegetables. "They are old," Moi said, "as old as me! Look, I cannot eat this!" She spat out the green fibrous mass of bok choy.

"So why did you buy it then?" Auntie Yee taunted. "Just to complain?"

"That old man Sing, he cheated me!"

"Old man Sing is almost blind! How could he cheat you when you picked what you wanted?"

"He handed it to me," Moi said, as she lifted the rest of the bok choy and tossed it towards Auntie Yee. "He knows a good or bad bunch by touch. He is a tricky one!"

"Aii-ya!" Auntie Yee sighed as she lifted her hands above her head.

"A tricky one!" Moi continued, mumbling her displeasure to Auntie Yee. With almost everybody else in the house, Moi remained silent. She made herself noticed in other ways, by suspicious stares and slamming doors.

Auntie Yee had found Moi living on the streets. Moi had been with her since the beginning of the girls' house. For a place to sleep, Moi became her cook and housekeeper, even before Auntie Yee knew if she could cook or clean. The truth was, she felt sorry for Moi, and began watching the way Moi limped from street to street, always holding her head up so proudly. And unlike others who made their lives on the street, Moi had managed to keep herself relatively neat and clean.

Auntie Yee once watched Moi digging through some garbage for food. When she found some scraps, Moi wrapped them carefully in a handkerchief. Then, rather than eat them herself, she fed the few precious scraps to a starving dog. When Auntie Yee finally approached her, Moi eyed her suspiciously and spat on the ground next to where she stood. When Auntie Yee didn't move away, Moi dropped her bedding and listened to what Auntie Yee had to say.

"I need a cook," Auntie Yee had said.

"What is it to me?" asked Moi.

"The job is yours if you want it," Auntie Yee answered.

"Why?" Moi's eyes narrowed as she stared at Auntie Yee.

"Because I can offer you nothing more than a warm room and a cot to sleep on."

Moi shifted. "How do you know if I can cook?"

"I don't," Auntie Yee answered.

"How do you know I won't rob you blind?"

"I don't."

Moi laughed. Several missing teeth left darkened holes on one side of her mouth. She picked up her bedding and followed Auntie Yee back to the girls' house.

Auntie Yee couldn't have managed without Moi. The last time she had offered to hire a new cook, Moi refused with anger. "No!" she snapped. "Moi is the only cook here, unless Moi is not good enough for you!" Auntie Yee would then waste the next hour soothing her. After so many years, Moi still worried about ending up on the streets again. She had little trust in anyone, not even Auntie Yee.

*

Auntie Yee had been seven years old when she was given to the silk work. She lived in a girls' house until she was twelve, and then was made to marry. Like many girls, Auntie Yee was forced into marriage against her will. Her father knew that if no daughter was sent out in marriage, her brothers would receive no wives in return. Auntie Yee left the silk work and was sold to a struggling farmer. Before him, the only males she had known were her father and brothers. The farmer was decent enough and did not force himself on her when he saw how scared she was. He only laughed and said, "There will be plenty of time for more later!" For the first three nights of their marriage, he seemed satisfied with touching her and having her touch him. She felt only fear when he grabbed at her, but when she touched him long enough in one place, his body would tighten and arch with a low moan, as if he were in pain. Then he would leave her alone for sleep.

Before her marriage, Auntie Yee had heard stories of married life from the older girls at the girls' house. "Some girls are beaten into submission," they had said. "But the worst are the 'stone girls' who are made to take bitter medicine by their mother-in-laws. They are ridiculed and scrutinized from morning until night for not fulfilling their wifely duties. It is a fate I would wish on no one, not even my most hated enemy!"

Following custom, Auntie Yee was allowed to return home to visit her family three days after her marriage. She knew if she were allowed to leave the farmer, she would never return to him and his family. There was no telling when he would force himself on her. She couldn't bear the thought of sleeping in the same bed with him ever again. She decided then to return to the sisterhood and remain celibate. She simply returned to the village and resumed her work at the silk factory. There were few objections from her husband and his family. She was never very nice to look at, and could do much more for them by working to support her husband, the concubine she procured for him, and their children. In return, Auntie Yee would be able to remain celibate and her husband's first daughter, Chen Ling, would come to her when she was of age.

Auntie Yee knew she had been a fortunate one. Even now she believed her good fortune to be the result of the lucky charms given to her by the girls at the girls' house to ward off her husband's advances. She had kept them hidden away from his sight. To this day she kept the few tarnished trinkets and withered herbs carefully wrapped in silk underneath her pillow.

Over the years, Auntie Yee had many difficulties, both in starting her own girls' house and in supporting her husband's family. She worked long hours and borrowed from her sisters at the silk factory until she had enough money. The girls came afterward, one by one like stray cats, filling the house with bodies and voices. Chen Ling came to Auntie Yee soon after. Auntie Yee was her other mother, and Chen Ling was a young girl who already seemed old.

After evening meal, Auntie Yee watched Chen Ling take the precious volume down from the shelf in the reading room. Chen Ling's body was thick and square like hers. It was amazing how alike they looked, even though Chen Ling didn't have one drop of Auntie Yee's blood. She had never seen Chen Ling's hand caress anything but this book. With low whispers the girls eagerly waited for Chen Ling to begin reading the ballad of Kuan Yin to them. Kuan Yin was the goddess of mercy. It had always been the girls' favorite among the ballads in the book.

"Kuan Yin alone fought against all the objections of her family to become a nun," Chen Ling said with great enthusiasm. Her voice resonated against the walls of the room as she read. Chen Ling had a talent for speaking. Auntie Yee still wondered where it came from; certainly not from her or from Chen Ling's sad-faced father and mother.

Chen Ling wasn't like the other girls. She had always kept her distance from everyone, ever since she was a young girl coming to live with Auntie Yee. How resistant and cautious she was at first, and so self-sufficient that Auntie Yee's heart sank at not being able to do the small motherly things she had thought about. Chen Ling reserved her enthusiasm for the great volumes in which she read of the religious life. Even so, Auntie Yee had come to love Chen Ling, despite her religious beliefs and her rigid ways. She loved all the girls, but Chen Ling was her own. But whenever Chen Ling spoke of equality between men and women, Auntie Yee shook her head and didn't listen. It was enough to keep the girls' house running without all this other nonsense!

Chen Ling had made Auntie Yee proud. She quickly established herself as an efficient, hard worker and in a short time had risen within the ranks of the silk factory. What mother could ask for more?

Auntie Yee indulged her when allowed, buying for Chen Ling the religious books and pamphlets she read one after another. It was through them that Chen Ling had come into her own. With great fervor she spoke to the girls after evening meals, telling them of the advantages they had in remaining pure in the sisterhood.

"Why do we need a husband to mock us and a mother-in-law to beat us? This way we can dictate our own lives and remain free!" Chen Ling said.

Suddenly the girls who had sat quietly listening would clap and chant, "Kuan Yin! Kuan Yin!"

Chen Ling paced the floor, her arms rising up and down in quick, jerky movements. Sometimes Auntie Yee could hardly recognize this young woman who was her daughter.

Auntie Yee knew that many of the girls, afraid of Chen Ling, remained at a safe distance from her. Lin and the new girl, Pei, watched with interest, but Auntie Yee knew they would never conform to Chen Ling's way. It was not in them, as it was not in her.

But Chen Ling had captured a small group of girls who followed her without reservation, especially one girl named Ming. Auntie Yee could only shake her head when she saw how Ming followed Chen Ling around like a puppy dog. Ming was a thin, serious girl who was on the plain side and appeared very intelligent and eager to please. She and Chen Ling were almost inseparable, spending hours together reading the good books. For the most part, Auntie Yee was happy that Chen Ling had found such a friend.

The Pond

In the waning light Yu-sung packed the last of the mulberry leaves in a basket. Then, looking up, she shifted the baby Yu-ling into a comfortable spot on her back and looked for any sign of Pao coming up from the ponds. Since Pei had gone away, Pao worked longer and harder than ever. Their days and nights were filled with a thick silence, no longer burdened by Pei's curious chatter. Yu-sung kept Li and the baby out of Pao's way and simply let him work his way toward his own peace.

Once, when it was still dark, Yu-sung awakened to find Pao no longer beside her. Her sleep had become as haphazard as his. Through a crack in the curtain she looked hard to see the shadowy outline of her husband sitting in the dark. Neither of them made a move. Pao had aged in the past few months, and even in the darkness he was stooped over as though some great weight bore down on him. They remained frozen in this position until something foreign reached her ears. Yu-sung strained to make it out. She turned quickly around to make sure it was not

Yu-ling, who was still sleeping soundly. The strange muffled sound cracked through the silence. When she looked again, Pao's face was buried in his arms and she could tell the soft whimpering was coming from him. Her first instinct was to comfort him as she would her children, but she didn't move, remembering that, before anything, he was her husband.

Outside, the air was cool and sharp. In the hollow darkness, everything seem to echo around Pao. He could just make out the faint glow of the ponds and the dark brooding mulberries that surrounded them. It was because of the ponds and groves that he found a place on this earth, a reason more powerful than blood. Long after he was gone, they would remain.

Pao wandered instinctively down to the largest of his ponds. He often did this when he could not sleep. Sitting on the dry dirt, he waited for something, but he was not quite certain of what. He tried not to think of Pei or hear her voice, which sometimes followed him into his sleep. In one moment of weakness, he had thought of taking Pei's arm and running from the girls' house, but he had stood firm as she turned into the house with Auntie Yee. He could only hope she was happy there among the other girls.

Suddenly Pao turned his attention back to the pond. In its blackness he looked hard for any movement, the smallest flicker of life. Then out of the corner of his eye he saw a ripple in the calm surface. Quickly Pao stood up and looked harder, but nothing stirred in the empty pond. Still, he felt a warmth spread through him. He stood there waiting for some movement to return.

Then slowly Pao lowered himself into the cold water, feeling more alive than he had in months. The cold spread the length of his cotton pants, but as Pao pushed against the water he felt like a boy again. He imagined the invisible fish, hundreds of them, almost knocking him off balance. Still, he persisted, and step by step Pao moved closer to the center, reliving those days of abundance, when he pushed the metal net and took the frantic fish towards their certain death.

The sky had lightened considerably by the time Pao made his way back to the house. The first stirrings of the day began with the waking birds. It would be another mild day. He paused just a moment outside the door and listened for Yu-sung's quiet movements. Then he went in. She stood by the fire stirring the jook as the thick steam filled the room. Neither of them said a word. Yu-sung's hair was pulled tightly back into a knot. His eyes caught hers and he saw the weariness in them before she turned away. Pao sat down and watched as she placed a bowl of jook in front of him. He wanted to say something of how he felt about the fish and the ponds, but he kept silent.

Chapter Four

1925

Pei

Pei's days at the silk factory were very long. The girls arrived every morning at five thirty. When the horn wailed its low cry for them to stop working at seven thirty each evening, they left the factory wilted and drained from the wet heat. Most of the time they were given half an hour for lunch and ten minutes off for every three hours they worked. Sometimes, if they were behind their quota, these breaks never came. The male managers hired by the owner, Chung, waved their sticks and shouted, "Keep working!" The girls reluctantly obeyed.

Many of the girls argued and complained bitterly among themselves. "We are here before the sun rises," said one girl, poking at the mass of cocoons dropped in her basin, "and they won't even give us time to relieve ourselves!"

"Let's see how they feel standing all day in this heat!" another voice said.

Still, they bit their lips and kept working.

Like all the new girls, Pei had begun in the sorting room. The dim, hollow room filled with cocoons smelled stale and musty. She tried very hard not to ask too many questions of Lin, but every step was like a new adventure, from transporting cocoons on wooden carts from one room to another, to standing behind the long wooden tables sorting out the mountains of white. The girls who once whispered secrets about her now spoke in the same secretive hush with her. Soon Pei could tell a good cocoon from a bad one simply by touch, by the texture and the firmness of its shell. A year later she was promoted to standing before a metal basin of steaming water soaking the cocoons. With her forked stick she poked the white mass of cocoons, which floated to the surface like tiny islands. The steam and the slightly sweet smell of the cocoons boiling soon became a familiar part of her new life.

In the beginning Chen Ling watched over her from a distance, like a bird hovering. But when she saw that Pei could hold her own, Chen Ling disappeared back into the tiny hole of her office and was rarely seen.

The first few months were miserable for Pei. She missed her family terribly. Sometimes, after everyone was asleep, she let her tears flow freely, her face pressed into her pillow. She often fell asleep exhausted by grief. Gradually, with the help and kindness of Lin and Mei-li, she grew accustomed to the rigorous routine and the long hours of standing.

Pei slowly began to feel comfortable working in the silk factory and living at the girls' house. Everything was new and exciting. She saw and felt things she had never dreamed of. Every other month, Lin took Pei to the theater, where a traveling troupe of actors would paint their faces white and portray both the men and women in an opera. They sang in high, whiny voices and moved gracefully across the stage. Pei sat on the hard wooden bench, completely still, captivated by the splendor of light and music. Afterward, she would ask Lin question after question. "Was it really a man who portrayed the woman?" Or, "Why would he have killed himself over such a little thing?" Lin always laughed and patiently answered Pei as well as she could. At other times, Pei might go with Lin and a group of the girls to visit the village temple, its vibrant red-and-gold altar the biggest and most ornate she'd ever seen.

During the first year of learning the silk work, Pei realized there was very little time for memories. Some evenings she was so tired she could barely stand, but the faces of her family still appeared in her dreams, only to grow more vivid each year during the Dragon Boat Festival. Even now, after almost six years, Pei still felt a pain in the middle of her stomach whenever they were given a Jong for evening meal. She tried hard to imagine how Li and her mother must look, but the years had dimmed their colors. Sometimes, Pei was afraid she would one day pass her sister Li on the street and they would be strangers. And, unlike those of some other girls at the girls' house, Pei's family never came to visit. Occasionally, she made up small excuses for them: Her father could not leave his ponds; or, her mother was not up to traveling so far. But deep inside, Pei knew they would never come; they had given her to the silk work. It was as if they no longer had a daughter.

Since coming to the girls' house, Lin and Mei-li had become Pei's closest companions. Pei's most private feelings were saved for Lin, but lately Lin was always so busy at the factory. She had moved from reeling silk to supervising the girls in another building. Pei missed her terribly. She knew that it was an important step for Lin, but she'd begun to feel abandoned by her. With Mei-li, it was enough that they laughed and had fun together.

Mei-li was always good-natured and laughed with a high, tinny shrill. She had come to the girls' house two years before Pei, fitting in without any major complications. With her easy disposition, Mei-li had no problems making friends. Even when there were bad feelings between the girls at the house, their long silences and violent bursts of emotion didn't touch Mei-li, who remained neutral and friendly to all.

Mei-li's parents came to visit her religiously every month.

They brought her gifts of dried beef, pickles, and sugar candy. She shared most of this with Auntie Yee and the girls—all except the sugar candy, which she saved and shared only with Pei.

On one occasion, when Mei-li and Pei were walking back to the girls' house from the silk factory, Pei asked, "What do your parents talk about when they come every month?"

"About our family mostly, my brothers and their wives. My mother complains of their laziness!" Mei-li laughed.

"Don't they obey her?"

"They're sly, my mother complains. When she turns her back they do the opposite of what she tells them."

"What does your father say?"

"Nothing, really."

"My parents say very little. They have always had to work very hard. That's probably why they never come to visit." Pei paused, realizing it hurt just as much to say this aloud as to think it. "Do you ever want to go back home with your parents?"

"In the beginning, but now I'm glad to be here." Mei-li stopped. From her pocket she produced another candy for herself and Pei. "There are many more rewards to being here. Besides, not only do I get presents from my parents, but we can take trips to the temples and theaters, and how else would we have met?"

"Yes," Pei said after a moment.

"Do you wish you were back home?"

"Sometimes."

They walked in silence.

"Were you so happy there?" asked Mei-li.

Pei considered the question. The thought of happiness had never come into her mind. Her life was made up of her parents and Li and the dank smell of the fish ponds. Happiness was a feeling of lightness when they were finished with chores and free to wander down to the pond.

"I don't know, I suppose it was all right, sometimes," Pei answered. "It would be nice to see my family again, just once, so I could see how they all are."

Mei-li nodded. She pulled out another candy and handed it to Pei. Every night they walked back from the factory to the girls' house in groups, looking like scattered flocks of white birds along the road. The laughter from the group of girls ahead of them rang out in the soft night air. Soon it would be summer, and the clear, sweet air they breathed would once again turn hot and sticky.

Not all the girls working at the silk factory lived in a girls' house. Many, from the village, remained at home with their families. Pei's friend Su-lung was one such village girl. Su-lung worked beside Pei soaking cocoons. She lived with her family in one of the small, dark houses that lined the narrow alleyways. In the maze of cramped spaces, entire families lived side by side.

Even though Su-lung lacked the freedom Pei and her sisters had at the girls' house, Pei envied the fact that Su-lung lived with her family. Pei sometimes thought she would gladly give up her freedom at the girls' house if it would mean staying with her family. So when Su-lung invited her and Mei-li to meet her family and share an evening meal with them, Pei was only too happy to go. When she looked for Lin to tell her the news, Lin had already left for a meeting at work.

Su-lung's house was not far from the silk factory. Through a cool alley they walked happily. To each side of them, narrow passageways splintered off into darkness. On the way they gathered even more than their usual share of stares, triggered by their uncontained laughter. On several occasions, jealous villagers stopped and pointed at them. "Who do you think you are?" they said vulgarly. "Living together with all your money!" The villagers had no idea that most of the girls' earnings went to their families and for room and board. Usually, they were bothered by this thoughtless hostility, but tonight nothing could upset them. Only when Su-lung slowed down and stopped in front of a low wooden door did their voices become silent.

With a small push, Su-lung opened the door easily. They were greeted by the smell of something frying and chattering voices coming from an inner room. As her eyes adjusted to the murky light the one oil lamp gave off, Pei saw very little in the way of comforts. There was only a small table and a few wooden chairs filling up the tiny room.

"Come this way," Su-lung said happily.

Pei and Mei-li followed her into the inner room and were immediately introduced to Su-lung's parents, brother, and sister. When Su-lung's brother, Hong, stood, he was almost as tall as the ceiling and automatically stooped to avoid hitting his head. Pei could not remember the last time she had been in the same room with a boy. Hong, appearing just as awkward and uneasy at meeting them, remained standing. Then, quickly, almost embarrassedly, he sat down. Mei-li giggled and nudged Pei with her knee.

As usual, Mei-li felt no shyness and spoke of the girls' house and of her own family with an air of authority.

"My family is from Fukien," she said happily. "I have two brothers who are married, though now I feel as if those at the girls' house are just as much my family."

Pei was content to listen to the noisy chatter of a family so different from her own. So she smiled and kept silent, and so did Hong.

After a simple meal of rice, steamed fish, pork, and vegetables, Su-lung's mother brought out star fruit and melon. For the first time since Pei had arrived at the girls' house, she didn't feel out of place in the company of others besides her sisters. She felt a warmth she had never felt as a child. "Eat, eat," said Su-lung's mother, as her father smiled attentively; Hong relaxed enough to answer Mei-li's questions.

"What are you studying, Hong?" Mei-li asked without shame.

"I am preparing for my university entrance exams. I hope to be studying economics."

"That must be very exciting," she continued.

"It's a great deal of work," he said, beginning to show interest in her interest.

"Yes, it must be. I could never do it."

"I'm sure you could if circumstances were different."

Hong spoke in a quiet, serious manner, his gaze fixed upon the person he spoke to. His eyes were narrow and suspicious, and while Pei soon lost interest in him, Mei-li listened to every word he said without taking her eyes off him.

When they left, the night air felt cool and welcoming. Pei was anxious to return to the girls' house, hoping to see Lin, but Mei-li moved slowly and spoke in a strange, dreamy way.

"I thought Su-lung's parents were very nice," Mel-li said. She stooped down and picked up a flower. Very systematically she began pulling off its petals.

"Yes," Pei replied. "They're very different from my parents."

"Mine, too." Mei-li let the stem of the flower blow away from her hand. "What did you think of Su-lung's brother, Hong?"

"He seems nice."

"Do you think he thought I was nice?"

Pei looked at Mei-li and saw the pink flush of her cheeks. "Why wouldn't he?"

"I don't know."

She laughed and put Mei-li's mind at ease. "I think he thought you were very nice."

Mei-li smiled happily and said nothing more about Hong.

All night Pei hardly slept for fear that she wouldn't awake in time to see Lin. Every morning Lin and Chen Ling left early for

the factory and didn't return until late. It was as if Lin made no
effort to see her anymore.

Above the rhythmic breathing of the girls, Pei listened for the
door across the hall to open and close, followed by the muted
footsteps making their way down the stairs. At last the first
creakings of the house brought her out of a half-sleep. Pei
quietly rose, careful not to wake the others. As she opened the
door, the dim light from downstairs entered. Moments later the
door across the hall opened and Lin appeared.

"What are you doing up?" Lin whispered, tying a red piece
of yarn to secure the bottom of her braid.

"I wanted to talk to you," Pei said, trembling, the cool morning air moving right through her cotton gown. She had grown
so much in the past years she now stood a half a head taller than
Lin.

"Go back to bed, you're cold, we can talk later."

"I haven't seen you in so long—are you angry with me?"

Lin's face softened into a smile. "How could I be angry with
you?" Her eyes looked away from Pei's. "I've been angry with
myself for feeling things I shouldn't."

"What things?"

When her dark eyes turned back to Pei, Lin said softly, "I was
jealous because you have had Mei-li and Su-lung and haven't
needed me."

Pei was stunned by Lin's words, no longer feeling the cold.
She had been so afraid that Lin no longer wanted to have
anything to do with her. "How could you ever think that?" she
finally asked.

"Word gets around," answered Lin, but then she smiled at the
sight of Pei's distress and said, "I can see I have been foolish. I'm
sorry if I have upset you. Now go back to bed and we'll talk
later." Lin pushed back a wavy strand of loose hair from Pei's
face.

"Ever since I came here, you've been my only family," Pei said.

"Go back to bed, we'll talk later," urged Lin. "I have to go." Lin let her hand rest momentarily on Pei's shoulder and then she was gone.

The next day at the silk factory Chen Ling approached Pei in her businesslike manner and asked to speak with her. Just as quickly another girl stepped in and took over for her as they walked towards Chen Ling's office. This was a small, cluttered room behind the sorting room. Pei was relieved to see Lin waiting inside. When Pei looked toward her, Lin smiled reassuringly; Pei relaxed and leaned against the heavy wooden desk. Chen Ling immediately claimed her chair and with an air of calm and authority leaned back, folding her arms across her chest.

"I've been watching your work, Pei, and you've done very well," said Chen Ling.

"Thank you," she answered, lowering her eyes.

Pei had never gotten over being timid with Chen Ling, even though most of the girls had credited the quiet Ming with helping to soften Chen Ling. It was well known throughout the factory that they were inseparable outside of the silk work.

"We have decided that it's time for you to move on to reeling the silk. You've shown that you can handle whatever work we've given you, so I don't see why you should have any trouble moving on."

Pei looked toward Lin, who was smiling, then back to Chen Ling. "I would like that very much," she said eagerly.

"Good, then it's settled. You'll begin tomorrow and Lin will work with you until you are able to do it sufficiently well on your own. Congratulations, I'm sure you'll continue to do good work."

For a moment Chen Ling almost smiled before looking down at the papers on her desk, signaling an end to their conversation.

When they were safely out of Chen Ling's office, Lin took Pei's hand and with a small squeeze said, "Congratulations. This will mean more money for you and your family."

"Will it?" Pei said absently, not quite believing her good fortune. It sometimes took other girls eight to ten years to become reelers, and she had accomplished it in five, when she was only fourteen. "It's pretty good, isn't it?" she then asked.

"If you ask me, it's long overdue!" Lin said enthusiastically.

But their joy quickly vanished when a high, piercing scream came from the far end of the room. Several muffled screams followed as Lin moved quickly toward the noise and away from Pei.

At the far end of the room a group of girls was gathered. Their machines were left to operate by themselves. The whizzing sound of the bobbins spinning without the connected cocoons filled the air. The screams that had pierced the normal rhythm of the machines were suddenly reduced to low moans. Pei moved quickly through the thick crowd of girls until she reached Mei-li, who stood on her toes trying to see over the heads of the other girls.

"What happened?" Pei asked.

"Someone's been burned!"

"Who?"

"I don't know, I can't see a thing," said Mei-li, pushing forward against the girl in front of her.

The moans grew louder. Pei heard Lin's voice call out for someone to get Chan the herbalist, who was called upon whenever accidents occurred at the silk factory. Mostly these were routine, the slight burns that the girls suffered from the hot water and heated metal basins. Almost immediately the girls moved back to clear a path. Then in the clearing, she saw Ming lying on the ground, her clothes soaked as the spread of water worked its way outward. The vat of boiling water, which was usually secured to the cart, had somehow fallen on its side, the rush of steaming water hitting Ming before she was able to move out of its way.

Ming lay on the floor in obvious pain, the skin of her face and arm pink as if she had been scoured with a brush. Lin hovered over her, placing her hand under Ming's head to give her what little comfort she could. The hushed whispers of the girls sent Pei into motion, and without hesitation she found a discarded cocoon bag and covered Ming's shivering body with it.

"What's happened here?" the irritated voice of Chen Ling demanded.

The crowd of frightened girls stepped back to allow Chen Ling through. But not until Pei stood and moved out of the way did Chen Ling see the injured Ming lying on the ground.

"It was an accident," Lin said softly. "I've sent for Chan."

Immediately Chen Ling was on her knees, gently cradling Ming's head in her arms. She whispered words of encouragement to Ming. When Chan arrived and saw the seriousness of Ming's burns, he instructed that she be taken back to the girls' house immediately. At first, Chen Ling would allow no one to help. "Stand back!" she demanded, pushing away from Ming those who tried to help. Carefully she lifted Ming's thin body into the protection of her arms.

After Chen Ling and Ming left, there was an eerie emptiness amid the noise. For a moment Pei and Lin didn't move. Then, with a sudden burst of energy, they were both on their knees, mopping up the excess water. Even though Pei tried, she couldn't bring herself to meet Lin's gaze.

Y u - s u n g

Yu-sung no longer had any children. They had given Pei to the silk work and Li to marriage. Her youngest daughter, Yu-ling, had gone into the other world less than a year after Pei left. She did not think Yu-ling had suffered—there was no fever like those the others had had—she simply lay stiff one morning and did not wake. Her death seemed as quiet as her life. Pao buried her next to the others, and for several days after Yu-sung felt nothing. Then, when she could feel again, Yu-sung came down with a fever and lay in an endless dream in which her eldest daughter, Li, cared for her. Pao remained silent and hovered over her like a dark shadow.

Now Li was gone. She had been given in marriage to a farmer on the other side of the hill. He had sent Sing Tai, the village matchmaker, after seeing Li one day in the village. Yu-sung was in the groves with Li when the matchmaker approached Pao. Pao listened to what the old woman had to say and returned to his work. It was not until that evening, when they had finished their evening meal, that Pao spoke for the first time of the matchmaker's visit.

"Sing Tai came to see me this afternoon," he told Li. "There is a man named Chin, a farmer on the other side of the hill, who wishes to marry you." Pao picked his teeth with a small, sharpened piece of wood.

Li looked up at him, surprised.

"The farmer is a widower," Pao continued, his eyes avoiding Li's and Yu-sung's. "His wife has died in childbirth, along with the child. He has two other young children."

Yu-sung's heart stopped, though Li did not seem to flinch. Li cleared her throat and asked, "He wishes to marry me?"

Pao nodded.

Yu-sung looked from her husband to the quiet, serene face of her eldest daughter, her last child. The day Yu-sung had dreaded and feared since her daughter's birth had come and she could do nothing but remain silent.

"Is this what you would wish, Ba Ba?" Li then asked him.

Pao turned and paused for a moment, then said, "The decision is yours. I have told Sing Tai we will have an answer in two days."

Li stood up and cleared the table, saying nothing more. She remained silent the next day, and as much as Yu-sung wanted to say something to her, the words stuck to the roof of her mouth like sticky rice. The next evening, before Li stood up to clear, she simply said, "I will marry the farmer, then."

Pao grunted his answer, and Yu-sung grieved.

The day the farmer was to come, Li went about her duties as always, as if her marriage day were no different from the rest. That morning Yu-sung opened the chest at the end of their bed and breathed in the years of her youth. Layer by layer she removed the white paper that separated one precious possession from the next, removing the red silk dress and slippers, and the silk scroll-painting she could not bear to look at after Pei had gone. In the back corner she found the lace handkerchief given to her by her grandmother. This she took out and placed on the bed before replacing everything else. When Yu-sung went to find Li, she was carrying water in to wash the morning bowls.

"I can do that," Yu-sung said, gesturing for her to sit down. Li placed the bucket on the floor and did as she was told. Li seemed so young still, looking up at Yu-sung and waiting for her next words.

"Are you all right, Ma Ma?"

"I want to give you this," Yu-sung said, letting the words slip out before she felt herself choke on them. She held out the lace handkerchief wrapped in the milky-white paper.

Li looked at her, surprised, and then reached up for the gift. Her fingers clumsily unwrapped the paper and stroked the finely woven designs.

"It belonged to Tai Pao," Yu-sung said, "my mother's mother."

Li looked up shyly, her face as relaxed and curious as a young child's, but just as quickly she caught herself, and her thin lips whispered, "Thank you."

The house rattled hollow in the strong, persistent winds. At night, when the winds blew, they were like voices coming through the house. Yu-sung lay in bed for hours listening to what they were saying. Sometimes she imagined them to be the voices of her daughters, returning to tell her of their lives. "It is all right, Ma Ma," they told her. But when she sat up slowly, so as not to disturb Pao, and listened harder for their distant voices, the noise was simply the winds of a storm approaching.

The Monsoon

A week after Ming's accident, the rains came. Auntie Yee and Moi boarded the windows and secured everything of importance against the furious winds. For a day and night the girls lived within the tomb-tight atmosphere waiting for the winds to gather their strength and sweep through the village. For centuries the winds and rain had left their mark on Yung Kee, showing no mercy, toppling anything not secured by brick and mortar. One year the ancient Hing Wah temple was torn from the ground piece by piece. Its ornately carved door was found in splintered sections down by the river, while other remnants were found miles away, several weeks after the winds had stopped. For months after, people worshiped in the large, empty cavity left in the temple's place.

And now they again waited, as the sky darkened and rumbled and the rain came down slowly at first, then built into a constant, sometimes violent flow, neither stopping nor pausing to take a breath. The entire village of Yung Kee stood in the bleak, gray daylight waiting for the howling winds to come or for the rain to let up, but neither happened. The earth drank in all it could until every crevice filled up and the land bloated.

Two days after the rains began, the girls were ordered to return to work at the silk factory. Convinced that the winds would grow no wilder than a swift breeze, Auntie Yee allowed the girls to bear the rain and return to work.

Each day out, Pei, Lin and Mei-li could easily see the damage the rain alone was causing. The river swelled and soon poured over the banks onto the streets. Hundreds of boat people left their floating houses for dry land, carrying whatever possessions they could.

"What's that?" Mei-li cried, pointing to every stray object that floated by as they walked.

"It's just a piece of wood," Pei said, taking her arm and leading her forward, past the begging men and women in the streets.

"Why do they stare at us like that?" Mei-li whined.

"Because they're hungry and cold!" Lin snapped.

Pei surveyed the misery around her with a heavy heart. Most of the boat people were forced to live like squatters in the doorways of buildings or under makeshift shelters as the rain continued. With the roads washed out, food became scarce. Entire families begged in the streets, pulling at Lin's clothes and her own as their children clung to them crying with the cold and hunger. Each day there were more bodies lying lifeless along their path. Pei and Lin gave all they could from their own lunches, but it was never enough to satisfy the hordes of hungry boat people.

The girls themselves suffered the effects of the constant rain. Most of the girls arrived at the silk factory muddy and soaked through, with no choice but to work in their damp clothing the entire day. Sandbags and large pieces of cloth were placed against the doors of the factory and wrung out constantly by girls who stayed all night to keep the water from entering and damaging the reeling machines.

Then one day amid all the noise of the reeling machines came the high-pitched voice of Mei-li screaming "Get it away, get it away!"

Lin and Pei arrived to find an unconscious, gray, almost black rat floating belly-up in her basin. Directly above them others scurried across the rafters. Mei-li looked up, and seeing the army of rats fainted where she stood. From that day on Mei-li would go nowhere in the factory without a large wooden stick for protection.

"They are sly devils, they ravage through everything," said an unusually talkative Moi, making the soup that evening. "I tell you it is only the beginning of the rats you will see come out because of the flooding. I have seen them a foot long or more!"

"It can't be!" Mei-li screamed.

"I remember when I was a young girl in Tientsin, I saw villagers hanging their babies in nets strung from the ceiling for fear the rats would eat their children while they slept," said Moi, dropping the wooden spoon and turning toward her audience. "It makes no difference, the rats persist no matter what. They dig their claws into the walls or climb down the thinnest of ropes to get to the child. I have seen it myself, back in Tientsin, a baby's face half eaten by rats as it hung from netting above the floor!"

Mei-li hid behind Auntie Yee as some of the girls cowered at Moi's stories.

"Moi, why do you tell such stories?" scolded Auntie Yee.

"I speak only the truth! Why, at least here we can be certain that some of these rats will find themselves skinned and roasted over the open fires of the less fortunate!" Moi snapped as she went back to her cooking.

Auntie Yee rolled her eyes and lifted her hands up in the air before leaving the room.

As Mei-li lay in bed listening to the falling rain she came to a decision. When the time came for her to marry, it would be to Su-lung's brother, Hong. From the first moment she saw him, it had been as if her fate was set. Nothing anyone could do or say would change her mind. The only one she dared to confide in was Pei, and even then, not everything could be said. Despite the rains and her intense fear of the dark, ugly rats, Mei-li disobeyed Auntie Yee and deliberately walked out of her way past Su-lung's house in hopes of catching sight of Hong.

Most evenings she caught a glimpse of him returning from his studies, books in hand as he hurried into the two dark rooms she had visited. What was it about Hong that made her want to be with him, even from a distance? She had never had these feelings for anyone before, not even her own family, whom she preferred to have at a distance. But as she watched Hong's long strides take him quickly out of her sight, she felt a sinking in the hollow of her stomach. Mei-li kept up this secret ritual night after night without exception. She arrived home only a short time after the others, always ready with an excuse if Auntie Yee should question her. "I stopped to speak to a friend," she would say, or "I had to finish some work." So far, Mei-li was relieved not to have had to tell Auntie Yee any of these lies.

On one of these nights Mei-li did not see Hong. She waited as long as she possibly could before hurrying back to the girls' house. The disappointment stung her as she walked quickly through the pouring rain, her thoughts focused on her own misery. Even the darkness, which would usually frighten her with all its unimaginable creatures, couldn't deter her. As Mei-li turned the corner, she didn't realize someone was following her, the dull footsteps muffled by the water. On instinct Mei-li turned around to find Hong a few steps behind her. She had not seen him come up from behind the stone wall that usually hid her from his sight, so he must have come from the opposite direction. Then Hong did something very unexpected: He grabbed Mei-li's arm and led her down the street, away from the girls' house.

Mei-li let herself be taken away, her heart pounding wildly. Even soaking wet, she felt a warmth spread through her body as Hong held tightly onto her arm. She hoped he would never let go, but as they turned into a small dark building, he released her in the narrow passageway.

Hong fumbled with the lock, then opened the door to a small, dark room whose damp smell made Mei-li shudder. For a moment she thought of the rats, and of all the other hidden creatures that might lurk in a place like this, but she quickly put them to the back of her mind.

"Where are we?" Mei-li finally gained the courage to ask.

"It's a friend's room. He's away visiting his family."

Hong lit an oil lamp, which set the small room aglow. There was little in the way of furnishings, just a chair, a table, and a bed against the far wall. Mei-li stood and waited. She had known from the beginning that Hong was the only man she would be with. And she did not resist when she felt his hand search for hers, then move up her arm to the nape of her neck.

"You've been watching me," he said.

"Yes," she answered.

"Why?"

Mei-li remained silent.

"Come this way, you must be cold," he whispered.

Slowly Hong removed her outer clothing and lowered Mei-li

onto the hard bed. She could faintly see Hong removing his wet jacket before he slowly lowered his body next to hers. They lay side by side like this for a few moments before Mei-li felt Hong's warm fetid breath against her neck as he fumbled with her clothes and slipped his hand underneath. His damp hair gave off the oily scent of flowers. Mei-li shivered when his fingers found her breasts. Then, awkwardly, Hong tipped her head back and groped for her mouth, and when he found it pressed his lips heavily against hers. Mei-li closed her eyes and let her body mold tightly to Hong, following his every move.

"I love you," Mei-li said afterward. She had not felt all that he did, but then she assumed making love was always more pleasurable for a man. It certainly was not what Chen Ling had hinted it would be like, she did not feel like she would burn in a fire for all eternity. It was just wonderful being so close to Hong.

Hong was sitting up on the side of the bed, putting back on his wet clothing. He did not answer.

"Do you love me?" asked Mei-li.

"It doesn't have to be all that serious," said Hong, his eyes avoiding hers. "No one has to know anything; it will only cause trouble."

"What do you mean?"

"Only that no one has to know about this yet." He looked toward Mei-li and smiled. "My passing these exams is very important to my family. I can't burden them with anything else until they are all over with."

Mei-li said nothing.

"And how will it look for you to have been with a man when you're still at the girls' house?"

"I don't care how it looks, I love you!"

"Well, I care," Hong said, grabbing her arm and giving it a

quick squeeze. "No one must know about this, do you understand?"

Mei-li nodded, swallowing hard. She remained quiet. The light flickered as she watched their shadows dance against the stark brick wall. The damp, sour smell of the room seemed to suffocate her. Somewhere, beyond the falling rain, Mei-li thought she heard the muffled sound of a child crying.

Chapter Five

1925

Pei

Outside the rain continued to fall as Auntie Yee and the girls gathered in the reading room to wait for Mei-li. It was after evening meal, and Mei-li had not returned from the silk factory with the last group of girls. Pei watched helplessly as Auntie Yee grew more and more agitated.

Now and then Moi peeked in, finally emerging with a tray of tea and biscuits which no one touched.

"Mei-li should know better. Where can she be?" Auntie Yee said, pacing the floor. She stopped short to wait, and Pei could see her worried face scanning theirs for an answer. Anxiously, Auntie Yee moved toward her, hoping for any small clue as to Mei-li's whereabouts.

"She may be with Su-lung," Pei finally gained the courage to say. "I'm sure she's just waiting there with Su-lung's family until the rain lets up."

"With Su-lung? Why would she be with Su-lung? Mei-li knows that I want all you girls to come directly back here from the factory!"

Pei remained silent. Ever since Mei-li began having all her foolish thoughts about Su-lung's brother Hong, Pei had listened to her ramblings with a touch of uneasiness. She was sure Mei-li was walking past Su-lung's after work. Every night Mei-li hurried back to the girls' house just after everyone else, always breathless, her face flushed. Auntie Yee didn't seem to notice, but when Pei asked her where she'd been, Mei-li would always smile and change the subject. Still, Pei had never dreamed that Mei-li would go so far as to disobey Auntie Yee's rules.

"I'll go to Su-lung's house immediately!" Auntie Yee said, moving frantically towards the door. But before she could put on her coat, the front door creaked open and Mei-li hurried in, wet and dripping on the shiny wood floor.

"I'm so sorry, Auntie Yee," said Mei-li apologetically. "I hadn't realized—"

"Where have you been?" Auntie Yee interrupted, her voice trembling. She walked in quick circles around Mei-li. "Do you know how worried we've been?"

"Su-lung was frightened so I walked back with her to her house. I didn't realize the time, and then the rain became so strong," Mei-li whispered, wrapping her arms around her shivering body.

"You know you are to come directly back here from the factory! You frightened all of us terribly!"

"I'm very sorry," Mei-li said, wiping her eyes.

Immediately Auntie Yee softened. "Well, I don't want it to happen again! As long as you're safe now, I'm thankful. Come now, you'd better get out of those wet clothes, then come down and have something to eat. I'll have Moi get you a bowl of hot soup."

Auntie Yee hurried toward the kitchen, waving her arms to urge the rest of them to get along with their business. "Go, go!" she said to Mei-li.

Mei-li moved toward the stairs, glancing in Pei's direction. There was a sly smile on her face that confused Pei about where she'd really been.

*   *   *

In the darkness of the room Pei could only see the shadow of Mei-li's white nightgown moving up and down as she quietly got into the bed next to Pei's. "Where were you?" Pei whispered.

"I was with Hong tonight," Mei-li said ecstatically, turning towards Pei.

"You saw him?" Pei asked.

"Yes, we met each other on the street close to his house. He knew me immediately."

"Are you crazy!"

"He has the most beautiful hands, the hands of a scholar."

"How would you know?"

"I saw them when we were together."

"How could you be together? Where did you go?" Pei questioned, suspicious of Mei-li.

"To a room that belonged to a friend of his."

"I think you've been standing in the rain too long," Pei said skeptically. "That is, if you're telling me the truth!"

"Why wouldn't I tell you the truth? I was safe with Hong tonight, and now I must marry him." Mei-li then whispered: "It's gone too far."

"What are you saying?"

Mei-li hesitated, and then, giggling, said, "Some things are fated to be."

Pei paused and watched her friend apprehensively. She wanted to get up and shake Mei-li awake from her dreams, but Mei-li's strange behavior had taken on a new dimension, and in the hazy darkness, something cold and frightening moved through Pei. In the next moment the feeling was gone, but Pei was shaken.

"Please be careful," Pei said.

Mei-li giggled. "Why are you so serious? I've never been happier."

Pei stared hard at her talkative friend, then fell back into a comfortable position for sleep. She had so many questions to ask Mei-li, but it was late, and they would have to wait until another time.

"I'll leave you to your dreams, then," Pei whispered wearily. "Good night."

The lulling sound of the rain continued, now and then accented by small violent bursts scattered against the window.

"Do you think the rain will last much longer?" Mei-li suddenly asked.

"No, I don't think so."

"That would be so nice," Mei-li said, turning back into her own bed.

Auntie Yee

Every morning since the rain had begun, Auntie Yee came downstairs and opened the front door to see if the sky had shed its final tears. It became a habit she'd grown used to, like the dull mumblings of Moi to herself.

Only, on this particular morning Auntie Yee still felt unsettled. Mei-li's lost hours last night filled her with a dull dread. What if Mei-li had been hurt somewhere? What would she tell Mei-li's parents if she were never to be found? These thoughts of what could have happened to Mei-li left her tossing and turning all night. But as Auntie Yee pulled open the door she was greeted by an unexpected surprise. The rain had ended, leaving a strange quiet along with the flooded earth, which smelled of rotting plums.

"The rain has stopped!" Auntie Yee said, entering the kitchen.

Moi glanced up at Auntie Yee from her cooking, barely acknowledging her presence. "Early this morning," Moi finally said, stirring her pot of steaming jook.

"I thank Kuan Yin," Auntie Yee said happily. "Now we can get back to our lives!"

Very carefully Auntie Yee took the bowls down from the shelf.

"There will be a mess to deal with now," Moi said. "If they think they've seen rats, just wait!"

"The girls don't need to hear that kind of talk!" Auntie Yee said sternly.

"The truth shouldn't frighten anyone," mumbled Moi. She stirred the jook and said nothing more.

As Auntie Yee set the table, she looked up at the first sound of someone coming downstairs, though she knew it was Chen Ling. Even when Chen Ling didn't have to work early at the silk factory, she was the first girl downstairs each morning. She took her usual seat at the table, but this morning she asked Auntie Yee to sit with her.

"Second Mother," Chen Ling said, "I have something of importance to tell you."

Auntie Yee took the seat across from her, wondering what could be weighing so heavily on her daughter's mind. Chen Ling's formality was unusual, even for her. Auntie Yee knew that Ming was recovering nicely from her burns and would be back on her feet in a few days, so it must be something else.

"What is it?" she asked.

Chen Ling cleared her throat and looked Auntie Yee directly in the eyes. "Ming and I have decided to go through the hairdressing ceremony."

For a moment Auntie Yee was speechless, but not out of surprise. She had always known Chen Ling might go through the hairdressing ceremony, which was the final declaration from a young woman that she wouldn't marry, but instead would remain in the sisterhood of silk workers. As with a marriage, an auspicious day was chosen and a banquet was held with family and friends, who gave lucky money to the nonmarrying woman. It wasn't that Chen Ling was too young—she was almost twenty—but the words coming from Chen Ling's mouth sounded too flat. Auntie Yee had expected them to ring out at her with the same intensity as Chen Ling's evening talks to the girls, thrilling her. But instead, Auntie Yee felt as if she wasn't hearing anything she didn't already know.

"I'm very happy to hear this," Auntie Yee said. "I know it's something you've both thought about deeply."

"It is," answered Chen Ling, allowing herself to relax and smile.

It was only then that Auntie Yee's heart filled with a motherly warmth. Chen Ling looked so grown-up sitting across from her, and when Auntie Yee reached over and touched her daughter's hand, Chen Ling didn't move away.

The next day Chen Ling and Ming gathered the girls together in the reading room and announced that they were going through the hairdressing ceremony. There was the buzz of voices and congratulations as Auntie Yee watched the girls gather around her daughter and Ming. And for the first time Auntie Yee realized that Chen Ling would really be leaving the girls' house, and moving to a sisters' house with other women committed to the silk work.

As always, Auntie Yee found solace in keeping her hands busy cleaning. She began to clean the girls' house from top to bottom. With Moi's help, she quickly took down all the heavy boards and opened every window and door to allow fresh air to move freely through the stale house. Pei followed her about, full of questions.

"After Chen Ling and Ming go through the hairdressing ceremony, will they ever be able to marry?" asked Pei, finding Auntie Yee dusting the reading room alone one day.

Auntie Yee laughed and shook her head. "That is the choice

they've made. Actually, the hairdressing ceremony is very similar to a marriage ceremony, only it's a celebration of choice."

"Is that what it was like for you?" asked Pei, lifting objects out of Auntie Yee's way as she dusted.

"It wasn't quite so simple for me, but yes, it's just as important as a marriage ceremony. While a bride is assisted by an elderly woman who has had many sons, the nonmarrying woman is assisted by an elderly celibate woman. Someone such as myself." Auntie Yee laughed.

"What if the woman should change her mind after going through the hairdressing ceremony?" Pei asked.

Auntie Yee stopped dusting and turned in all seriousness towards the tall, curious Pei. "It's a choice that cannot be taken lightly. It must be a way of life that you want more than any other, and to wander from it will bring great shame to your family and anger the gods."

Pei took in every word she said, and nodded slowly.

"Listen to me," Auntie Yee said, laughing, "I sound just like Chen Ling!"

After the Monsoon

After the rains ended, the girls' house came alive with laughter and activity. Chen Ling and Ming's upcoming hairdressing ceremony brought a new excitement to everyone. It felt like the recovery from a long illness. Yung Kee once again survived what might have been a disaster, and Auntie Yee's voice sang victory throughout the house as she continued to clean up the results of the storm.

The second morning after the rains stopped, Pei left the house before the other girls, hoping to see Lin, who had already left for the factory. With the arrival of fair weather, Lin and

Chen Ling were back to their old schedule of working long hours.

Outside, the air was thick and pungent with the water-soaked earth. The sun shone weakly from behind the clouds, but Pei was excited. She wrinkled her nose against the rank, rotting smell and walked happily toward the silk factory.

Everywhere there were signs of cleaning up, as the villagers worked with buckets and pots to rid their homes of mud, and the boat people waited anxiously for the water to recede. Their few precious possessions—bowls, sandals, and scattered clothing— lay along the road, washed up by the flooded river from the boats. Rat carcasses lay bloated along the soggy road. Next would come the slow and arduous task of rebuilding what had been washed away, while the few unfortunate ones who had lost their lives in the flood could be burned or buried.

Yet, even as the remnants of this storm were swept away, Pei began to hear the news of another kind of storm brewing within China, a struggle for power that blew like a whirlwind into every corner of the country. With the death of Sun Yat-sen, China looked towards a new leader named Chiang Kai-shek. Old and young alike swept and shoveled, while in teahouses and on the streets they argued their positions on their country's fate.

"It's time for change in China!" some would say.

Others would spit and shake their heads. "What do you know? China doesn't need the likes of you causing trouble! We have the Japanese devils for that!"

Pei walked the streets and listened to the voices, her happiness dampened by what she heard. China was so large and forbidding. The struggle for power all felt so remote from Yung Kee and her life at the girls' house. She looked up to the sky and let her mind clear of all the disheartening thoughts. Soon she would be safely back with Lin at the silk factory. Ming was well enough to return to work, and everything would be as it had been before the rains.

*   *   *

A few evenings later, the girls' house received an unexpected visit from Mei-li's parents. Their monthly visits usually took place on every first Thursday, so their unannounced arrival caught everyone by surprise.

"I'm sorry," said Mei-li's father, a heavyset, balding man. "We have come to see Mei-li about a matter of great importance."

Mei-li's mother followed mutely behind and nodded solemnly toward Auntie Yee.

"Of course, of course. We are honored by your visit, Chun Sen San and Chun Tai," said Auntie Yee, leading them into the reading room. "I'll send someone to get Mei-li."

Pei went upstairs to find her. Mei-li remained expressionless upon hearing that her parents were downstairs waiting. She said nothing, simply tossed aside the book she was reading and went down to them.

Downstairs, Auntie Yee moved nervously around the kitchen, preparing tea for her unexpected guests, while Moi poured dried plums and nuts into small bowls.

"Have they no manners to come so late?" complained Moi.

But before anything else could be said, they heard louder and louder voices coming from the reading room.

"I will not!" screamed Mei-li.

"Please, Mei-li, calm down," her father begged.

The rest, inaudible, was followed by Mei-li's crying and the muffled voices of her parents trying to calm her.

When the tea was ready, Auntie Yee hesitated, then knocked firmly on the double doors and waited for them to open. When they did, Mei-li's father appeared apologetic and readily accepted her presence. From the small crack left open between the doors, Pei could see Mei-li in Auntie Yee's arms, crying. Every so often Mei-li would look up at her parents to say between her tears, "I will not marry him . . . I will not!"

Mei-li's crying persisted, but to no avail, for when her father finally flung open the double doors, his angry voice rang throughout the house. "I am your father and you will do what I say!" He stormed out of the house with Mei-li's mother following quickly behind.

Mei-li remained in the reading room with Auntie Yee. Pei knew only too well what had taken place. Another girl at their house had been visited by her parents with the news that a husband had been chosen for her. A week later, the girl had left, accepting her fate without argument. Pei knew this wasn't the first time Auntie Yee had been left to comfort a girl whose parents wanted her to enter into a loveless marriage. As with the others, Auntie Yee could only stand helplessly by. Every year it was the same story, as she watched certain families return, blind to the fact that their daughters were no longer the young, obedient children who had been left at the girls' house. The silk work provided them not only with money, but with the independence of working and living on their own. And for many girls, there could be no turning back.

Pei waited in the darkness for Mei-li to come to bed. Long after her parents had left, Mei-li remained in the comforting arms of Auntie Yee, not to emerge even when the lights were put out. At last the door to their room opened and the single figure of Mei-li quietly made her way to the bed next to Pei. Across the long room a girl coughed and another moaned in her sleep.

Pei watched as Mei-li quickly undressed and slipped into her cotton gown, then whispered, "Are you all right?"

"Yes."

"Your father was very angry when he left."

"Not as angry as I was."

"Will you marry, as your father wishes you to?"

Mei-li didn't answer right away, but sat silently down on Pei's bed.

"Only if my father wishes me to marry Hong."

"Have you told them of Hong?"

"No, I've only told them I won't marry the one they've chosen for me."

"Who have they chosen?"

"The son of a family they know."

Pei leaned closer to Mei-li. "But what do you really know about Hong?"

"I know all I need to know, Hong is the only one I will ever marry!"

"What are you going to do, then?"

Mei-li paused, her round face half hidden in the darkness. She rose slowly and moved entirely into the shadows, then whispered: "I don't know yet."

Chapter Six

1926

Pei

When they reached the main road, Pei wished that she and Lin had walked in another direction, away from all the noise and the suffocating crowds. Her mouth felt dry and sour. It was a week before Chen Ling's and Ming's hairdressing ceremony, and the girls had been given a rare day off from the factory while waiting for a new shipment of cocoons. Pei felt she'd seen so little of Lin in the past year that it was as if they had just awakened from a long sleep, still awkward and shy. After Ming's accident, Lin had been given all Chen Ling's duties. Lin pleaded with the owner, Chung, for help, but he refused to bring in another girl, fearing it would cut into his profits. Then the rains came with a vengeance, leaving everything and everyone in three feet of water. When they finally dried out, Lin had withstood the storm.

"How could you stand it?" Pei asked, as they recounted the year. She stepped quickly to the side, avoiding an oncoming cart stacked high with bamboo cages filled with ducks and chickens.

Lin simply laughed, as if it were someone else's life they were talking about. Work never seem to frighten her, and she never complained, though in the past year she'd grown thin and haggard.

In the white light of late winter, Lin looked frail. She said very little, and her hands shook slightly when she brought them out in front of her. Her eyes met Pei's for a moment, then looked away, anxious. For months Lin had been receiving letters from her mother in Canton. Lin hadn't said anything to Pei about them. She simply read the letters, then tucked them away as if they had never existed. Pei hoped Lin might finally tell her about the letters without her asking.

What Pei really felt ashamed of was how little she knew about Lin. Lin had taken care of her for the past seven years, but Pei knew very little about Lin's childhood, or her mother and two brothers, who lived in Canton. Lin held tightly onto her family secrets, and for once, Pei's questions made no difference. At fifteen, Pei knew little more about Lin's family than she had at eight.

Suddenly, Pei was distracted from her thoughts by a loud crashing noise coming from a nearby fish shop, followed by the high shrieking of a woman's voice. "Devils! I want you out of here!" The front door flew open and a woman chased out several stray cats that had crept into her shop. Pei and Lin stopped to watch, laughing.

When everything was calm again, they walked slowly away. They turned down a dusty street, quieter and less crowded. Pei decided it was time to satisfy her curiosity. "Were you thinking about the letters from your mother?" she asked.

Lin paused, then looked up at her with a smile. "Yes," she answered.

"Why haven't you ever told me anything about your family?"

"There was never anything to tell."

Pei waited for Lin to continue, feeling a cool wind send a chill through her. Lin appeared as calm as usual, but as Pei looked closer she could see Lin's tightly pursed lips and the dark, dry eyes, which carried a hint of sadness.

"Is anything wrong?"

Lin sighed and then relented, in one breath: "My mother has found my brother a suitable wife to marry."

"What's wrong with that?"

"Now she wants me to leave the girls' house and return home to marry."

"What!" Pei said, stunned.

"My mother's health has returned." Lin swallowed. "And she has found the right girl for a favorable marriage to my brother Ho Chee. The marriage will also help to advance my brother's career, so that he can carry on the good name of my father. But since I'm the eldest, something must be done about my own unmarried position, in order to clear the way for him." Lin paused for a moment, as if something were stuck in her throat. "My mother has even suggested I leave the silk factory and return home as soon as I can."

"You can't," Pei whispered. She wished they had stayed on the main road, where the crowds might distract her. The thought of Lin's leaving felt too large and dark for her to understand.

Lin smiled wearily. "Don't worry, I've known too many girls whose families have made them marry against their will. I won't be trapped in a loveless marriage with a total stranger. I can't allow that to be my fate."

"What are you going to do?" Pei asked.

"I've been at the girls' house for almost ten years now, and I'm past the age of marrying well. Who would want to marry a woman of twenty-one? I'm too old for a match of any worth." Then, as an afterthought, Lin said, "There's always the hairdressing ceremony."

"But you could still have any husband you choose. You're so beautiful! The hairdressing ceremony would mean you could never marry!" Pei's throat felt dry as she looked away to avoid Lin's eyes. For the first time, Pei saw Lin struggling with a decision that would affect both their lives. She didn't want Lin to see how frightened she was.

"It makes no difference to me now. I don't think it ever did, not really. Marriage was always what my mother wanted for me. My only concern has been to help my mother and brothers. After my father died, I just wanted to protect them from anything else that could harm them. The silk work provided me with a quick means to do that."

Lin stopped beside a wooden sign whose faded red characters listed herbal medicines; she was quiet, as if remembering something painful. "Did you know," she finally said, "that some families keep a daughter aside just for the silk work?"

Pei nodded her head. Over the years Pei had wondered if she herself was one of these "silk daughters," or if her parents really had no other choice but to give her away. She always hoped it would be the latter.

"It was never my mother's original intention for me," Lin continued.

"I know," Pei said. She was certain of this, and said it so softly it was almost lost in the wind.

Lin looked at her curiously. "And what do you suppose my fate was to be?"

At first Pei couldn't say anything. From the moment she laid eyes on Lin, she had known Lin was not like the others. Besides having a smooth, even beauty, Lin carried herself differently, with quiet, graceful movements. She didn't have the clumsy country ways of the others. Lin's dark eyes seemed to have seen more of the world than the rest of the girls had.

"I think you could have presided over a very great house, with a husband and children who adored you," Pei finally answered.

Lin laughed. "You have predicted what was my mother's fate, or at least part of her fate."

"Did she have a very great house?"

"Yes," Lin answered thoughtfully. "My father was a very high official in Canton, and we lived in a good district near the

European settlement. My parents were always entertaining, especially my mother, who was so beautiful I . . . "

Lin lifted her hand to touch her own face.

"Are you all right?"

"I don't know what I'm going to do now," Lin suddenly said, defeated.

"You won't leave, will you? You know I'll do anything to help you stay," Pei said, with renewed vigor. Her voice sounded strangely foreign to her.

"I know." Lin paused, looking away. "At first, being here was only for my mother and my brothers, and there was a simplicity to it. Even with all the loneliness, I was helping them. But now, there's you. What will become of you?"

Pei remained quiet, trying to think of some rich scheme that would return everything to the way it had been. Pei knew that "clearing the way" meant Lin must either enter a loveless marriage, or go through the hairdressing ceremony and move from the girls' house to a sisters' house. Either way, Pei would lose her. Over the years, Lin remained her closest friend. Pei had come to love her entirely, as a sister and teacher. Without Lin, she would be lost. Pei suddenly felt so cold she could barely stand the small ache growing inside of her.

Before Pei could say anything else, Lin turned back to her and suddenly pulled Pei's arm, looking up and smiling at her height. "Come now," Lin said, "let's not waste this wonderful day!"

But as awful as Pei felt, Lin seem to relax as they walked on. Coming toward them was a family returning from the marketplace. The daughter and her two younger brothers each held a bag of fruit. Lin smiled and watched them pass. Her voice was calm when at last she broke her silence and began telling Pei about her life before the girls' house.

* * *

"I have never dreamed of my family, they're much too real for that," Lin slowly began. "I was born the eldest child, and only daughter, of Wong Hung-Hui. Much of my early life was spent taking care of my two younger brothers and learning the household duties that would prepare me for marriage and my future in-laws. We lived in a large brick house in one of the better districts in Canton, with two old servants and three dogs. I knew from early on that we lived a privileged life. My father was a high official in the government, and men dressed in uniforms or Western suits often came to our house. The women who accompanied them had heavily painted faces and wore bright, Western-style clothing. My brothers and I would watch from the top of the stairs as they entered, but always my mother remained the most beautiful woman in the room as she stood beside my father in her red lace cheongsam.

"As a small child, I worshiped my mother. She was the only daughter of a scholarly man who had little wealth, but the intelligence to know that Wong Hung-Hui would make something of himself. Knowing that my mother had the gift of great beauty, her father quickly went to Wong Hung-Hui's family and made the match between my parents. It proved to be a successful pairing, for my mother's beauty would always be an asset to my father's career.

"My father proceeded to prove himself successful as an official in the government and quickly climbed the ranks. Along the way, he made enemies who thought him too brash and idealistic. My father always believed that China, in all her glory, was still a country whose vastness left her far behind the other foreign powers; it was from foreigners that she would learn, and one day stand alone in greatness. And it was this belief that was to cause his death."

Lin paused and inhaled. Pei wanted to say something, but remained silent as they continued on. Even the endless bargaining voices of the crowded marketplace couldn't touch them as they walked by the makeshift stalls of fruits and vegetables. As a child, Pei had loved the market, filled with people and surprises. Now, as they moved through the thick crowd, she felt completely alone.

"I loved my father," Lin continued. "While my mother concerned herself with entertaining my father's important guests, my father would often take me on long walks and buy me small gifts and candy. My mother was always someone to admire from a distance, but our old servants gave us love and care. You must remember, before my father died we were used to the best of everything. It would be nothing for us to have six dishes, including duck, pork, and fish, grace our table every evening, just for us children.

"By my tenth birthday, I had everything a young girl could ever dream of having. Not only did I learn all that I might need to become a dutiful wife, as my mother wanted, but my father allowed me to be educated with my brothers by a private tutor who came daily to our house. I couldn't have wished for a better life.

"But my childhood ended less than a year later, when my father was murdered. He had long been a thorn in the sides of the traditionalists, who believed he was simply kowtowing to the Western powers. One quiet afternoon on his way home from his office, someone stabbed my father again and again, not more than twenty feet from our house. No one admitted to seeing anything."

Lin stopped as if there were no more words, and looked up at Pei with tears in her eyes. Pei felt caught, trapped in Lin's unleashed words, but even as she tried to think of something to say, Pei knew no words could ease Lin's pain. So she kept silent as Lin's thin voice strained to continue.

"Everyone along his path knew my father, or had grown used to the sight of him, since he'd chosen to dress always in a Western suit, rather than a long silk gown. Many people disapproved of this, but my father felt he would have to be flexible with the foreign powers in order to benefit the Chinese people. It was our gardener, on his way home, who found my father, but by the time he was brought back to our house, my father had bled to death.

"My brothers and I were forbidden to see his body until the day of his burial. But I did see him when they first brought him in. His eyes were half-open, so I could see there was still some life left. Then the gardener put his head down close to my father's heart, and rose slowly, shaking his head from side to side. With his thick, callused fingers, stained with my father's blood, the gardener closed his eyes and let him go. Just like that, they said my father was dead, and they wouldn't even let me feel the last bit of warmth in him."

"I'm sorry," Pei said softly, remembering her own silent father, whom she could never please. Lin grew paler and didn't seem to hear her words.

Lin swallowed hard. "My mother, who was by then mad with grief, stayed in the room with my father. She washed and scented his body, dressed him in his finest silk gown, and wouldn't speak to anyone. It was as if she had lost her voice, simply retreating into herself. Our old servants cared for us children, and at night I lay in bed crying, trying to imagine that nothing had changed, that my father would be sitting in his chair at the table the next morning.

"But nothing was the same after my father was buried. My mother trusted no one, closing both her mind and heart to the outside world. We were forbidden to leave the house unless it was of absolute necessity. My mother grew more and more detached from us, preferring to live with her memories. Most of the time, she stayed behind the closed door of her room, dressed in her silk finery, staring out the window, waiting for my father to return. This continued for almost a year. Along with our two servants, I ran the household from day to day. My father had left some small savings, but not a great deal. There should have been plenty of time to put away money for the later years. We began by cutting every unnecessary expense from the budget. And toward the second half of the year, we were eating rice and vegetables for our main meal.

"I tried to talk to my mother about our situation, but she simply sat gazing out the window. When she did speak, it was of bad omens and of past events that I knew nothing about. So, at the age of eleven, I was forced to adopt all the responsibilities of our household. I had no choice but to let our two servants go. There was no one to turn to. My father's family had not been wealthy, and my mother's family carried no responsibility for her from the day of her marriage. Luckily, our two servants, who had long been part of our family, preferred to stay on without compensation. I don't know what I would have done otherwise. It was one of our servants, Mui, who first spoke of the silk factories.

" 'Yes, Missy,' Mui said. 'Many girls are given to the silk work for the money they can make for their families. I worked in a silk factory for a short time as a young girl, before being bought from my family and brought to Canton to work as a servant.'"

" 'Could I work at one of these factories?' I asked.

" 'Oh, no, Missy, a girl of your family and breeding cannot work among village girls!'

" 'Why not? It seems to me that we are in the same position as many village families. Even though we have this big house to hide in, our empty stomachs are no different from theirs!' I argued.

"Mui reluctantly agreed. At my request, she sought out more information about these silk factories. Mui had known Auntie Yee when they were girls. She'd heard through other servants that Auntie Yee was now running her own girls' house. And it was Auntie Yee whom Mui turned to when I made my final decision to work at a silk factory. It was only to be until my mother felt better. Auntie Yee sympathized and accepted me immediately even though, at twelve, I was already several years older than most who entered a girls' house. I left, knowing that Mui and our other servant would look after my mother and brothers, while the money I made at the silk factory would be sent home monthly.

"The last time I saw my mother . . . I remember the faint scent of lavender as I entered her room. My once-beautiful mother was only a shadow, frail and thin in her silk gown. The curtains had not been drawn back yet, so the room was bathed in semi-darkness as my mother lay on her large bed, her eyes open and staring up at the ornate ceiling.

" 'I have to go away for a little while,' I told her. I was to make the journey to Yung Kee that morning with Mui. I remember bending over and quickly hugging my mother, which felt very strange, since she rarely touched us.

" 'You know your Ba Ba doesn't want you roaming the streets by yourself,' my mother said.

"I remember smiling. 'Don't worry about me. I want you to take care of yourself and get out more. I'll write every month.'

" 'Don't be silly,' my mother said, sitting up. 'Go and tell Mui I'm ready for my tea now.'

" 'Yes, Ma Ma.' I rose from the bed and pulled the heavy drapes open. I remember how the sunlight filled the room as my mother lifted her hand to shade her eyes."

Lin stopped and looked up wearily at Pei.

"Did they ever find your father's murderer?" Pei asked.

Lin shook her head slowly.

"Would you like to stop and sit for a while?" Pei realized they had walked all the way to the river. Its stale smell surrounded them.

"Can we keep walking?" Lin asked.

"Yes, of course."

They moved on side by side in silence. Pei was filled with so many questions, but thought better of them and simply said, "It must have been awful for you."

"I missed my family terribly," Lin suddenly continued. "But I learned to keep the loneliness to myself. I thought nightly of my past life with my parents and brothers. The girls' house was clean and comfortable. Auntie Yee was pleasant and the money and freedom that came with the silk work were like nothing I had ever imagined. The most difficult part was having no one to talk to. Most of the girls were nice enough, but many came from poor farming families with little or no education. In the beginning, many shunned me, or made rude comments behind my back because I didn't mix with them. 'Doesn't she have a tongue?' they said, or 'Who does she think she is? Her work is no better than ours!' Only Chen Ling approached me with kindness, but her stubborn beliefs and abrupt ways have always kept me at a distance. Through those early years I learned to blend in, but there was always something missing, until the evening Auntie Yee asked me to go upstairs and bring you down. How unlike the others you were, so full of pride and curiosity."

Pei stopped walking and allowed Lin's words to sink in. After so many years of keeping everything inside, Pei knew, Lin's words now flowed freely for the first time. The urgency of Lin's past had returned like an open wound, the ghost of her father filling her. And for the first time, Pei felt really needed. It was like a gift in her life to realize she could be of some importance to Lin, if only to listen.

"Go on," Pei said.

Women Who Dress Their Own Hair

The day chosen for Chen Ling's and Ming's hairdressing ceremony dawned wet and humid. All day the girls' house was abuzz with excitement as Auntie Yee and Moi ran around making last-minute preparations for the banquet. They gave the same care and concentration to the hairdressing ceremony as they would have to a marriage ceremony. Betrothal to the sisterhood was just as important as that to a man, and both were binding on the young woman for the rest of her life.

Chen Ling knew this particular hairdressing ceremony would be extra-special for Auntie Yee, since this time it was she who had chosen her second mother's path. Chen Ling smiled to herself, knowing Auntie Yee was across the hall putting on the new white silk tunic made for the occasion. When she was dressed, Auntie Yee would come to assist them.

The heavy aroma of flowers and incense that filled Ming's and Chen Ling's room was almost overwhelming. The windows and curtains were open to let in the weak daylight. Chen Ling and Ming sat patiently in front of a large mirror, waiting for Auntie Yee's assistance. Their dark hair hung unbraided in small waves down their backs. Since early morning they had changed into the long black silk skirts worn during the ceremony. For weeks they'd talked and bargained with shopkeepers and the restaurant in preparation for the ceremony and banquet. Now, neither of them said a word.

Chen Ling turned and looked anxiously toward the door. She had been waiting months for this day to arrive. Since the first day she had come to Auntie Yee at the girls' house and had the dark strands of her hair cut evenly across her forehead, Chen Ling had felt as if she had never belonged anywhere else. At the girls' house, Chen Ling found strength and courage from the stories of Kuan Yin in the precious volume. From them, she developed her own voice and found her rightful place. She adapted to the silk work immediately, as if it were second nature, and was now just moments away from the final step toward dedicating her life to the sisterhood. Some girls went through the hairdressing ceremony by themselves, while others went in small groups. Chen Ling thought about Ming beside her, and was filled with joy.

Auntie Yee knocked once and entered, bringing with her a clean, cool smell, which would soon disappear in the thick air of the room. She looked younger in her white silk tunic. Auntie Yee circled the room once, then smiled at them nervously. "It is a good day," she said.

Ming nodded.

"Were you this nervous at your hairdressing ceremony?" Chen Ling asked. It was the first question she had ever asked about Auntie Yee's life before the girls' house. Until now, Chen Ling had never found the time to ask. She was too busy learning the life of the sisterhood.

Auntie Yee moved closer to Chen Ling. "Even more so, but mine was not half as grand as yours will be." Without a pause, she said reassuringly, "I've never regretted my choice."

"Neither will I."

Auntie Yee stood behind Chen Ling and looked at her daughter in the mirror. Chen Ling caught her eyes for just a moment before Auntie Yee looked away. Auntie Yee leaned over and lit another stick of incense before straightening and rubbing her hands together. "Are you ready?" she asked Chen Ling.

"Yes, Second Mother."

Auntie Yee laughed nervously. Chen Ling watched as she picked up the strong wooden brush lying on the table in front of them and ran the stiff bristles quickly across the palm of her hand. Auntie Yee took a step back, and Chen Ling felt the brush slide smoothly through her hair. With each stroke Auntie Yee combed the straight bangs of Chen Ling's hair, smoothing it back with a lacquer made from wood shavings, and chanting the ritual words stressing felicity, prosperity, longevity, and purity of body and soul. Then, with careful, experienced hands, Auntie Yee divided Chen Ling's hair into three parts and braided it tightly. Chen Ling heard Auntie Yee inhale deeply as she lifted the thick, glossy braid and coiled it into a chignon atop Chen Ling's head, signifying her marriage to the sisterhood. Chen Ling looked at herself in the mirror and felt a warmth move through her body. She looked different with her hair coiled up: older, yet more serene. Auntie Yee laid her hand gently on Chen Ling's shoulder and smiled proudly. Then, without saying a word, she stepped behind Ming to repeat the ceremony.

When the first part of the hairdressing ceremony was complete, Chen Ling and Ming rose and kowtowed in respect and gratitude toward Auntie Yee. Then it was Auntie Yee's turn to sit as they poured tea for her. She sipped the hot tea slowly as they stood and watched. In return, Auntie Yee gave each of them a red envelope of lucky money to begin their new lives. Chen Ling and Ming again bowed their heads in reverence and thanked Auntie Yee profusely. Afterward, they all went downstairs to the reading room to pour tea and burn incense before Kuan Yin and worship their ancestors. Later that evening, Chen Ling and Ming would celebrate their good fortune at a banquet with family and friends.

The banquet was to be held at a restaurant close by the girls' house. As the time approached to leave, Pei began to worry about Lin's absence. Lin had been gone since early morning without telling Pei where she was going, only leaving a short note saying she would return in time for the banquet. But as evening fell, Pei began to think something was terribly wrong. Lin was rarely gone for so long without telling her. Pei tried hard to think of where Lin might have gone, but these fearful thoughts were interrupted when another girl approached her.

"Pei, you must talk some sense into Mei-li. She refuses to go to the banquet."

"What's wrong?"

"Who knows? She has been acting strangely ever since that night with her parents."

"Where is she?"

"Upstairs."

Pei found Mei-li staring out the window of their room. She had slowly withdrawn from everyone since the evening her parents came to the house.

"Auntie Yee expects us to leave now for the banquet," Pei said gently.

"I have something else I have to do," Mei-li said.

Pei touched her arm lightly. "I'm sure it can wait until tomorrow."

"No, it can't wait until tomorrow," mimicked Mei-li.

Pei had never seen Mei-li like this before, and something inside told her to approach the situation cautiously. She knew Mei-li had been terribly upset by her parents' visit and their desire for her to marry.

"But this evening is very important to Auntie Yee," Pei finally said. "She has planned this banquet with a great deal of care."

"It doesn't matter," Mei-li said, her voice hard and flat.

"It does matter!"

Mei-li suddenly turned around and with an expression full of hate said, "I'll go where I want to go! Nobody can make me do what I don't want to!" Then Mei-li lifted her hand upward as if to strike Pei, but instead swung at the air.

Pei stepped back, almost falling. She thought of what Lin might do in this situation, and after a moment said calmly, "Chen Ling and Ming will be very hurt if you don't go to their banquet."

Mei-li stared wide-eyed at Pei, taking quick breaths, her round face flushed.

"It will be all right," Pei said. She reached out and gently took hold of Mei-li, her arms encircling Mei-li's stiff body until she felt her friend's weight give in to her.

In Pei's embrace, Mei-li calmed, her face softening when she finally pulled away from Pei. Then, in a strangely quiet manner,

Mei-li said, "Yes, you're right. We better go now before they wonder where we are."

Pei stood puzzled and apprehensive a moment longer. When Mei-li turned back toward Pei, she smiled, showing no hint of anger or unhappiness.

The restaurant was alive with voices and the clatter of dishes, which echoed through the steamy room. For the banquet, Auntie Yee had taken the entire restaurant, which was festively decorated with the red and gold symbols of double happiness. Extra tables were squeezed into the crowded room to accommodate all the guests. Chen Ling's father, now a vague memory in Auntie Yee's life, declined to come from his small village, though he sent along a red package of lucky money and his blessings. Ming's parents, who were poor farmers, traveled for two days by oxcart to see their daughter go through the hairdressing ceremony. They sat proudly at a front table with her seven brothers and sisters.

Chen Ling and Ming sat at the head table with Auntie Yee and Moi. To Pei's surprise, Lin had returned and was also sitting in their midst, speaking easily with some of the older girls. Immediately, Pei felt relief—and anger at seeing Lin there enjoying herself, while she had been left to worry. But she swallowed hard and decided to let nothing more mar the evening.

Chen Ling and Ming no longer resembled all the other girls with long thick braids. They appeared older without bangs and with their hair coiled meticulously atop their heads. Each was dressed in a long black silk skirt and white shirt and smiled happily as Auntie Yee stood and began the celebration with a small speech for them.

"Honored guests, I thank you for coming to celebrate this special day with Chen Ling and Ming. We at the girls' house will miss them, only gratified by the knowledge that they are continuing their lives in the sisterhood. Now I would like to drink a toast to Chen Ling and Ming!"

Auntie Yee raised her cup of tea, followed by every guest in the room.

The evening moved slowly on, one course after another, until the ninth course, of steamed fish bathed in oil and green onions, was served. Mei-li sat beside Pei as if nothing had ever happened, and ate heartily as each dish was placed on the table. More than once Pei tried to capture Lin's attention, but it was as if Lin deliberately avoided meeting her gaze.

When at last the banquet was over, the girls rose from their tables in a wave of black and white. Pei moved quickly forward, hoping to reach Lin before she slipped away again. But as Auntie Yee, Chen Ling, and Ming rose to receive the girls filing through with their congratulations, Lin remained seated.

"Where were you today?" asked Pei, taking the chair next to her.

"I went to see my mother," Lin answered.

"In Canton?"

"No, she was here in Yung Kee with my brother."

"Why didn't you tell me?"

"I didn't want to upset you."

"What did she come here for?" Pei asked.

"She wanted me to go back to Canton with her."

Pei sat quiet and tentative. "What did you say?" she finally asked.

"I told her that I didn't want to return to Canton, and that I've chosen not to marry."

Pei sat upright in her chair. "What did she say?"

"She wasn't very happy about it, but I have to clear the way for my brother, one way or the other."

Pei looked out toward the deserted tables and the picked-over remains of the banquet they had just feasted on.

"Does this mean you'll go through the hairdressing ceremony?"

"Yes," Lin quickly answered. "Don't you see, it's the only way I'll still be able to see you. If I were to return home to Canton and my family, we might never see each other again."

"And what about me?" Pei asked softly.

Lin said nothing.

They both knew that going through the hairdressing ceremony meant Lin would move from the girls' house. After that, it might be days before they saw one another, except at the silk factory.

Without looking at her, Lin took hold of Pei's hand and gave it a slight squeeze.

Chapter Seven

Auntie Yee

After their hairdressing ceremony, Chen Ling and Ming moved to a sisters' house near Auntie Yee. They lived among other young women who chose to do the silk work. In the beginning, Auntie Yee tried hard not to notice the emptiness, but the silence was deafening, so she washed and scrubbed everything in the girls' house after Chen Ling and Ming left.

"Why are you washing those windows again?" Moi taunted.

"Because they're dirty."

"No dirtier than yesterday!" Moi laughed, giving nothing of her own feelings away. She turned back toward the kitchen and let the door fall heavily behind her.

Auntie Yee knew the girls also missed Chen Ling. Her voice no longer rang through the house, reading and speaking to them each evening about the sisterhood and the struggles within China. At night the girls tried to keep themselves busy around the house. Lin and Pei read, while others tried to paint or sew. The emptiness seem magnified after Chen Ling and Ming returned for their first visit; voices filling the rooms.

"What is it like at the sisters' house?" the girls repeatedly asked.

"There are women from all over the southern province. They have come to Yung Kee to do the silk work for one reason or another. Some have gone through the hairdressing ceremony, while others are there only temporarily to work while their husbands find work overseas," Chen Ling answered enthusiastically. "We have a small room to ourselves, but it's not as nice as here," she added, looking in Auntie Yee's direction.

"We do all our own cleaning and make most of our own meals," Ming added shyly. "Each person must be responsible for herself; we don't have Auntie Yee or Moi to look after us."

Then Chen Ling laughed deeply. "That's why we've returned to visit at evening meal!"

The girls laughed and whispered to one another in excitement.

Of all the girls, it was Pei whose voice rang out with question after question. Pei seem to cling to each answer as if her life depended on it.

"Do you have many new friends?" she asked. "Are you happy there?"

"Yes, we're very happy at the sisters' house," Chen Ling and Ming managed to answer before another question came hungrily their way.

Chen Ling had returned often since her hairdressing ceremony. And each time, Auntie Yee noticed a change in her daughter. There was an ease about her that hadn't been there before. Auntie Yee felt both proud and envious of her, because Chen Ling had found her way so easily in life. Soon Auntie Yee's other girls would be forced to make a decision concerning the direction of their lives. She knew that for some it wouldn't be an easy one. Chen Ling and Ming were blessed by Kuan Yin in having had their own choice. Auntie Yee had never been that fortunate and, she feared, neither would many others.

When Pei and Lin came to tell Auntie Yee of Lin's decision to go through the hairdressing ceremony, Auntie Yee was not the least bit surprised. Unlike Chen Ling, who was born to the silk work, Lin had grown into it, with ease. But Auntie Yee's first thought had to do with Pei. She turned toward her and immediately knew it was Lin's absence Pei was grieving for. Her face was expressionless, her pale, thin lips pressed together so tightly they almost disappeared.

Auntie Yee called for Moi to bring them some tea. As she sat across from Pei and Lin, it was almost as if she could feel Pei's grief move through her. But how could they know? To them she was Auntie Yee, too old and fat to understand what went on in their young bodies and quick minds. How could they know that the same grief had once played in her own life? It stung her memory even now, though it seemed a lifetime ago.

Auntie Yee had told only Moi her story, back in the early days when she wasn't sure the girls' house would succeed. Auntie Yee had been sick with worry about how to support her husband and his family. And it somehow made her feel better to remember a loss which made everything else seem smaller and dimmer. Moi had listened uncomfortably, then excused herself, going out to draw water from the well.

Yee was nine when she was given to the silk work. She was taken from the warmth of her childhood bed and thrown into the stark reality of another world. It wasn't as if one life was much better than the other, but in her old life she did have her eldest brother, Chan. He was her half-brother, born to her father and his number one wife. Yee was his third daughter by his second concubine, and quite useless to anyone. Only Chan took notice of her; in return she adored everything about him.

Chan was nine years older than Yee, with a thick, muscular body. He moved with a graceful ease, though you wouldn't think it simply by looking at his bulk. Often Yee would watch for him coming up from the fields, his cropped hair shining with sweat, as he squinted against the sun in her direction.

"Who are you looking for?" he would yell up from the incline.

"You!" she would yell back, running down to meet him. Yee would jump up into his arms, her cheek resting against his sweaty neck and shoulders. There was something mesmerizing about this daily ritual. She never forgot the strong smell of his maleness, along with the swift, gentle way in which Chan would lift her into his arms.

At night, they would sit on the front porch and tell stories, or listen to the night sounds, the constant music of the crickets filling up the darkness. It was their own private world they existed in, with the dim lights of reality behind them, and the unknown shadows of their future before them. In all her life, Yee would never again feel the same happiness as in those clear unhampered dreams of a child.

Days and nights would pass in this way, and Yee realized her childhood was made up of these small moments with Chan. The others must have seen that, too, only to disapprove, especially their father, who thought his oldest son was being too distracted by Yee and their foolish dreams. After their father spoke to him, Chan began taking a different path up from the fields and would no longer pick Yee up when she greeted him. Instead, he would rub his arm as if it were sore and say, "You're too big for that now."

After he said that, nothing was the same between them. Chan seemed to purposely stay away from her, though once in a while Yee caught him watching her with a familiar tenderness in his eyes. Then one night, when she could no longer stand it, Yee stole out of the house to the small storage shed where Chan slept.

"Who is it?" Chan's voice shot out from the dark.

She let the creaking wooden door close all the way before she answered, "It's me."

"Yee?"

"Yes."

"Is there anything wrong?" He fumbled in the dark to light the oil lamp. "Are you all right?"

"Why do you hate me?" Yee had asked.

Then her tears came. Yee had not meant to cry, but just being so close to Chan made her miss him more.

"I don't," she heard Chan whisper. Almost simultaneously, he reached out and took Yee in his arms, and she fell against him, crying in a low moan. Chan's quick kisses on her head and against her forehead began to soothe her, until her crying stopped. She lay in his arms for what seemed a very long time, neither of them saying a word. Then Yee fell asleep, only to be awakened some time later by Chan, still holding her in the same position.

"You must go back in now," he whispered.

"I want to stay with you," she said, clinging tighter.

Chan shook his head and slowly pushed her away, his eyes avoiding hers. Auntie Yee's only experience of love as a child was because of Chan, and it seemed too cruel to have it taken away. At first she fought him, pushing her young body against his, but she was no match for his strength. She wanted to cry again but held back the tears until they burned inside of her.

Auntie Yee didn't know then that she would never see Chan again. The next morning he was gone, and the following day she was sent away to work in a silk factory. The grief she felt was hard and numbing. Sometimes, Auntie Yee still thought of Chan, and like a ghost he returned to her, young and strong. The memory still warmed her. Occasionally, Auntie Yee convinced herself it was a luxury to remember Chan in that way, when life was young and much more generous.

Auntie Yee awoke from her thoughts and urged Pei to drink some tea. Pei tried to smile, clutching the teacup in her hand. Auntie Yee watched the two young women sitting across from her. They were each beautiful in their own way. Lin had always been a classic beauty with flawless features, and Pei had grown so tall, her Hakka features softening into a quietly striking face. Unlike Auntie Yee's, their grief would only be measured in the short distance they would have to live from one another. Auntie Yee smoothed back a fallen strand of hair from her forehead and cleared her throat.

"Let me tell you a story," she began.

Pei

Pei decided she would never marry. She would go through the hairdressing ceremony and move to the sisters' house with Lin. From what she knew of marriage, it only brought unhappiness. Her own parents rarely spoke, and even a marriage as strong as Lin's parents' had come to an unhappy end. But every time Pei tried to tell Lin this, she only smiled sadly and said, "You're too young to know what you're saying."

"I know I want to go with you," Pei pleaded.

They would then argue until Lin ended it by telling her to wait a few more years to make her decision. Pei vowed never to give up.

Little by little, Pei began to feel Lin's absence from the girls' house. Lin went about moving her things so quietly, it was days before Pei realized that small items belonging to Lin had disappeared from their usual places. Pei first noticed the polished silver mirror missing. Since her first day at the girls' house, Pei had felt an attachment to the mirror. She had looked into it and caught the first glimpse of her new life. When Pei ran upstairs to see if Lin's set of combs was still beside her bed, she felt both relieved and annoyed to see that they were. It was as if Lin were deliberately keeping secrets from her.

Pei sometimes wished everything would go faster, only to be terrified when it did. Each time Pei found something of Lin's missing, she felt as if she were losing a little bit more of her friend. Pei began to collect her own objects in their places: a small enamel bowl filled with colorful pins; a silk cushion the color of the sky; and a white porcelain bird which could never fly away. No one knew how much better this made her feel.

While Pei worried about Lin's leaving, she was also entertained by a host of strangers who suddenly found their way to the girls' house. They seem to come from everywhere, descending upon the house like flies. Some said it was because of the struggles up north. More and more hungry people arrived in Yung Kee. Moi got rid of the unwanted, screaming at the beggars who somehow came in from the main street. "Get away from here, you stink more than a dead dog!" she would scream at them as they lingered by the back door, their foul stench filling up the kitchen. But almost always, Moi then stepped out and called them back, sending them away with a bit of hard rice and vegetables.

Auntie Yee laughed and said, "Moi will never forget where she came from!"

The vendors also came, one after another, old women with herbs that could cure any ailment, from the physical to the emotional. They carried everything in glass jars, and measured the dark twigs and dried leaves into white pieces of paper folded neatly into perfect squares. The old women were usually followed by ancient-looking men carrying heavy basketloads of fruits or vegetables. The baskets were balanced evenly upon bamboo poles that fit securely along the men's backs and shoulders. Each morning they came singing "Or-anges! Ba-na-nas! Or-anges!" in a chorus of mismatched voices.

Chen Ling and Ming also came over often, and each time Lin

turned to Pei with a smile that said, "You see, we won't really be far apart."

While Pei never saw her family, the girls' house was constantly full of family and friends, but none came as often as Mei-li's parents. Mei-li had become strangely docile and accommodating about her arranged marriage. While her behavior frightened Pei, Mei-li's father happily invited the entire girls' house to the wedding. Her parents had rewarded Mei-li with small gifts, which she left to accumulate unopened in the basket beside her bed.

Pei had begun to worry more and more about Mei-li. "Are you all right?" she asked, one night when they were alone.

"Of course, why shouldn't I be?" Mei-li answered.

"Because you've been so quiet," Pei said hesitantly. "And your parents keep coming with their plans for your marriage."

There was a long pause. Pei was afraid Mei-li would become upset, but instead she answered calmly. "Everything will be fine in time."

"What do you mean?" Pei asked.

Mei-li refused to tell Pei anything other than she was now happy about the marriage, and Pei didn't dare push. Sometimes, when Pei mentioned Hong's name, Mei-li turned around and glared at her as if he were a stranger. In her heart Pei knew that Mei-li was still keeping secrets. At least twice a week Mei-li slipped away to go for a walk. Pei followed her once, only to be led through a maze of streets and back to the girls' house, as if Mei-li knew she was there. At other times, when Mei-li returned from her walks, there was a glow in her eyes that didn't die for days.

One evening Pei returned to the girls' house late from picking up some tea for Auntie Yee. She was not surprised to hear from Moi that there were visitors in the reading room, but was shocked to learn that the visitors were Lin's mother and brother.

She stood stunned for a moment. Nothing gave them away, neither loud voices nor low murmurs. She felt a knot tighten in her stomach. As a child waiting by her father's empty pond, Pei had learned to bury her anxiety at not seeing any fish. She would close her eyes and imagine the glittering fish moving across the surface of the water, like small flashes of light. She could actually feel their presence. Pei sat on the stairs and waited. She closed her eyes again and tried to see Lin's face behind the closed door, but failed.

The doors finally opened, liberating Pei from the darkness, yet she felt scared. She heard Lin's familiar voice first, though it was Lin's mother who suddenly stepped out into the hall. She was so beautiful Pei wanted to climb back up the stairs out of sight. She was wearing a fancy tight dress, buttoned up the side, with a high collar, and when she turned at just the right angle, parts of the dress sewn with shiny beads caught the light and flickered. Her skin was as white and smooth as Pei's porcelain bird, and her large dark eyes darted back and forth anxiously. It was easy to see from whom Lin had received her gift of beauty.

Then came the next surprise. Lin's brother stepped out into the hall. Pei felt an immediate twinge of disappointment. He was not very tall, nor handsome in comparison with Lin and her mother. He was dressed in dark Western clothing and stood with the same erect bearing as did the white devils Pei had seen passing through Yung Kee. But he did have the same gentle smile as Lin.

When Lin emerged, Pei slowly moved farther up the stairs, so that she was partially hidden, but could still hear what Lin was saying.

"Will you be returning to Canton directly?" Lin asked. She stepped closer to her mother.

"We'll pass the night here and return tomorrow," her mother answered curtly.

"I'm glad; it'll be a much easier trip for you." Then Lin leaned over and let her lips quickly brush her mother's smooth cheek. "I don't want you to get too tired."

Her mother's face softened. "Are you sure you won't change your mind? There's still plenty of time."

"I'm certain of my decision," Lin answered.

Lin moved toward her brother and, with a smile that carried some childhood secret, kissed him on the cheek. Then, as if knowing Pei was there, Lin looked up toward her on the stairs. For a moment Pei was frozen with fear, until Lin broke the spell and motioned for Pei to come down and meet her mother and brother.

"This is Pei," Lin said. "Pei, this is my mother, and my brother, Ho Chee."

Ho Chee nodded his head shyly.

Pei felt something cold and sharp move up her spine as Lin's mother eyed her from top to bottom. Pei was not sure if this was a nod of acceptance or not, but she tried to smile, and whispered a hello that sounded hollow and childlike.

"Pei will be coming to the marriage ceremony with me," Lin continued, "if that's all right with you."

"If that's what you wish," her mother answered coolly. With a sideways glance, she seemed to take note of Pei's presence without actually looking at her.

"Yes, it is."

In Lin's voice there was a slight edge of defiance Pei had never heard before.

"We'd better go, then," her mother said sharply, turning toward her silent son. "There's still a great deal that must be done, and it's getting late."

Ho Chee turned around once to catch Lin's eye, then took his mother's arm possessively. Pei watched mesmerized as Lin's mother slowly walked out the door and down the front steps in her tight, glittering dress. Her perfume lingered even after she was gone, a sweet, flowery smell that was new and quite different from anything Pei had ever smelled before.

Pei's own mother had never smelled so sweet, only of the sweat that came from the long hours toiling in the small, endless world of the mulberry groves. After dark, her mother would slowly make her way back to the house, her figure concealed beneath the coarse white clothing she wore. This was the rank, spare world of Pei's childhood, which now felt so far away.

Pei hoped Lin's mother would turn around once more. She wanted to see her flawless, milky-white skin, which seemed to glow in the dark. Her eyes burned from not blinking, but Lin's mother never turned back. When they closed the gate behind them, it was like blowing out a candle.

Lin took Pei's arm and led her back inside. Moi was filling a bowl of rice for each of them when they entered the dining room. Pei had forgotten all about eating when she learned Lin's family was in the reading room. Now, she was starving. Moi didn't like it when girls came in late for evening meal, and she dragged her bad leg with exaggerated heaviness to make her point. When Lin and Pei thanked her profusely, Moi mumbled, "Quick, quick, eat then, before it gets cold!" and disappeared into the kitchen.

Pei and Lin ate quickly without words. When they finished eating, Pei leaned back and asked, "What ceremony did you tell your mother I would go with you to?"

"My brother's marriage ceremony."

"Oh, no, I can't go!" Pei said, half-rising from her chair.

Lin laughed. "You can and you will. It will give you a chance to see Canton. Besides, I'll need the company."

"I won't know what to do in a big city like Canton," said Pei. The thought provoked more excitement than fear in her.

"You'll do what I do."

"Is that why your mother came here? To talk to you about the marriage?"

"Partly. She also hoped I might have changed my mind about the hairdressing ceremony."

Pei remained silent.

"You have to understand my mother. She believes that a husband will be my savior, and that only through the right marriage can honor and power be restored to our family."

"What did you say to her?"

"That I'm past the age of marrying well, and that no honorable family would want me."

"That's not true!" Pei quickly said.

Lin smiled shyly, and simply answered, "Honor is everything to my mother."

"What about me?" asked Pei. She had wanted to say something else, but the words slipped from her mouth before she could catch them.

"You have time."

"Why can't I go through the hairdressing ceremony with you?" Pei asked. It was a question she had grown tired of asking, and it hung in the air, flat and tasteless.

"You can't," Lin answered wearily.

"Why not?"

"Because you don't really understand," Lin almost whispered. Then she said loud enough to fill the room, "It means choosing not to have a husband and children."

"I don't care about any of that!" Pei said, realizing for the first time that she was angry at Lin for not taking her seriously. "Don't you think I've thought it all through? I've made my decision, I know what I'm saying!"

"You don't know," Lin said tenderly. "You're only just sixteen, the age when most girls are chosen for marriage. There could be a good marriage waiting for you."

"What makes you think I want to marry?"

"How can you be certain you don't?"

Pei looked away from her. Lin stopped, and waited for Pei to turn back and face her. When she didn't, Lin stood and began to gather their bowls.

"I just want you to take some more time to think this over, to be really sure of what you want," Lin finally said.

"I want to go with you."

"That isn't reason enough!" Lin drew a breath. "When and if you decide to go through the hairdressing ceremony, it has to be because that's what you want, and you alone."

"Don't you care about me anymore?" Pei asked.

"Of course I care about you—why do you think I'm telling you to wait? We'll still see each other afterward."

"It won't be the same."

"Don't you understand? The sisterhood isn't for everyone. It's a commitment for life and there's no turning back!" Lin looked down at Pei. "I don't think you're ready to make that kind of decision."

Pei felt hurt, almost crushed, by Lin's words, but she wouldn't give in to them. Instead, Pei remained silent. Only time could show Lin how much she was really committed to the sisterhood. It would have to come slowly, like a wind from far away, but when it did, Lin would know.

The Meeting

Mei-li knew Hong was waiting for her. When her bare feet touched the cold wooden floor she wanted to cry out, but she remained careful not to make a sound to wake Pei, or any of the other girls. The murky light of morning was just entering the room, which meant Mei-li would have to move quickly before the house awoke. In the past month, she had learned to dress and undress in quiet, swift movements. But this morning there wasn't much time. She wouldn't be able to braid her hair, so instead she gathered it up into a waist-long ponytail, tying it together with a red ribbon.

Downstairs a light was already shining from underneath the kitchen door. Mei-li could hear Moi's movements as she began preparing their morning meal, humming quietly to herself. Above, the heavy footsteps and creaks began to announce another day. In a matter of moments Auntie Yee would be coming downstairs, pulling open the wooden shutters that kept the house dark and cool. Auntie Yee had become suspicious, and Mei-li was running out of excuses for why she was leaving the house so early and returning late. The excuses of work and Su-lung wouldn't go any further, and Pei was asking more and more questions. There were so many times Mei-li wanted to tell Pei everything, but the words caught in her throat, and she could hear Hong's words threaten her into silence. Her stomach felt queasy, then calmed. Everything would be taken care of soon enough, when she and Hong were married. The thought soothed her. Mei-li didn't have any answers this morning, but it was just a few more steps before she would be safely out of the house without being caught. "Hong is waiting for me," she told herself over and over again, as a flush of energy moved through her. Mei-li opened the front door and slipped out into the morning light.

Mei-li could find her way to Hong's house even with her eyes closed. They met once or twice a week when time permitted, when he could take time away from his precious studies. Hong was the smartest person she had ever known.

Most of the time they would go to small, squalid rooms that belonged to classmates of his. They were all dark, damp-smelling holes resembling the first room he took her to. But when Mei-li was with Hong nothing else mattered; if he was unable to get a room, then she suffered not seeing him at all. Lately, they hardly spoke, and when they did, she always said something wrong or wanted too much.

But what Mei-li felt with Hong was close to perfection. He had taught her how to make love, what to do to please him. There were times when Mei-li knew she was making him happy. Afterward, he would lie back and stare at the ceiling with a quiet smile on his face. At those moments, Mei-li would know what he was thinking. And then, Hong would turn and stroke Mei-li's hair, or kiss her lightly on the neck. They would be all hands then.

Mei-li lived for those moments, which always seemed to end too soon. Afterwards, Hong would return to his sullen, silent self, barely acknowledging her presence. Mei-li wondered if she had been dreaming to be so happy. Sometimes, she was terrified at the thought of never seeing Hong again. Mei-li knew she would die if that happened. And when she thought of her mother and father, Mei-li got so angry she couldn't catch her breath from the choking sensation. They had absolutely no interest in what she felt. It was as if she had been born an empty box, only to be filled by their desires. Mei-li had decided to let her parents think she was happy with the match, to let them proceed with their marriage plans, though she knew that that marriage would never be her fate. Very soon she would tell them about Hong, even if she had to suffer the worst punishment.

Mei-li leaned heavily against the wall across from Hong's house, waiting. Hong was unusually late. She stayed half-hidden in case Su-lung suddenly emerged and saw her. Hong had told her over and over again that they must be very careful about being seen together.

Lately Mei-li had not been feeling well. A twinge of queasiness moved through her again, just as it had for several mornings. She could no longer deny the child growing inside of her.

Mei-li had heard horror stories of girls who grew big with child and then died in terrible pain at childbirth. This scared her, but she tried not to think about it, knowing a child belonging to Hong couldn't hurt her. Sometimes when she closed her eyes she felt better. Mei-li had heard other girls speak of bitter herbs, sold by old women at the market, that might put an end to this feeling, but thinking about that only made her sicker to her stomach.

It seem an eternity before the battered wooden door finally opened and Hong's tall, familiar figure stepped out into the street. As always, he clutched a book tightly under his arm. The first thing Mei-li wanted to do was call out his name and run up to him, wrapping her arms around his neck, but she knew it was impossible. Mei-li watched as Hong looked cautiously from side to side and walked across the street toward where she was waiting. A feeling of warmth filled her, but it disappeared quickly when Hong hesitated and stopped, then turned around and walked in the opposite direction.

Mei-li leaned against the wall, her heart beating furiously. She couldn't understand what was happening. She had seen Hong only two days before, when they had set this day and time to meet. Could she have been mistaken?

Then, not knowing what possessed her, Mei-li began to follow Hong's quick, long strides. She found herself pursuing him with a vengeance, though she didn't dare call out for him to wait for her. When Hong turned into the marketplace Mei-li could almost reach out and touch his back. But as they moved deeper into the square she began to lose him in the crowd of men and women bargaining at fruit stalls, or eating their morning meals of jook or dumplings in noodles. The greasy, stuffy air made Mei-li feel sicker to her stomach.

Mei-li found Hong waiting in line at one of the stalls. She moved quickly next to him, but when he still didn't notice her, Mei-li tapped him lightly on the arm.

"What are you doing here?" he asked. His stare was stonelike.

"Don't you remember, we planned to meet this morning? I was waiting outside your house. I have to talk to you," Mei-li found the courage to reply.

"Not here."

"It can't wait any longer," she pleaded.

Suddenly Hong grew angry. He grabbed her arm and pulled her away, squeezing so hard it hurt.

"Don't you want to eat?"

"I'm not hungry anymore," Hong answered.

Not until they were well out of the marketplace did Hong stop and look at her. But it wasn't with a look of happiness that he gazed down upon Mei-li. Hong was so angry his dark eyes narrowed, and his face seem to belong to a stranger.

"Why are you following me?" he asked suspiciously.

"I didn't mean to, I just wanted to see you so badly, like we planned."

"About what?"

"About . . ." Mei-li began, but then stopped when she saw Hong coldly looking down at her. She shifted from one foot to the other, and decided then against telling Hong she was with child.

"What?" he angrily asked.

"It doesn't matter."

Hong began to pace back and forth. Each time he crossed a small patch of water on the ground, he barely missed being hit by water dripping from the laundry hanging above.

"Anyway," he said, suddenly calmer, "I've been wanting to talk with you."

"You have?" Mei-li was surprised by the quick change in his behavior. There were very few occasions on which Hong let her know he really did care for her.

"I've been thinking," Hong then said, clearing his throat, "that we should stop seeing each other. It's not because of you, but my exams need my total concentration if I'm going to pass them. I just can't do it any other way."

Hong let out a small sigh of relief when he was done. At first Mei-li couldn't say anything. She could only think of this as being the most Hong had said to her in the past few weeks.

"Do you mean until your exams are over?" Mei-li finally asked.

Hong began pacing again. "You really don't understand, do you? I think it would be better if we stopped seeing each other for good. There's no future in it."

"I love you!" Mei-li blurted out, still not believing what she was hearing.

"But I don't love you," Hong said, without turning around to pace back toward her.

Hong's words were like ice. Mei-li could hear her own voice pleading at first; then she began to cry and couldn't seem to stop. When Hong placed his hands on her shoulders, she suddenly felt sick at his touch. Without thinking, she turned and swung, hitting him as hard as she could. The force of her blow was so unexpected Hong fell backward and onto the ground. Through her tears, Mei-li could see the surprise on his face as he struggled to get up. Then, before anything else could happen, she turned and ran as fast as she could away from Hong.

"Mei-li! Mei-li!" she heard Hong yell after her, but she couldn't stop running. Even when his voice grew fainter until it disappeared, and a sourness rose in Mei-li's mouth, she didn't stop.

Mei-li walked for miles. Hong's voice continued to haunt her. Her body felt numb and stained forever by his touch. She kept moving until she could go no farther. The rancid, stale smell of the Pearl River reached Mei-li and sucked her toward its murky waters. On the river, sampans and barges moved rhythmically toward their destinations, as the high-spirited voices of the boat people filled the air. Mei-li was calmed by the sight of the water and open space. Everything felt so light, even the child she knew was growing inside of her. She followed the river's edge, walking with renewed energy until slowly the people disappeared and the narrow strips of land became barren. Finally, the river belonged just to her.

For a moment Mei-li felt comforted. Then voices began to grow loud in her head. Her own weak voice seemed smothered by Hong's sharp words and the foolish words of her father. Mei-li covered her ears with the flat palms of her hands, and the voices dimmed but didn't leave. She slowly walked down to the river's edge, letting the cool water absorb her tiredness. The life inside of her was so quiet, wanting only to sleep, just as she wanted to sleep. Mei-li walked deeper into the water, feeling nothing, neither sorrow nor fear. The slight current rocked her back and forth, pulling her evenly forward. Very calmly at first, Mei-li began to laugh, her laughter echoing off the surface of the cool water. She suddenly felt free of all restraints. As the water filled her body and stifled her last breath, all the other voices died, and she was alone at last.

Chapter Eight

1927

Pei

Mei-li wasn't discovered missing until the spinning and grinding of the machines began at the silk factory. Lin noticed Mei-li's empty spot at the reeling machine and went immediately to Pei.

"Have you seen Mei-li?" Lin asked, her voice rising above the steady grating.

"No, isn't she at her machine?" Pei answered, looking toward the other end of the room.

Lin shook her head. "No one has seen her."

"She was already gone when I woke up this morning. I haven't seen her since last night," Pei said, a feeling of dread coming over her. She swallowed her suspicions about Mei-li and Hong and simply shrugged her shoulders in ignorance, hoping Mei-li would return any minute, full of smiles and apologies.

But Mei-li did not return. The day dragged on with Pei's eyes wandering the gray room for any sign of Mei-li. The heat and steam felt oppressive as Pei's worry turned to anger, and then to worry again.

In the evening, Auntie Yee frantically sent the girls out in small groups all over Yung Kee to search for Mei-li. The guilt of silence stung her with such a pain, Pei knew she would have to immediately go to Su-lung's to see if Mei-li was with Hong.

She thought about telling Lin the whole story, but decided to wait until she returned.

In all the confusion, it wasn't hard for Pei to leave the girls' house unnoticed. She walked quickly down the almost empty streets. Pei hadn't been to Su-lung's house since the dinner, and it looked different, smaller and dirtier. Pei's thoughts of what to say still weren't complete when she reached up and knocked on the rough wooden door. To Pei's complete surprise, Hong appeared before her, his head stooped at the low doorway. The oily smell of cooking escaped from the dark room behind him. He glared at Pei blankly and said, "Su-lung's not home."

"I'm not here to see Su-lung," Pei snapped back. "I wanted to speak to you."

Hong's eyes focused hard on her. "Why?"

"I wanted to know if you knew where Mei-li was."

"I don't know any Mei-li," Hong answered calmly.

Then Pei took a chance and said, "She knows you."

Hong shifted his weight, and his face appeared flushed. "Then she's telling lies."

"Do you know where she is?" Pei asked again.

Hong looked harder at her, then answered abruptly, "I can barely tell one of you from another, much less know where your friend is."

Then Hong stepped back, his face half-hidden in the darkness. He closed the door so quickly that Pei didn't have the chance to say anything else. She hesitated a moment, then turned to leave, having seen the answer she was looking for in his narrow eyes. Hong was guilty of other things, but Pei thought he didn't know where Mei-li was; and for the first time, she realized what it was to really feel hate. It was hard and cold as stone, and she couldn't have hated Hong more if he were a Japanese soldier.

*   *   *

The news of Mei-li's death came unexpectedly the next morning. No one at the girls' house had slept much the night before, especially not Auntie Yee. She answered the door and received the news with the pain of a fresh wound; then she gathered the girls together and told them the sad news, before taking full responsibility for Mei-li's drowning. "I should have seen it," she said, despondent. "I've known of so many girls who have taken their own lives rather than face a marriage they didn't want. How could I have been so blind!"

Mei-li's body would be brought to the girls' house sometime that morning. She might have been lost forever, if she hadn't gotten caught on some branches at the side of the river, and been brought back by a boatload of fishermen.

"At least we know Mei-li's spirit can be laid to rest without drifting aimlessly out to sea!" Moi finally said, the only one daring to speak. She moved about the room slowly, refilling each cup of tea.

Pei could feel her heart beating so fast, she thought she might faint. Her first thought was that it wasn't true: Mei-li couldn't be dead; her laughter still rang so loudly throughout the house. Pei suddenly felt as if she would suffocate if she didn't do something. She stood up and moved toward the door, but she wasn't sure if she would make it. Then, without saying a word, Lin took hold of Pei's arm and helped her outside.

"Mei-li was in love with Su-lung's brother, Hong," Pei finally said, breathing in the fresh air. She swallowed hard.

Without a word, Lin put her arms around Pei and hugged her. Then, pulling away, Lin pushed Pei's hair away from her face and said softly, "It's not your fault, Mei-li was old enough to know what she was getting into."

"But I could have done something, stopped her . . ."

"No one could have stopped Mei-li, not if she didn't want you to."

Pei nodded, her eyes burning with tears. "I think I'll wait out here for them to bring her back," she simply said.

"If you need me, I'll be inside," Lin said.

It was a cool, cloudless day. Something inside of Pei still expected to see Mei-li come bouncing up the steps, offering her a piece of sugar candy, and laughing at all the fuss she had created. But when Mei-li's body was brought back to the girls' house, lifeless and covered with a dark blanket, Pei swallowed hard and began to cry openly in small gasping breaths.

Auntie Yee wouldn't let any of the girls near Mei-li. Her body lay alone in the reading room until her parents arrived. Pei hovered around the door, until she was sure Auntie Yee had gone upstairs, before quietly entering. The room was dark and secret, illuminated by two candles, with tiny flickering glows of incense burning in the corner. Pei moved slowly toward Mei-li. When her eyes adjusted to the light, Pei could see that Mei-li's body had been washed and was now wrapped tightly in white cloth, her head uncovered. Auntie Yee had combed her hair and rebraided two even coils, which lay neatly to each side. Pei leaned over, just close enough to see her friend one last time. Mei-li's face appeared calm and familiar, just bloated a bit from her time in the river. She appeared healthy and asleep. Pei could almost convince herself that this was simply all a bad dream, but when Pei lifted her fingers to Mei-li's face, she felt nothing. The coldness of death pushed her back, filled her with a dread that spread throughout her body and remained with her for days.

When Mei-li's parents came the next morning, they were solemn and silent. Her father spoke in low tones to Auntie Yee and showed little emotion, while her mother wept quietly to herself. Not long after they arrived, two men came to take Mei-li's body away. The girls watched in silence as her body was carried out. Then they lined up by the door to offer their condolences when Mei-li's parents left. Mei-li's father kow-towed and accepted their gesture with gratitude. "It was an accident," he mumbled. "A stupid accident!" he said again to himself as he walked out, not daring to lift his eyes to meet theirs.

Pei found out later that Mei-li's funeral was small and had been kept very quiet. Mei-li was buried alongside her ancestors in their village not far from Yung Kee. No one from the girls' house had been invited to attend, not even Auntie Yee, who had grieved as much as any mother would. On the day of Mei-li's burial, the girls worked at the silk factory as usual, each one of them in a somber state of mourning, with thick black armbands tied tightly around their arms.

Afterwards, vicious rumors about Mei-li spread through Yung Kee. Some said she was unhappy and opposed her parents' marriage match, while others whispered that she was with child, and had no choice but to end their lives. Auntie Yee and the girls quietly grieved.

Pei lived through each day in a dull trance. She ate very little and hadn't slept well since Mei-li's drowning. Only Lin could offer her comfort, which Pei gratefully accepted, even if no one could take away the pain. She couldn't understand how Mei-li's life could mean so little, how a thing like love or marriage could end a life. If it could hurt so badly it killed, then it wasn't something she needed in her life.

Then early one morning, several weeks after Mei-li's death, Pei's sleeplessness brought her to a final decision. She would go through the hairdressing ceremony with Lin. It was as clear as any light. Pei couldn't wait to tell Lin. Very quietly she entered Lin's room, careful not to wake any of the others. Pei spoke Lin's name softly until she slowly awakened.

"Lin, please get up," Pei whispered, her warm breath close to Lin's ear.

Lin didn't stir awake until Pei's fingers gently pressed against her shoulder. "What is it? Is everything all right?" she asked, groggy with sleep.

"I need to speak with you," Pei said softly. "I've come to a decision."

"What is it?" Lin asked, closing her eyes and opening them again to get a clearer vision of Pei.

Pei looked down so that Lin couldn't see that she had been crying, her face flushed and swollen. But it was futile to hide anything from Lin. Lin reached over and touched Pei's warm cheek.

"I've decided to be with you at the hairdressing ceremony," Pei whispered to her.

Then Pei was crying again. A silent swelling of tears gathered in the corners of her eyes, even as she fought against them. She waited for Lin to say something, to tell her to wait until morning to see how she felt. But when Pei looked into Lin's eyes, she knew Lin had finally understood that nothing would change her mind.

Women Who Do Not Go Down to the Family

Pei and Lin's hairdressing ceremony was postponed for several months after Mei-li's drowning. All thoughts of bad omens were put away, and never mentioned in order not to mar the ceremony. Still, there were times when Pei could feel Mei-li's presence in the empty bed next to hers, or almost see Mei-li coming toward her on the street. But it was always just a shadow, or a cruel trick of the mind. Pei didn't dare speak of these omens to anyone. Mei-li had chosen to go into the other world, even if her ghost lingered. So when the date of the ceremony was finally chosen, Pei felt relieved that they would soon be leaving all the memories that were still so painful.

Auntie Yee was not surprised at Pei's decision to join Lin in the ceremony. They had been almost inseparable from the beginning. She smiled, and cocked her head to the side for a moment, but whatever doubts Auntie Yee might have felt about Pei's joining the sisterhood, she kept them to herself.

Pei and Lin's hairdressing ceremony was small and simple. Mei-li's death was still too fresh in their minds. Unlike Chen Ling and Ming's, their ceremony included no large banquet and no prolonged wave of excitement led up to it. On the morning of their hairdressing ceremony, Pei sat down and faced the large mirror used for the ceremony. Thin sticks of incense burned in front of her. The long black skirt she wore felt hot and uncomfortable. She looked around the room, crowded with empty beds. It felt as if an entire lifetime had gone by since that first day she arrived at the girls' house eight years ago. Little had Pei known then, that having her hair cut would change her life so drastically.

When Auntie Yee came, she said little and laughed nervously. She stepped behind Lin and tapped her shoulder. Pei watched closely as Lin smiled and nodded her head for Auntie Yee to begin the ceremony.

It felt like a dream at first, as Pei closed her eyes and listened to Auntie Yee's soft chanting. She felt calm and happy, knowing that this time she wasn't alone, but with Lin, as she entered upon a new life. When Pei felt the warmth of Auntie Yee behind her, she glanced up and smelled Auntie Yee's clean, open scent. Without saying a word, Auntie Yee smiled and began chanting and combing through Pei's hair. Pei felt a small twinge of pride move through her. And when Auntie Yee's quick fingers braided her hair and pulled it gently into a chignon, Pei knew she was right to take this final step in joining the sisterhood.

Auntie Yee had arranged a wonderful dinner for them at the girls' house. The dining room was transformed with the glitter of red-and-gold banners hanging from the walls. Trays of candy and favors lay waiting for all the guests on each table. Auntie Yee and Moi had created a pleasant, happy atmosphere, even though Mei-li's death still cast a silent sadness among all of them.

Lin's family did not attend the dinner, much to Pei's relief. Instead, Lin's mother sent fruit and lucky money to Lin as a small token. Pei's own family remained silent. She had asked Auntie Yee to let her family know of her decision to go through the hairdressing ceremony, but no reply was ever returned from them. After the ceremony, Pei would no longer be bound to them financially, but there was no doubt in her heart that the money she earned would continue to go to her family. It was the only tie she still had to them.

Chen Ling and Ming had arranged for Pei and Lin to stay at the same sisters' house as they did. When the dinner was over and the last girl had congratulated them with red packages of lucky money, it was time for Pei and Lin to leave the girls' house. In all the excitement, Pei had forgotten how difficult it would be to leave Auntie Yee and all the girls she'd come to know as her family.

In the cool, clear evening Pei and Lin stood at the front gate with the entirety of their belongings folded into two small baskets. They slowly hugged each one of the girls, even Moi, who usually kept her distance and stood awkwardly to one side. Pei would always remember the muted, humming sound of her younger sisters' weeping, and of Auntie Yee's childlike voice rising above the rest, saying, "Remember to keep warm—you won't get sick if you keep warm!"

*   *   *

The sisters' house was older and larger than the girls' house. It was no more than half a mile away, but on a secluded street that they rarely walked down. Once they were through the gate, Pei and Lin stood silent for a moment. They looked up in the semidarkness and saw the house's elaborate carved woodwork and large open terrace. According to Chen Ling, it was once the house of a very wealthy family from Canton who had come to spend summers in Yung Kee. Upon the marriage of his children, the father found no need for such a large house and had sold it to the silk factory.

When they approached the large, ornate door, Pei's eyes searched the dim outlines for any hint of what lay beyond it. When Chen Ling reached to open the door, it was helped along on the other side.

"Welcome!" said an older, gray-haired woman. She introduced herself as Kung Ma.

As they entered the large hall, the first thing to catch Pei's eye was an arrangement of glass hanging from the ceiling. She had never seen anything like it before in all her life. Its large bulk was made up of clear shiny pieces encircled by lighted candles. Not until Lin nudged Pei on the arm did she wake from its enchantment.

"It's much like the chandelier that hangs in our house in Canton," Lin whispered to her.

Pei remained speechless.

"I would like you to meet Pei," said Chen Ling, continuing with her introductions to Kung Ma.

Kung Ma smiled kindly and nodded her head.

"Hello," Pei said, looking shyly at the silver streaks that ran through Kung Ma's hair.

"My, you are a tall one." Kung Ma laughed warmly. "Welcome to our humble house." She pointed toward a set of richly carved double doors. "Come now, let's go meet some of your other sisters."

Kung Ma opened the doors to an enormous room. It was at least three times the size of the reading room back at the girls' house. Their new sisters were scattered throughout the room. To one side were bookcases, filled with more books than Pei had ever seen before. On a table in one corner was a large statue of Kuan Yin with sticks of incense burning before her. Their sweet aroma filled the air. Unlike the spare, sterile walls of the girls' house, these walls and tables were covered with paintings and small statues.

"Most of those were painted by us," Kung Ma told them, pointing to the wall covered with paintings. "I'm afraid we have a long way to go." She laughed.

Pei looked away from the crowded walls and tables, only to suddenly realize they were being carefully scrutinized by their new sisters. The sisters were of all ages and sizes, simply dressed in white shirts and dark trousers. Each one had her hair pulled back. Some whispered back and forth to each other, while others gave the newcomers curious sidelong glances. Pei immediately felt their eyes directed toward her.

Then, as if Lin could read her mind, she turned to Pei and whispered, "I think it's your height they find so curious." Pei swallowed hard and lowered her shoulders. Even when the women pulled their eyes away, Pei could still feel their curiosity burn through her.

Their new room at the sisters' house was toward the end of a long hallway. Like Chen Ling and Ming, they shared a small, inexpensive room. Each month their rent and family obligations would be subtracted from their pay with still enough left over for essentials and pleasure. Unlike the rest of the house, the room was surprisingly bare and plain. It contained two beds and a small table separating them. At the far end of the room there was a window, whose frame was littered with flaking paint. Pei moved instantly toward it. In the darkness, she looked down to what she guessed was a small garden.

"It's too dark to see," Pei said.

"What?" asked Lin.

Pei turned around to see Lin sitting on one of the beds, an oil lamp cradled in her hands. For the first time since all the festivities began, Pei really looked hard at Lin's face in the white glow of light. She could see that despite how exhausted Lin was, she looked beautiful with her hair pulled back, exposing the smooth, even lines of her face. As strange and uncomfortable as Pei felt in their new life, Lin seem to fit into it perfectly.

"I think there's a garden down there," Pei said.

Lin smiled wearily. She placed the lamp on the table and looked up at Pei. "It's nice here, isn't it?"

"I've never seen a house so big." Pei looked around their new room. "It'll take days just to discover where everything is!"

Lin laughed and stood up. "So which bed do you want?"

At first, Pei was almost shy at the thought of sharing a room with Lin. "I'll take this one," she said quickly, choosing the bed closer to the window.

They lay in their beds, tossing and turning, trying to get used to the strangeness of the room and the constant shifts of wind, which sent a whistling sound through the large, hollow house. Neither them said a word in the darkness. The light of day would bring the beginning of their new lives, and it was almost morning when they finally slept.

The next evening Kung Ma closed the black book that contained the neat row of figures she painstakingly kept in separate columns. Across the room, a group of her sisters sat patiently waiting for her to look up. This occurred every month when she balanced the month's funds.

"It looks very good this month," Kung Ma said, looking up at the attentive faces, including the new faces of Lin and Pei.

"Will we have enough for the New Year's celebration?" Sui Ying, a younger sister, asked.

Kung Ma smiled at the young woman's enthusiasm, and her thick, dark brows seemed to form a line of charcoal across her forehead. Her dark hair, which was now evenly streaked with gray, gave her an air of authority.

"Yes, it looks that way," she said, placing the black book safely back in the desk drawer.

Sui Ying jumped happily up from her seat and went to tell the good news to the other women of the house.

For almost six years Kung Ma had kept the books at the sisters' house. She had been approaching her thirty-seventh year when the position was handed down to her at the retirement of an elder sister. Kung Ma was honored to be chosen and had readily accepted, fully realizing the importance of her duty and how much it meant to the survival of her sisters.

A few of the sisters in their house were no longer young; though they were not ready for retirement, a fund had been set up for monthly contributions toward a home to which they could retire. With careful planning, this could be done for each of the sisters. Each sister also made other monthly contributions in case of family deaths, emergencies, or if unexpected expenses should arise. If there was any money left over, it would be used for festival and New Year's celebrations. These elaborate arrangements were now solely in the hands of Kung Ma.

She was just one of a large group of women at the house who didn't return to their new families after marriage. They lived together at the sisters' house and worked at the silk factory. Every month they sent part of their earnings to their families left behind. Those who went through the hairdressing ceremony had fewer financial burdens, while others, like Sui Ying, were young grass widows. They stayed at the sisters' house, waiting anxiously for the day when they could be reunited with their overseas husbands. Kung Ma felt satisfied. With the arrival of Lin and Pei, their sisters' house was full.

Kung Ma had little memory of her real family. For as long as she could remember, the word "family" had meant her sisters, first at the girls' house and now at the sisters' house. They provided all the love and nourishment she had never received from a father and mother, and consequently, they received back all that was in her power to give. Occasionally, in some odd moment of the day, Kung Ma thought of her family, though she no longer saw their faces clearly. She had been given to the silk work at the age of seven, and had flourished. Still, with each passing year, Kung Ma felt her memories seem to sharpen. They seemed to move through her with every throbbing beat of her heart.

It had been on one still, unexpected night that Kung Ma's life changed for the second time. At fourteen, she was suddenly taken from the silk work and made to marry. Out of nowhere returned the father she barcly knew; he sold her again into another life. She'd been taken by such surprise that by the time the realization of the situation hit her, Kung Ma was already in a rough, poorly constructed wagon with the stranger who was her father, heading away from the girls' house.

But the bigger surprise came later, when they entered a small, rundown farmhouse in the middle of nowhere: Her new husband was a boy of six. Kung Ma stood waiting, frightened and anxious as a pent-up animal, when the child was brought in from outside. His face and scanty clothing were covered with dirt; he peered up at her with curious, cautious eyes, as if to say "Who are you? What do you want?"

"This is your new husband, Wa Ming," her father announced.

Kung Ma looked down at the little boy and began to laugh, at first quietly, and then without restraint. Her father grew red with rage, while the little boy soon grew impatient with all the

adult games and wandered off to play in the corner of the filthy
room.

For the next three days Kung Ma stayed with her new husband and his family. Afterward, she returned to the silk factory
to work for her husband's family until Wa Ming had grown into
a young man who could carry out his husbandly duties. This was
the agreement worked out with her father, in which Kung Ma
had had no voice. During her time at the farmhouse, Kung Ma
said little to her new family, doing what she was told and
ignoring everything else. She would remember that time like a
bad dream, leaving a bitter taste in her mouth.

The one sweet moment Kung Ma remembered fondly was
playing with her little husband. They looked like brother and
sister squatting on the ground. Wa Ming innocently watched his
new wife throw a handful of twigs on the ground, and then try
to pick them up one by one without moving another. He tried
again and again with uncontained laughter. She never forgot the
laughter that filled the air, pure and free, or the little boy, who
must be a father himself by now. Kung Ma never went back to
her young husband, and never failed to send money monthly to
support him, his concubine, and his family. It was all they asked
from her.

Kung Ma closed the door to her room. Unlike those of some of
her other sisters, her life had been relatively undamaged. From
the top drawer of her old bureau Kung Ma extracted a large
red-and-black book in which she wrote every day. In it she
recorded her life and the lives of her sisters as the words were
passed to her in daily conversations.

"Don't you ever want to see your husband again?" Sui Ying
once asked.

"Others have returned to their husbands after the silk work,
and some have even borne them children," Kung Ma said, more
to herself than to Sui Ying.

"Is that what you'll do?"

Kung Ma looked up and laughed. "I doubt we would know what to do with each other!"

But in the quiet of her room Kung Ma recorded it all. The smallest detail was saved, like some precious gift. The boy-husband she barely knew was a total stranger now. He was not like the husband for whom Sui Ying waited, the husband who traveled overseas trying to make a better life for his family. It was each one of their fates that brought them husbandless to the sisters' house. Hers was a life she accepted without regrets, collecting small tokens of its existence along the way.

Sometimes, after long, busy intervals at the silk factory, when Kung Ma reached for her book her hand would unconsciously move past it, stopping at a white box buried deep within her clothing. The box contained the only remnants of her marriage: a handful of brown twigs.

Chapter Nine

1928

Pei

The rhythm of their days had changed after they moved to the sisters' house. The days were fuller and faster, and sometimes filled with more surprises than Pei could have dreamed of. The women who lived at the sisters' house came from all over China. Those who hadn't gone through the hairdressing ceremony stayed at the sisters' house as residents. Like Auntie Yee, some had chosen the silk work over husbands, while others worked until their husbands returned from overseas jobs. Every evening Pei sat curious and attentive, listening to stories of the outside world. Chen Ling spoke about the atrocities committed by the Japanese soldiers in the north, while the Chinese Communists continued to fight and run for their lives. Other sisters, who had lived and worked in Canton or Hong Kong, spoke of the white devils and their strange ways. Pei learned of their infrequent bathing habits and of their love of drinking expensive liquors and eating large slabs of bloody beef.

At the sisters' house, every night was different. Sometimes laughter filled the room, and at other times voices rose above the others in disagreement, but always Pei felt something special when she heard these conversations; she was transported to faraway places.

During their first few weeks, Pei and Lin reveled in all the new books they could read. They were free to do as they wished after their assigned duties of washing and cleaning were finished. Many of their sisters painted, or wrote skits to keep them entertained. Pei had never known such laughter as when Sui Ying and another sister, Lee Moi, performed. It was usually an opera, and almost always about a broken romance. Sui Ying portrayed the man, and the slighter Lee Moi the woman.

There were fewer rules to follow here than at the girls' house, but more responsibilities. Lin began telling Pei they must start looking out for each of their futures. It made Pei's head spin just to think about financial arrangements, so she left all those decisions to Lin to take care of their extra money. Lin sometimes teased Pei about growing older, but Pei was delighted by the fact that each day she was learning more.

After their hairdressing ceremony, Pei also noticed they were treated differently by their old friends at the girls' house. The younger girls cast their eyes shyly downward as they walked by Pei at the factory, giving her the respect due an elder.

Sui Ying and Lee Moi were closest to Pei in age, yet most of the time Lee Moi was sullen and disagreeable, and spoke little to anyone except when she was acting. It was different with Sui Ying, who soon became a fast friend. Pei seemed to feed on the fact that their lives were so different. Sui Ying worked at the silk factory while she waited for her husband to send for her. She was just a few years older than Pei, but at twenty she looked much older, with her heavier, sturdier frame.

Through Sui Ying, Pei began learning about another life she knew very little about: love and marriage. Sui Ying and her husband had been promised to one another when they were small children, and as fate would have it, theirs was a perfect match. Though they both came from poor families, they found wealth in their love and marriage. But when the floods came, Sui Ying's husband, Lau Chen, was forced to join the hundreds of other men who went overseas seeking employment. Sui Ying was lucky enough to find work immediately at the silk factory and a room at the sisters' house. "I don't know what I would have done—we were penniless, and I couldn't stay with his family and do nothing!" said Sui Ying, throwing her hands up in the air as she told the story.

Often, when Lin had gone with Chen Ling to attend factory meetings, Pei and Sui Ying would sit in the small garden in back of the sisters' house, where Sui Ying spoke happily of her husband. The garden had become Pei's favorite place, with its calm light and sweet perfumes. In those quiet moments, Pei was grateful to have the friendship of Sui Ying.

"Lau Chen has found another position!" Sui Ying said jubilantly one evening in the garden. The heavy fragrance of jasmine seemed to intensify with the waning light.

Pei grew happy in her friend's joy. "What is it?" she asked.

"He's loading the large ships that leave Hong Kong harbor and travel all over the world," said Sui Ying excitedly. "It pays more than the other job on the fishing boat!"

The letter with its crisp blue pages crackled in her hand.

"Does this mean you'll be leaving the sisters' house to join him in Hong Kong?" Pei asked anxiously.

Sui Ying smiled. "It means that I'll be able to join him sooner, but it won't be immediately."

Pei smiled with relief. There were many reasons she enjoyed her talks with Sui Ying. One of the reasons she could scarcely admit, even to herself. Lately, Pei had been feeling things that were strange and foreign to her, as if her body as well as her mind had awakened. She was curious about what it was like to be married. When her sisters laughed and spoke of intimate details between men and women, Pei could only blush and leave the room. Only with Sui Ying could she dare to ask what a man and woman did with each other once they were alone.

"Does that mean when you're back with your husband you'll have children?" Pei asked. There was a small quiver of uncertainty in her voice.

"I suppose so," Sui Ying answered. "If it's to be our fate."

Pei remained silent for a moment, thinking of all the bad things she'd heard about childbirth. Besides the fact that it dirtied a woman, and could bring death to her, its polluting effects followed a woman into the afterlife and condemned her to punishment in purgatory. Chen Ling had said this more than once, and it seemed that Pei's own mother had suffered no less in her life on earth.

Pei looked at Sui Ying and couldn't imagine a life like that being her fate. "But aren't you afraid of being dirtied?" she asked.

Sui Ying laughed. "We can't run away from what's planned for us. Besides, we wouldn't be walking on this earth if our mothers didn't follow their fates."

Pei digested Sui Ying's words. This was something she hadn't heard before. Despite all the talk of the powerlessness women faced in childbirth, Pei couldn't deny the fact that new lives came into this life every day.

"What is it like?" Pei finally gathered the courage to ask.

"What is what like?"

"What's it like to be with a man?" A hot flush moved through Pei, and she didn't dare look into Sui Ying's eyes.

Sui Ying looked up at the darkening sky, as if looking for an answer. Then, in very precise words, she said, "If you're with someone you love, then it's something very beautiful. You're so close to that person that nothing else seems to matter."

"Is it painful?" Pei asked, having heard this over and over again from other women.

Sui Ying smiled at her persistence. "Sometimes, at first, but not all the time. It depends on each person, I think. It's different for each one of us, but I can tell you this, it doesn't matter if you're with the right person."

There was a stillness to the night that seemed to swallow their words. All of a sudden Pei thought of Mei-li, and something painful moved through her. Mei-li had thought she was with the right person. She had loved Hong, but still she died because of him. This kind of love would always be a mystery to Pei. She let out an unexpected sigh and asked, "But if you aren't with the right person, and you're forced to be with someone you don't want to be with, does that make it dirty?"

Sui Ying thought for a moment. She took a deep breath. The air felt like a cool, comforting caress. "Then it would be the most painful thing in the world."

Canton

It had been almost two years since the engagement of Lin's brother was first announced. The marriage had been postponed twice while the two families worked out matters of the dowry. When at last a final date was chosen, Lin arranged for some time away from the silk factory, then purchased the boat tickets for her and Pei's trip to Canton.

As the day of their departure neared, Pei grew increasingly nervous. Yung Kee was the largest village she had ever been to, and it seemed immense compared to her own small village. Canton was an entirely different story: It was a big city filled with people from all over the world. Pei could easily be swallowed up in its grip.

"Are there many white devils?" asked Pei.

"More white devils than you ever dreamed of," Lin said.

"What are they like?"

"You'll see for yourself," answered Lin.

On the morning they were to leave, Pei couldn't eat a thing. She checked her bag over and over again to make sure she hadn't forgotten anything. Her mouth felt dry and sour as she waited, and even Sui Ying's constant reassurances did little to help. Only when they finally said their good-byes and began their journey toward the river did Pei feel a small sense of relief.

The boat station was a small, crowded lean-to, roughly constructed out of mismatched pieces of wood, with a roof of woven straw. People jostled each other with their makeshift suitcases, baskets of food, and bamboo cages filled with live chickens and ducks. The constant drone of voices seemed to make everything vibrate, and the stench of food, fowl, and human sweat nauseated Pei. But as far as she was concerned, there couldn't have been anything more exciting.

When the boat finally arrived, creaking and puffing to a stop, Pei stood back and stared at the flat-bottomed monster in amazement. In the ten years she'd been in Yung Kee, Pei had never been on anything larger than the midsized houseboats docked by the side of the river. This boat had two decks and was enormous. The top deck held rows and rows of wooden benches, but the bottom level had no benches, and passengers there would have to either stand or sit on the wood-plank floor for the entire trip to Canton. Pei watched the hordes of people pour down the wooden ramps towards them, some looking anxiously for loved ones, others just trying to get out.

"Are you all right?" Lin asked, when they were finally making their way up the wood ramp toward the top level.

"It's so big," Pei said, stepping onto the large, open deck, which rocked gently below her feet.

"This is nothing," Lin said. "Wait until you see the ships in the Canton harbor!"

They made their way slowly down the narrow aisle filled with people pushing their way toward any available seat. Those already seated stared hard at them and their clean, white clothing as they passed. Pei had long since learned to cope with the rude stares of those who found the sisterhood strange and filled with too much freedom. Over the years she learned to stare back at them until they lowered their eyes or looked away. In this test of wills, Pei always won.

When Lin finally found them some seats toward the back of the boat, Pei sat down and waited for them to set sail. Below, they could hear the rumblings of those settling into the lower deck. Soon every empty space was filled, and they heard the scraping sounds of the chains lifting the ramps. At last, they felt the boat shift, groan, and begin to move.

From Yung Kee the boat moved slowly up the Pearl River towards Canton. On each side of the open boat, Pei could see the teeming river life. Small, almost naked children played games along its edge, while their mothers talked and washed clothes in the murky water. Beside them, their dilapidated boats swayed and creaked.

This scene slowly gave way to a quieter, less populated region. Pei saw the fertile farmlands where farmers worked to produce sugarcane and rice. It was the same flat, red earth of her childhood, and seeing it again provoked memories of the lost childhood Pei thought she'd buried.

Lin's familiar voice brought her back again. "It's beautiful isn't it? I never really noticed before."

"Yes." Pei smiled. "It feels strange, like a long-lost friend."

"Is it similar to where you grew up?" Lin asked.

Pei turned slowly toward Lin. She had said all that she could to Lin about her family life; that her father had fish ponds and they all worked in the mulberry groves.

"Yes, it's very similar," Pei finally said.

An older woman dressed in white wheeled a cart down the aisle; she was selling tea and sweet buns.

"I was always getting into trouble," Pei continued, "doing things I wasn't supposed to, like asking too many questions, and going out to play and coming back filthy."

Lin laughed and said, "We weren't allowed to dirty our

clothes. Our amah had to change my youngest brother six times one day because he dirtied his clothes. It made my mother very angry."

"We wouldn't have had any clothes if we'd had to change six times!" Pei laughed. "We only had two sets of clothes, one for summer and one for winter. If one was being washed, then we'd wear the other. I was always getting dirty. Sometimes, when the ponds were low and no one was around to see me, I'd wade into the water as I'd seen my father do when he harvested the fish. There were hundreds of fish back then, and they felt like tiny bristles of a brush swimming against my legs, strong enough to knock me into the water if I didn't plant my feet securely in the muddy bottom. It was like nothing else I've ever felt!"

"It must have been wonderful."

"No," Pei said quickly. "Those times were few and far between, and I had them only in secret."

"But what about your sister Li, didn't she share these secrets with you?"

Pei shook her head slowly. After all the years, it still stung. "We were very different. Li was more like my mother, very quiet and obedient. Most of the time she kept to herself, and never found trouble. I always wondered if there was something wrong with me, because I couldn't be more like them."

"Nothing's wrong with you," Lin said gently. "Don't ever think that just because you do things differently, you're wrong."

Pei lifted her head and smiled at Lin. Voices hummed all around them. She turned and looked out toward the overworked red earth, and suddenly felt like crying. From the distance, the land moved up and down along the waves of white heat.

More than six hours later the boat groaned and slowed as they approached Canton. Once inside the busy harbor they were surrounded by dozens of other boats. Pei looked around, wide-eyed. The port was bursting with movement; small sampans moved back and forth with dexterity, avoiding the larger Chinese junks with their flapping sails. Massive wooden ships stood large and imposing, with bold foreign writing on their sides. Pei had seen nothing like it before. The excitement of different people and strange voices surrounded her. The more pungent odors of salted fish and stale oil filled the air. Pei was quickly overpowered by the enormousness of Canton as the boat slowly made its way to dock. A crowd of people stood along the wooden pier and watched them approach. Many waved and shouted words Pei couldn't make out. She turned to Lin, who was watching just as intensely as she was. Neither of them spoke as the boat jerked and bumped heavily against the stone wall. Pei's heart beat faster as the horn sounded a low moan of arrival.

They slowly battled their way down the ramp through the thick and foreign crowd. Pei knew it would have been a nightmare for her if Lin hadn't taken her hand and led her through the maze of wooden piers. For the first time in her life, Pei saw the white-devil traders who came from faraway lands. Many of them were tall and heavy, with strong smells and hairy faces. They spoke in a coarse, vulgar fashion, and laughed and jeered at the young women as they walked quickly by. Shirtless coolies, glistening from the thin film of sweat that covered their lean bodies, jumped to the orders of the white devils, lifting heavy loads onto the large boats. And all around them, clustered in small groups, were Chinese soldiers dressed in gray uniforms, watching the coolies work.

"Who are they?" Pei asked, careful not to be caught staring.

"They're soldiers in the Kuomintang army of Chiang Kai-shek. My brother told me they are everywhere now, looking for Communist supporters who might be slipping in or out of Canton."

"Are many caught?"

Lin shrugged her shoulders. "Some, I guess."

Pei glanced over at them. Many of the soldiers were still so young they did not yet fit into their cotton uniforms. They stood proudly, showing themselves off. Some of them whistled and made rude comments.

"How much, sweet thing?" one young soldier called out.

"I'll teach you a thing or two!" another yelled.

Pei blushed and grew hot as she followed Lin's quick lead.

Voices seemed to buzz from every direction. Families that lived upon the docked boats went about their daily routines of living and selling their wares. They waved their arms and called out to them: "Missy, here, I have the best deals!" "Missy, the best jade in Canton!"

Women were perched upon their rocking boats, some with babies hanging from slings around their backs. They tried to sell Lin and Pei everything, from jade trinkets to dried fish and steaming bowls of noodles. Their older children, barefoot boys and girls dressed in dirty, tattered clothing, played beside them, oblivious to the world which revolved around them.

Pei sighed in relief when they finally emerged from the crowded pier and onto a wide, open street. Lin moved directly towards a line of sedan chairs waiting in a row at one corner of the street. The carriers sat beside their chairs. Several jumped up as they approached, while others sat glassy-eyed, smoking something sweet-smelling in thin, long pipes; still others, shoving rice into their mouths from small bowls, simply stared up at Lin and Pei and waved their chopsticks for the girls to move on. Farther down the street another group of carriers continued gambling, with no intention of leaving their game.

"What's that funny smell?" Pei asked.

"They're smoking opium," answered Lin.

"Why?"

"It helps them to forget."

"Forget what?"

"Their lives."

Without further explanation Lin stepped forward and spoke

to two of the more eager carriers. They wore beige tunics and short trousers, which exposed their muscular calves and the veins swollen from the constant pounding of their feet against the hard-surfaced streets.

When Lin settled on a price, she turned to Pei and said, "Let's go. I've talked them into letting us ride in one chair together."

The two men were already positioned at the front and back of the sedan chair. Between the poles was a small wooden structure with sliding windows on each side. Pei stepped between the poles and entered first, followed closely by Lin. She moved as much as she could to one side of the rough, flat seat so Lin would have enough room. Immediately Pei felt the chair being lifted. The chair bearers moved forward and broke into a half-trot as the girls sat snugly in their seat, floating several feet above the ground.

Pei slid open the wooden board as far as it could go and leaned out of the window. They were traveling down a broad street, crowded with other sedan chairs, a few monstrous vehicles Lin called cars, soldiers on horses, and merchants' carts filled with fruits and vegetables. Pei marveled at all the people and shops, especially the fancy-dressed white devils strolling down the street. They walked straight and erect, ignoring all the begging children who cried and followed them.

The busy street led to an area with larger buildings, which housed storefronts and factories with ornately decorated exteriors unlike any Pei had seen. In the flat open land of her childhood, Pei was lucky to have seen so much as another farmhouse miles from where they lived. Even the buildings in Yung Kee appeared miniature compared to these, whose massive walls seem to grow upward toward the sky.

A quick turn of the sedan chair suddenly sent Pei colliding into Lin, laughing. The bearers continued their steady trot for quite a while, passing numerous large gray houses, which, Lin said, belonged to visiting white devils. Then, before Pei knew it, they made another sharp turn onto a smaller, tree-lined street. Pei could barely see the large houses hidden behind the tall hedges and iron gates. There was something mysterious and almost menacing about their neatly manicured fronts. Pei felt a cold fear move through her, but kept this to herself.

The sedan chair slowed. It finally came to a stop in front of black iron gates. Pei nervously looked toward Lin, who was already climbing out of the chair. The strong smell of eucalyptus floated heavily through the air as Pei climbed out after her. While Lin paid the sedan carriers, Pei looked around at the lush greenery that imprisoned each house. The feeling of discomfort grew inside her. Pei stepped back and watched the sedan carriers swiftly lift their chair, leaving them suddenly alone.

"Come this way," Lin said. "There's nothing to be afraid of, Pei, I promise."

Pei tried to smile.

Lin rang the bell on the gate without hesitation.

Through the gate Pei could see the brown house of Lin's childhood. It looked large and imposing, like some tired beast. She looked hard beyond the last barrier that separated them from the house and Lin's family, but no one was in sight.

Without saying a word, Lin kept her finger on the bell. Pei swallowed hard and waited. She knew how much this day meant to Lin and her family. After more than twelve years, Lin had come home.

Chapter Ten

1928

Pei

"It's Missy come home! Missy come home!" the short, rotund woman shouted to the others as she struggled to open the heavy gates. "Missy, you have finally come home," she said joyfully to Lin, her face pressing through the iron bars.

Lin reached through the gate and touched her hand. "It's you, Mui," she said to the old servant.

Mui finally flung the gate open; Pei moved quickly out of the way as Lin rushed into Mui's open arms. Pei saw that Mui was older and grayer than Lin had described her, yet she still possessed the quick, light movements of a younger woman. Only Pei knew how much Lin had missed the old woman's maternal comfort during her years away. When Mui finally released Lin and was introduced, she hugged Pei with equal vigor.

By the time they walked through the garden to the house, Lin's brothers had gathered at the entrance, but her mother, Wong Tai, was nowhere in sight. The house itself was very old and large, made of wood and concrete; years of neglect showed on its fading brown surface. But when they entered the cool, dark interior, Pei saw that the house still maintained some of its past glories, with its large, dark furniture and ornately decorated vases. Lin looked all around in great excitement. She had told Pei that many of their better possessions, such as the rosewood cabinets and carved ivory vases, had to be sold after her father's death. When Pei looked up, she saw the most beautiful crystal chandelier hanging directly above them. She leaned over to Lin and whispered, "It's much more beautiful than the one at the sisters' house."

To the left of the entrance stood the majestic staircase which once played such an important part in Lin's childhood. It appeared just as Pei had imagined it; the polished, intricately carved dark wood curved flawlessly upwards. She could almost envision young Lin and her brothers peering down from the top of the stairs as their parents greeted the many guests dressed in tall hats and fancy clothes.

Pei was so taken with the house that she barely noticed Lin's two younger brothers standing to one side. They wore dark, serious suits with starched white collars. The younger, Ho Yung, looked hot and uncomfortable in his Western clothing, and shyly lowered his gaze when he was introduced to Pei, while Ho Chee, whom she had met once before at the girls' house, greeted her with familiarity. At first meeting, Pei had been so captivated by Lin's mother she hadn't even realized she stood a good inch or two taller than Ho Chee. The brothers now watched her closely and seemed as intrigued with her height as she was with their clothing.

Lin appeared surprised and happy to see her younger brother Ho Yung again. After so many years, it must have been like greeting a stranger. Gone was any resemblance to the small child she had once described to Pei. She stood back and laughed at his height. He had grown to be the taller of the two brothers, and easily the more handsome. With his straight, even features and dark serious eyes, he bore a closer resemblance to Lin than Ho Chee did.

"Come, come, you must go to greet your ma ma; there will be time for your brothers later," Mui said, clapping her hands.

"You two find something else to do. The girls must rest after their long journey."

Then Mui, in all her excited happiness, guided them upstairs to Lin's old room. As they moved soundlessly down the long hallway, Pei stepped carefully on the soft red woolen carpet that covered most of the shiny wood floor. Mui stopped, opened the door to Lin's room, and motioned the girls inside.

"You see, Missy, nothing has changed since you went away," Mui said happily. "Everything has been kept the same as when you left."

Mui had managed to keep the original contents of Lin's room. Everything stood as she had once described it to Pei. Lin's doll collection sat erect and dusted on the bureau; her books were in order on the white shelves; even her childhood clothes were still neatly hung in her black lacquer wardrobe. And there, to one side of the room, was the four-poster bed Lin's father had ordered from Europe. Its smooth white satin cover awaited Lin's body once again.

As Lin surveyed her childhood, Pei stood stiffly beside her. Every small detail seemed to be in place, yet for a moment Lin seemed surprised, as if she were seeing everything for the first time.

Then Lin smiled and gave Mui another hug. "No, nothing in this room has changed at all."

Mui nodded her head. "We have been waiting such a long time for your return, this room and your old Mui," she said, patting her own chest with the palm of her hand.

"So have I," Lin said.

"I know that everything will be as it was now that you've returned, Missy," said Mui.

Mui fluttered around the room, touching objects and reminiscing about Lin's childhood. Then, with the same air of busy happiness, she left to bring them tea and some fresh towels.

"I'm sorry," Lin said, turning toward Pei. "I'm afraid she's excited at seeing me home again."

Pei smiled. "I would be too, if I were she."

Lin looked around the room slowly, then turned back to Pei and said, "I have to go and see my mother for a short time. Why don't you rest here for a while?"

"Will you be gone long?"

"No, it shouldn't take long." Lin paused, her face pale and weary. She smiled anxiously and then asked, "Are you sure you'll be all right here?"

"I'm fine," Pei said.

Pei felt childlike standing in the crowded room. She picked up one of the many dolls sitting on the bureau, a doll with light-colored hair that felt soft and silky. It was so fine compared to her own thick, coarse hair. Pei rolled the doll over carefully in her hands, her fingers lifting the pink frilly dress to see if it was real lace, then stroking the smooth golden hair in disbelief.

She walked slowly around the white room, her fingers touching the neat line of books on the shelf. Very carefully she opened a drawer and found several intricately embroidered silk vests, and in another, a neatly folded stack of girl's underclothing made of wool and cotton. Pei sat down hesitantly on Lin's large white bed, and didn't dare move. Everything about Canton seemed so large and confusing. Pei felt that if she were to leave Lin's room, she would easily be lost in the big dark house with its soft floors. Although Lin had told her all about her childhood, Pei still found it hard to imagine Lin having to leave all this for the girls' house. What must she have felt walking through Auntie Yee's bare, sterile rooms for the first time? Yet never once had Lin asked for more, or even made comparisons. Always, when Pei questioned her about her childhood, Lin simply said, "They're two different lives; you can't compare a chicken and an egg."

Pei let her hand sink into the soft cover of the bed, so that the dark of her skin disappeared into the white. Her head was still spinning from all that she'd seen since leaving Yung Kee. Lin's family, and this house with all its wealth and beauty, frightened her. Unlike Pei, who could never have returned home to her family, Lin could easily have come back to this comfortable life when her mother's health was restored. With her great beauty, Lin would have had little trouble marrying a man of wealth and power, bringing great honor to both families. Her mother would have certainly seen to it.

The sound of the door opening jarred Pei from her thoughts. For a moment she thought Lin had returned. Instead, it was the old servant, Mui, humming to herself and carrying a tray of tea and biscuits to the table beside Lin's bed.

"Missy has gone to see her ma ma?" asked Mui, her quick eyes darting around the room.

"Yes," Pei answered. Then gesturing toward the tray Mui had set down, she said, "Thank you."

Mui stood there, solid and smiling, intent on staying. She looked Pei over quickly, and then said proudly, "We are very happy Missy has finally come home. Did you know it's because of my Missy that this family has survived?"

"Yes, I know," Pei said in a voice so filled with admiration that it brought a toothless grin from Mui.

"I see you know my Missy well."

Pei smiled awkwardly. The truth was, sometimes she was frightened that Lin might no longer want to be with her. Because of her tall gangly body, Pei felt she must be an embarrassment for her friend when they walked down the street. And all her questions would tire anyone, even someone with Lin's patience. Pei didn't dare to think of life in Yung Kee without her.

"She has taught me a great deal," Pei then said quietly.

Mui moved towards her with a cup of tea. "I can see Missy has chosen her friends well."

Pei let out a small self-conscious laugh. "I'm the one who has been very fortunate."

The Marriage Ceremony

Lin knocked lightly on her mother's door and waited, entering when she heard a faint voice from inside. Her mother's strong, sweet jasmine perfume reached her first, followed by the distinct realization that her mother's room was smaller than she remembered. Unlike Lin's last visit, the room was awash in sunlight this time. Her mother stood looking out the window, radiant in an embroidered blue cheongsam.

"I hope you had a pleasant journey," Wong Tai said, turning toward Lin. There was a vague smile on her face, which disappeared when Lin's eyes met hers. Only then did Lin realize that her mother hadn't seen her since she'd gone through the hairdressing ceremony. How strange it must be for her mother to see Lin's hair exactly like hers, tightly coiled in a chignon.

"Yes, we had a very good trip," Lin said, moving closer to kiss her mother on the cheek.

"You brought your friend, then?"

"Pei is waiting in my room."

"I see." Her mother looked away. "Your brother's marriage has kept us all very busy. I've barely had the time to look at myself. I must look a mess."

"You look beautiful, as always," Lin said.

Her mother's face softened, though a hard edge of resentment moved through her words. "You could have chosen marriage, you could have easily had all the same things as Ho Chee, if you had returned home. Even more if you wanted!"

Lin was unprepared for her mother's words, yet in a voice so definite it surprised even her, Lin said, "I have everything I could ever hope for at the sisters' house."

Her mother was silent for a moment. The tiny lines around her eyes seemed to deepen before her face became smooth and distant again.

"Ma Ma, I just want you to understand that I'm happy with my life in Yung Kee," Lin said, hoping her mother would understand.

"Working in a factory?"

"It's enough for me."

"You were raised to be much more than a factory girl! Your father had great plans for you to marry into a respected family!"

"My father's dead, and being a factory girl has kept us all alive."

Wong Tai turned around and stared at Lin. In her eyes Lin could see the faintest hint of anger, but in a voice devoid of feeling her mother said, "Your brother will be honored that you have taken the time to return for his marriage ceremony."

"Ma Ma, won't you try to understand?"

"I understand perfectly."

Then, turning back toward the window, Wong Tai stared out into the sunlight.

When Lin left her mother's room, the sweet fragrance seemed to pursue her down the hall. She turned back once to see that there was no one there, only the imprints of her own steps in the soft carpet. Just a few doors down, Pei was waiting for her. When Lin reached the door of her room, she smiled and felt a lightness overtake her. It was as if some great weight had finally been lifted from her shoulders.

Even after dark the tropical heat lay sticky and still over everything surrounding the large, old house. The heavy perfume that rose thickly from the garden drifted in and out whenever the door was opened and closed. Inside the house it remained dark and cool, insulated by the tall ceilings and the large terrace, which bore the burden of the heat during the day. Lin had not forgotten the dank feel and faint moldiness of the rooms; they were almost as bad as suffering the heat itself.

That evening at dinner, Lin's mother presided over the table. Never once did Wong Tai look toward Pei to acknowledge her presence among her children. Pei kept silent as she sat wedged between Lin and her younger brother, Ho Yung, sneaking quick glances at Wong Tai. Every so often Pei shifted in her seat. Mui moved happily around the table, serving chicken and long beans on stacked cloisonné dishes that were changed after each course so as not to mix the flavor of the oyster and plum sauces. Both a large silver serving spoon and chopsticks were propped beside each person's plate on an enamel holder. Pei's eyes followed every move as Lin ate slowly and precisely, giving Pei direction.

The conversation quickly focused on the marriage ceremony, which was to take place in two days. Lin spoke often, laughing freely as she involved herself in the family discussion, refusing to let her mother exclude her.

"Shall I see if everything has been prepared at the restaurant?" Lin asked.

"It has been taken care of," Wong Tai answered.

"Is there anything you need me to do?" Lin persisted.

Her mother was silent for a moment, then said, "I'm sure Mui will need your help."

Then, as if catching something distasteful from the corner of her eye, Wong Tai abruptly turned her attention toward her younger son, Ho Yung, who was speaking in quiet tones to Pei.

"Ho Yung, did you arrange for the roast pig to be delivered on the day of the ceremony?" Wong Tai interrupted from across the table.

Ho Yung looked at his mother and answered calmly. "They've promised to have it at the restaurant on time."

Wong Tai stared at him for a moment, then turned away to ask Ho Chee if he'd ordered the plum wine. Lin turned toward Pei and smiled, letting her elbow touch Pei's arm for reassurance.

On the morning of the marriage ceremony, Lin's mother and her brother Ho Chee left the house early to worship their ancestors at a nearby Buddhist temple. The house itself was abuzz with preparations. Mui ran wildly from cleaning the house to preparing the ceremonial tea. Soon the courtyard would be filled with family and foreigners alike, coming to honor the marriage of Wong Hung-Hui's elder son. Wong Tai had seen to it that all her husband's old colleagues would attend, if only out of respect for her fallen husband. Through them, along with Ho Chee's marriage into a wealthy family, honor and dignity would be restored to the house of Wong.

The ceremony would take place at the house and would be followed by a large banquet at Wing Lee's, one of the finest restaurants in Canton. Wong Tai had spared no expense in making this day memorable, using credit and her good name to get what she wanted. Within hours the house's courtyard was transformed. Thirty long tables were draped in red cloth, while lanterns with the gold symbols of double happiness were brought out and strung up. On each table sat a plate containing dried dates, dried winter melon, and dried water chestnuts, along with two types of lotus seeds, which signified many children for the newly married couple. To one side, on the ancestors' table, were plates of oranges, star melons, and bananas.

Then, in the afternoon heat, with guests and family waiting in the courtyard, the distant sounds of the wedding party could be heard. Wong Tai turned to Ho Chee, who was dressed in a long blue silk gown; he stopped his pacing, cocked his head to the side, and took a deep breath when he heard the approaching horns and drums of the wedding party. The music, which at first seemed imaginary, soon grew louder as it floated toward the courtyard. The loud hum of voices from the waiting guests quickly gave way to a quiet anticipation.

Mui hurried down the path to open the iron gate as the music grew louder. The thick smell of incense filled the air as they stood waiting in the suffocating heat. Pei stood with Lin towards the back, straining to see down the road, while Wong Tai remained calm and smiling, her eyes fixed on the opened gate. Ho Chee waited nervously beside her, small beads of sweat slowly making their way down the sides of his face.

Then the bridal procession came into view. First to arrive were several sedan chairs carrying the bride's possessions and dowry. Next came the red bridal chair, raised so high by the carriers that it seemed to be floating in the air. The bride inside was hidden by its sealed door and windows. And behind her chair marched a string of musicians who announced the arrival of the bridal party with the beating and clanging of their drums and cymbals.

Pei's heart beat faster. As the sedan chairs entered the gate, everyone moved back to allow the bridal chair a central position. Pei slowly moved away from Lin and through the crowd, hoping to get a better view of the emerging bride, but the box remained closed. The musicians assembled, and according to custom began the three songs that had to be played before the bridal chair could be opened.

When at last the music came to an end, a silence fell over the crowd. Pei watched motionless. One of the woman attendants accompanying the bride tapped several times on the bridal chair and then began tearing the seals that lined the door. When it finally swung open, a sigh escaped the crowd. Pei stood silent, caught in the spectacle of tradition. The bride seemed to hesitate at first, as if, Pei thought, she preferred the small wooden box to the unknown. Slowly she appeared, wearing a long red bridal gown with an embroidered phoenix down the length of it.

A heavy jeweled headdress and veil prevented her from seeing. With the help of her women attendants, the bride was almost carried down from her chair, leaning heavily on them for balance. Unable to see and forbidden to speak, she was then led past the gawking crowd toward her new husband and his family.

The wedding rites began, led by the ceremonial master. The bride was led back and forth, kneeling and kowtowing, first to each member of her new husband's family and finally to the guests. Ho Chee stood by her side, also paying homage to his family, now as her new husband. The young couple then went inside the house to pour tea for both sides of their family and to receive the jewelry and lucky money that would help them to begin their new life. After the tea ceremony, the couple adjourned to a private room, where they would see each other for the first time. Pei's curiosity would have to wait until the bride emerged without her veil at the banquet that evening.

Outside, the festivities began with blaring music and the harsh, explosive sounds of hundreds of firecrackers squirming along the ground. A cloud of white smoke filled the courtyard. Pei's eyes stung as she made her way slowly through the crowd of people, looking for Lin. She listened in fascination to the strange language the foreigners spoke, but she didn't dare look too closely at the women's fancy clothes or at the men, whose faces were covered with hair. Suddenly, she felt someone take hold of her arm and pull her back. She turned to see Ho Yung.

"I hope you're having a pleasant time," he said, his hand on her elbow.

"Yes, thank you," Pei answered. "I've never seen anything so lovely."

When Ho Yung looked up and smiled, Pei was amazed at how much he resembled Lin. He had the same dark eyes and sharp features. Pei studied his face as well as she could without being obvious. The lines of his face were stronger and more prominent than Lin's, and whereas her smooth skin was without a blemish, the faint dark shadow of a beard formed an outline on Ho Yung's chin.

"Is this your first time in Canton?" he asked.

Pei was startled: Ho Yung had caught her watching him, his eyes holding on to hers. "Yes," she answered, looking down.

"It must seem very crowded and noisy to you, coming from a smaller village."

"Yes, it is," she said. She wanted to tell him how fascinating everything was, yet remained tongue-tied.

"My mother loves these large banquets," Ho Yung continued, raising his voice.

Pei smiled. "I've never seen anything like it."

Ho Yung said nothing. The noise from the crowd seemed to increase, drowning out their voices. He greeted guests as they slowly moved past. Finally the smoke cleared a bit, and people helped themselves to the fruit and candy. Ho Yung smiled, and held on lightly to Pei's arm until he had led her safely back to Lin.

The banquet at Wing Lee's restaurant was the grandest and most lavish Pei had ever experienced. The tables filled the large dining hall to capacity. Each table had a numbered card on it that directed who was to be seated where, along with bottles of French champagne and a potent Chinese plum wine.

Wong Tai had found the perfect means of expressing her dislike of Pei's presence. While Lin sat at the head table with her family, Pei had been placed at a table, whose occupants were all white foreigners, toward the back of the room. Wong Tai had known there would be no time for Lin to change the arrangements. Pei was nonetheless captivated by what she saw, even if she did feel conspicuous in her own simple white tunic and pants. The white-devil women around her were dressed in colorful finery made of silk and lace; their faces and lips were painted bright colors. The men wore dark, handsome suits with tall hats. They spoke in low tones, long cigars clenched between their yellow teeth. The stench from the cigar smoke was almost unbearable, and the cigars left their mouths only long enough to make room to drink down the bubbly champagne. Yet they seemed to be taken with Pei's lone presence and treated her kindly, though she understood only a little of what they said to her.

"What is your name?" one very painted woman asked, in broken Chinese.

"Pei," she said, when she finally understood what the woman was asking.

"Isn't that charming?" the woman cried out, telling the rest of their table. "Her name is Pei, isn't that charming?"

Pei simply smiled and shifted in her chair.

One male foreigner said hardly anything. He drank a great deal and simply stared at her for an embarrassingly long time. Pei felt hot and uncomfortable, though since coming to Canton she had grown used to this bad habit of the white devils. Their eyes seemed to have followed her unceasingly since her arrival.

Wong Tai smiled pleasantly from the head table, having already greeted each guest with grace and charm. Pei had stood with Lin and watched as Wong Tai welcomed her husband's former colleagues, now once again connected to her through Ho Chee, who had acquired a position in the government among them. Pei watched Wong Tai's expression change from a look of control to one of gleaming happiness. In that moment, forgotten were the lean years, when there was little money and Wong Tai sat ill in her room.

When the bride emerged, the hum of voices and clinking glasses stopped. Pei forgot about all the strangers around her and turned to get a better view of the bride without her jeweled headdress and veil. The bride walked slowly, her head slightly bowed, still denying Pei a good look at her face. She made her way toward the front of the room to join her new husband in toasting their guests. Ho Chee appeared pleased with his new wife as she stood small and unassuming beside him.

Almost immediately the newlyweds began their arduous rounds of toasting each table. The guests seated with Pei were well into their last courses of salted chicken and steamed fish when the couple finally arrived. As Pei stood with the others to toast the couple, she was able to have her first close look at the bride. Her small dark eyes seemed expressionless, her skin as pale and smooth as porcelain. The new bride lifted her cup of tea, which appeared almost too heavy for her.

"Thank you, thank you all for coming," said Ho Chee, lifting his glass.

The young bride smiled slightly, detached, as if she were thinking of other faraway secrets. Pei caught the girl's eye for just a moment. She seemed to give back a glimmer of life, until Ho Chee's sudden laughter pulled her away and just as quickly she was gone.

When the banquet was over, Pei returned to the house with Mui. It was Wong Tai's wish that Lin stay on at the restaurant with her family to thank the departing guests. And rather than wait to the side by herself, Pei thought it would be much more comfortable for all if she just followed Mui back to the house.

Alone in Lin's room, Pei felt she was barely breathing. The quiet of the room was so inviting after the noise of the day that she fell heavily on the bed and closed her eyes. She lay motionless while the events of the past few days moved through her mind. It seemed such a long time ago that she and Lin had first stepped onto the ferry that brought them here. She didn't exactly miss Yung Kee and the silk factory, but its dusty streets and the heavy grinding sounds of the machinery provided her with a sense of reality. Here in Canton, Pei felt as if she were trespassing into a world which didn't belong to her, and wouldn't miss her if she were to leave. She knew it was an entirely different story for Lin, who had been born into this life and probably still belonged to its world of luxury and white devils. Pei opened her eyes and was greeted by the sickly smile of one of Lin's dolls across the room. It reminded her of Wong Tai that night at the banquet, sitting high above everyone at the head table, staring out into all those endless faces.

When Lin finally returned, Pei watched as she let down her tightly coiled hair, which fell like a snake down her back. She shook her head from side to side, loosening her hair into a tangled web, and combed it out in even strokes. As many times as Pei had seen Lin comb out her hair, watching it never failed to intrigue her.

"I'm sorry you had to sit by yourself" were Lin's first words as she moved toward Pei.

"I was all right."

"She had no right to do that," Lin said, her voice carrying a hard edge.

Pei looked into Lin's eyes. "How can you blame her? You could have easily returned to all this, married into a good family, and brought great honor to her and your family. But my presence only reminds your mother of your decision to go against her."

Lin looked down at Pei without saying anything. Then she sat down on the bed beside her and gently began to remove the pins from her hair. As Lin did every night, she slowly began to brush through Pei's hair from top to bottom and then from underneath. Pei let her head fall back just a little as the bristles tickled her neck. Then surprisingly, she felt the warmth of Lin's fingers touch her cheek from behind.

"What is it?" Pei asked.

At first Lin remained quiet, simply laying the brush down on the table. Then finally she looked at Pei and said, "I hated the way my mother treated you!"

"It doesn't matter; I was fine."

"All her life, she has always wanted to possess things. My father gave her the best of everything, but she always wanted more. When I told her I wasn't returning home to marry, I fooled myself into believing she could understand, but she has become selfish and spiteful in her hopes of regaining her past."

"It was really all right," said Pei again. She had never seen Lin so upset.

"She lives in this museum of a house, and she wants to keep it that way."

"You're just tired."

Lin paused, then asked, "Would you mind if we left tomorrow? I can't stay here any longer."

"Whenever you'd like," Pei said, only too happy to cut their stay a day short and return earlier to the simplicity of Yung Kee.

"After morning meal," Lin said firmly.

They both sat in awkward silence. Then, slowly, Lin brought her hand up to stroke Pei's hair. "What is it?" Pei wanted to ask again, but there was something so lovely about the way Lin's touch made her feel that she kept silent. In her entire life, Lin had been the only one ever to love her unconditionally, without the demands of her parents or the fear of her sister Li. When Pei turned around, she saw that Lin's eyes had filled with tears. She reached over and put her arms around Lin, feeling something she had never known before, the smallest hint of fear, gradually giving way to desire.

Pei woke up with Lin sleeping quietly beside her. It took her a moment to realize where she was as she gazed sleepily through the hazy mosquito net. The house was perfectly still. Then slowly, joyfully, the memory of being with Lin overtook her. Last night, for the first time, Pei had felt as if her body had come alive. For months she had been thinking something was wrong with her, with some inexplicable feelings inside her that she didn't dare talk about, especially not with Lin. It would have been too embarrassing. From the very beginning it had been so simple for her to love Lin, never dreaming she might be loved in return. Pei felt safe and comfortable in the soft, white bed. She turned around carefully and watched Lin sleeping, her breathing so faint Pei had to listen hard for it.

Pei closed her eyes again and tried to sleep, but all her senses were too awake to allow her the pleasure. She slowly slid her body to the edge of the bed, trying not to awaken Lin. When her bare feet touched the soft carpet, she let the rest of her body follow, then turned quickly to make sure that Lin had not been disturbed. Already the air felt hot and silent, the early-morning light revealing the crowded room as Pei moved toward the window and looked out. She glanced down at the courtyard and the stale remnants of yesterday's festivities. Covering the ground was a thin blanket of faded red paper, left over from the hundreds of firecrackers set off after the ceremony. The red lanterns and banners hung limp in the windless courtyard, now empty of the excitement and anxiety that had filled it.

Pei sighed, and let her forehead gently touch the cool glass. Her thoughts turned to Ho Chee and his new bride. After the banquet they had retired to their room, once the room of his childhood. There they would spend the first night of their marriage, separated by a locked door from the rest of the household. She thought of the young bride, frightened and demure. What must she have been thinking, alone in that room with the stranger who was now her husband? Pei couldn't imagine the young bride finding ways of trickery and wile to keep Ho Chee away from her, as she had heard some of the sisters had done. Still, it could be different. Sui Ying had loved Lau Chen and wanted nothing more than to be with him. Perhaps this young bride might feel the same, once she came to know Ho Chee. He was nice enough, though he seemed to lack the innate strength that Lin and even Ho Yung radiated.

Pei's attention was brought back toward the window by a muted sound from the garden below. She looked down again. This time she saw someone seated at the far corner of the wall. At first Pei thought it was Mui beginning the task of cleaning up, but upon closer scrutiny she saw that it was Wong Tai. Lin's mother sat huddled against the wall, wrapped in a dark, dreary robe, her face colorless as she tried to quiet her muffled crying. Pei stood motionless, watching, caught by surprise at Wong Tai's display of tears. She hadn't thought a woman like her ever cried. Pei knew this was a moment so private that she had no right to be there, yet she felt paralyzed by the sight. She glanced toward the sleeping Lin, who could offer no assistance, then turned back to the window and the sobbing Wong Tai. Immediately she knew something had changed, but it was too late. Wong Tai was looking up toward her, doing nothing to hide her red, tear-stained face. And in her eyes was a look so full of hate that Pei jerked back quickly, as if knocked by a hard blow. She stepped out of sight, her heart beating fast, not daring to return to the window.

Pei said nothing to Lin about seeing Wong Tai that morning. She felt it would just upset Lin more. When they gathered at the table for their morning meal, Wong Tai showed no signs of her early-morning tears. Her carefully made-up face smiled with a masked neutrality that led Pei to wonder whether the incident in the courtyard had ever taken place. Afterward, Wong Tai retired to her room and didn't emerge even when Lin went to tell her of their departure.

Pei didn't see Ho Chee and his bride again until they were packed and ready to leave. Now that the festivities were over, a certain flatness lay heavy in the air and over the entire house. Mui moved about nervously, her eyes watery and her voice full of concern.

"You must hurry, Missy, so you won't miss your ferry back.

I have packed some food for you and Pei to have on your journey back to Yung Kee," she said to Lin.

Lin smiled, hugging her old servant tightly.

A sedan chair waited for them at the gate. Ho Chee and his new wife appeared shy in their happiness. Pei saw something in the bride's eyes that hadn't been there the day before and understood her happiness. It was as if some hidden knowledge gathered in the night had, in both of them, taken the place of their fear.

"You have honored us by coming," Ho Chee said to them. "We wish you a safe journey back to Yung Kee."

Ho Chee had fully taken on the duties of head of the household, while his younger brother stood aside. But as they were leaving, it was Ho Yung who quickly stepped forward to help each of them into the sedan chair. He hugged Lin easily, and took hold of Pei's hand for just a moment before letting go.

As the sedan chair moved swiftly toward the harbor, Pei leaned back and closed her eyes. It was hard to believe that in a matter of hours they would be back in Yung Kee. The city moved past her like a dream. She felt as if all of Canton had been presented to her in a swell of pageantry, from her first sedan ride to the extravagant marriage ceremony with its unveiling of the bride. Nothing had been lost, not the cold, deliberate hatred of Wong Tai, nor the warmth and comfort of being with Lin. All of it unfolded before Pei like a sudden storm. It had come and gone so quickly she barely had time to catch her breath. Had it all really happened?

Pei opened her eyes and watched Lin looking silently out the window. Even in the heat and noise, Lin appeared serene and lovely. There were no signs of the anger she had felt toward her mother last night. A fine line Pei had never noticed before led downward from the corner of Lin's mouth in a perfect curve to her chin. It was almost as if Pei were seeing her for the first time. In the small cramped box, they didn't touch or say a word.

Chapter Eleven

1932

Pei

Even if no one dared to breathe a word, Pei began to see life change drastically at the silk factory. The past year had made conditions worse, due to the poor quality of cocoons coming in. They had to be soaked longer, yet they brought lower prices at the market. Chung, the owner of the factory, insisted the workers make up the lost revenue by working longer hours with no increase in salary. The new girls seemed younger and wearier as they worked at their metal basins. Like those of many older sisters Pei had seen, their hands would slowly become old and arthritic. Each day before the sun rose the girls were already immersed in the steamy, damp atmosphere of the silk work. Their fourteen-hour days didn't allow them to leave the building until it was well past the time for their evening meal. And the only sunlight they saw was what filtered in through the dirty, sealed skylights. What was once their means to freedom had turned them into virtual slaves for Chung. He knew that the girls would continue to work in silence, afraid to challenge the unfair hours for fear of losing their jobs.

"Where can you find other work?" Chung told them, his thick, short fingers waving in front of his balding head. "Who will have you? There are many more where you came from!"

Chen Ling and Lin were powerless to change the long working hours. They did what they could to ease the strain of the day-to-day operations, bringing the girls tea and secretly relieving them, but the rules were made by Chung and carried out by his male managers. These men moved up and down the aisles, slapping into the palms of their hands the long wooden sticks they carried. Pei hated their sarcastic laughter and smug looks as they grouped together watching the girls work. The managers complained loudly if something went wrong with production, but Lin and Chen Ling were never given any credit when Chung received his monthly reports.

"What can we do?" Pei asked.

Lin shrugged her shoulders and shook her head helplessly. "An answer will come soon, whether we like it or not."

Slowly many of the girls came down with illnesses due to fatigue and the bad ventilation. Each evening the girls, damp from the hot steam, left the factory to walk home in the chilly night air. It was a monstrous situation that would stop only when they gathered the courage to fight Chung.

Lin's prediction came true when a young girl working in another building died suddenly. The girl had been too scared not to work, even with a high fever and a bad cough. One morning, she collapsed in front of her basin and never regained consciousness. The news of her sudden death spread quickly through the factory, and with it came the courage to step forward before another life was senselessly taken.

Late that night, Chen Ling secretly spread the word of a meeting of the head silk workers at the sisters' house. Pei watched as they gathered in the reading room, most of them dead tired from their long day at the factory. The women appeared hesitant at first, fearful of being found out and fired by Chung, but this soon gave way to an urgency that spurred them forward. Pei knew they came hoping for some kind of change that would make their lives bearable again, even if they had to fight to get it.

Lin stood by Chen Ling, equally intent on finding a way to extract decent working hours from Chung. In the crowd Pei saw some faces she knew, and many she didn't recognize from the other buildings. One by one, the women spoke up and their grievances were openly stated.

"Shorter hours!" they said.

"Better ventilation!"

"More rest periods!"

The demands became so contagious that the voices began to blend together in a song, and it was all Chen Ling and Lin could do to quickly write the comments down. By the time the last voice had echoed through the air and fallen to a sudden silence, the list of demands had grown to two pages.

When the meeting finally ended the women stood around awkwardly, then began to disperse, promising to secretly recruit every silk worker into their ranks.

"Our only chance to fight Chung," Chen Ling said, "is for every one of us to come together and shut down the factory!"

The women remaining in the reading room stared hard and hopefully at Chen Ling; then, with low, cautious murmurs they emptied the room.

When Chen Ling was alone again with Pei and Lin, she relaxed and began to pace the floor. Across the room Ming was quietly straightening chairs and gathering teacups.

"Should we try to talk to Chung ourselves before going any further with this strike?" asked Chen Ling. It was the first time Pei could detect some hesitation in her voice.

"What difference would it make?" said Lin. "He'll just give us all his empty promises."

Pei watched as Chen Ling sipped her tea. There was something so familiar about the way her eyes closed tightly in thought. It suddenly reminded Pei of her childhood and the blind fortune-teller who had changed her life so long ago.

Then Chen Ling looked up and with carefully chosen words said, "We have no choice but to act quickly, before Chung gets wind of what we're doing. If he should, we'll have problems way beyond our long hours and poor working conditions!"

"It's a chance we'll have to take," Pei said eagerly. "One of us has already died because of Chung and our fear of him. It's our duty to make sure it never happens again!"

Chen Ling looked at Pei and studied her face for a few moments. "You've grown up," the older girl said simply.

"Pei's right," said Lin. "If change is to come, it must be now, regardless of the consequences."

"Yes," echoed Ming enthusiastically. It was the first thing she had said all evening.

"It's agreed, then," said Chen Ling. "We work to shut down the silk factory until they listen to our demands, no matter what the consequences."

"As quickly as possible," said Pei.

Chen Ling smiled at Pei and Lin with renewed spirit. "We fight, then!"

"We fight!" their voices repeated.

From the corner of Pei's eye, she could see the smiling Ming moving quietly around the room. Ming put a chair back into its place, then moved to close a window. She reached out into the night air and pulled the window shut with a flat thud, sheltering them for a time from the outside world.

The   Strike

It was still dark outside, but in the past year they had learned to differentiate morning from evening just by the subtle scents in the air as they walked to and from work. Sui Ying flinched just a little as they sat around the table, carefully formulating their plans to strike. Though she agreed wholeheartedly with everything they said, Sui Ying couldn't help but feel the smallest twinge of doubt about what they were about to do. She sat back and listened to Chen Ling's words about the strike. They seemed to go on and on, to pause for only a moment when Kung Ma came in carrying a tray with tea and the sweet buns they ate each morning.

Sui Ying and Kung Ma worked together in a different building at the silk factory. It would be up to them to unify all the girls in their building as quickly and quietly as they could. While Kung Ma readily accepted the task, Sui Ying was more hesitant.

"What if we should lose our positions?" she asked shyly.

"Chung won't have a leg to stand on if we all quit working at the same time," Chen Ling replied. "Just the time it would take for him to train new girls would lose him enough money to want us back on our terms!"

Pei looked over at Sui Ying and smiled reassuringly. Still, Sui Ying felt an emptiness inside her heart, whereas all the others were filled with rage. She thought only of what would happen if she were to lose her job when she was so close to being with her husband, Lau Chen, again.

"But what if something should go wrong?" Sui Ying continued.

"It's up to us to see that nothing does," Chen Ling said. "That's why it's so important that we all remain together through this."

Chen Ling's gaze softened.

Sui Ying looked down and thought of the small farm Lau Chen always spoke about. "It will have three rooms," her husband often said. "Enough room for all the sons we will have!"

Sui Ying smiled at the thought.

"Are you with us?" asked Chen Ling.

Sui Ying looked up at the eager faces of her closest friends. "Yes, I'm with you," she answered.

* * *

When they left the sisters' house that morning it was with a strong sense of commitment, which gave them the strength to face the long, laborious hours ahead of them. It was agreed that each of them would cover as much territory as she could, discreetly spreading the word of that evening's meeting at the sisters' house. Pei moved through the factory with a sense of purpose, but by noon she was disheartened at receiving more noncommital nods than the hoped-for enthusiasm.

The hours seemed to move with deliberate lethargy. Pei let her mind wander, her fingers continuing to reel the silk with quick, experienced know-how. If a thread was caught or tangled her fingers automatically solved the problem by swiftly taking another cocoon and reconnecting a new thread in place of the first. Others had not adapted so easily to the work. The young girl who stood across from Pei was no older than Pei had been when she first came to Yung Kee. Yet already there were burns on the girl's hands that would leave discolored scars throughout her life. Pei's heart went out to these young girls, who simply couldn't adapt to the silk work and had to suffer through each day, adding to their injuries. For others, it could be even worse. Some girls trained and retrained to no avail and were finally let go, returning to their families in disgrace. There, they were either forced into poor marriages, in which they were considered more a servant than a wife, or simply discarded by their families and forced to fend for themselves in whatever way they could. Complete failures had only occurred twice since Pei had been there; both girls were returned to their families and never heard from again.

When the evening bell finally rang, they were released at last from their steamy confinement. Pei and Lin quickly made their way back to the sisters' house. Over a hundred women, young and old, gathered there that night, spilling out into the courtyard. More than half the workers had come, but this was still not as many as they had hoped.

Chen Ling and Lin spoke to them, calling for total unity, stirring the crowd into cries for shorter working hours. As always, Chen Ling was the consummate speaker, full of fire and spirit, just as she had been back at the girls' house when speaking of religion. Pei watched her, mesmerized. Chen Ling's fists clenched as she moved her thick body gracefully from one side of the crowd to the other, capturing their total attention.

"What do we want?" Chen Ling cried out. "To be treated no better than the lowliest animal?"

"No!" the crowd cried out.

"What do we want—to work as slaves for the sake of Chung's greed?"

"No!"

"What do we want?" Chen Ling's voice rang through the air.

Then, from somewhere behind Pei and Sui Ying, came the slow chant, "We want shorter hours! We want shorter hours! We want shorter hours!"

Like a fire this quickly caught on until every girl and woman there shouted it at the top of her voice, filling the night air with a thunderous cry.

Chen Ling and Lin stood back, watching in total amazement. At first they raised their arms up in the air and tried to quiet the voices, for fear they would be discovered, but it was useless. Their own voices couldn't climb above the rhythmic chanting and they were soon mouthing the words themselves. Chen Ling and Lin turned to one another, and for the first time in their lives felt strength in their numbers.

Because of the growing number of women joining their forces, Chen Ling feared that word might get back to Chung about the impending strike. It was too dangerous to meet at the sisters' house in such big numbers, so several women were selected to represent the others. They would bring word to the others of when the strike would take place. Timing would be critical if they were to pull this off. Without wasting any more time, the leaders quickly decided that the strike should begin the next day, when the noon bell rang. They would spend all night, if need be, spreading the word.

The next morning came after a sleepless night for Chen Ling and most of the others. An undercurrent of fear and anxiety moved through them, but on the surface everything appeared as usual. They went about their work with the same quick dexterity, which gave away nothing to the male managers who watched over them. At times Pei wondered if Chung and his men knew and were just waiting for them to make a move.

The first bell rang exactly at noon. Its long, loud clang made its way up from the bottom of Pei's spine to the nape of her neck. For just a moment all of the girls seemed lost as to what to do. They stood glancing at one another, unable to move.

The few male managers patrolling the aisles tapped their long sticks along the metal basins, mocking them: "What's the matter, can't you hear? Or would you rather work than eat?"

Before they could say anything else, the men were confronted by a large crowd of workers moving toward them, led by Chen Ling and Lin. Pei waved her hand for the others to follow. One by one the girls followed them out. They poured out of the buildings and into the courtyard. Every single silk worker found her way out, leaving behind her any trace of fear or doubt. Within minutes the buildings stood empty. The quick buzz of the empty bobbins echoed within the hollow walls.

The managers placed in charge by Chung watched helplessly as the buildings emptied. They could only follow, wielding their wooden sticks and demanding that the women return to work. "Return now, and nothing will happen to you! Chung will not know of this incident!"

But their pleas could barely be heard above the roar of the girls, who shouted back, "We won't work!" "We want shorter hours!"

The men continued to shout until their faces grew red, and then they gave up. The tide of voices overpowered them. They simply stood back and watched in amazement as the girls shouted in victory.

Chen Ling raised her arms to gain control, but the tide couldn't be stopped. They had succeeded in shutting down the silk factory. As the first taste of victory moved through each one of them, Pei watched as Hing, the man in charge, whispered some words to his small band of men. One of them then turned around and hurried off, no doubt to tell Chung of their protest. A spark of fear moved through Pei, but it was quickly replaced by the sudden chanting of "Bring us Chung! Bring us Chung!" which she herself began to shout.

When the voices of the women finally calmed down, Hing tried again to persuade them to go back to work. "Return to work now and you will not be punished!" he shouted. But they simply laughed at his wasted efforts.

The crowd suddenly parted as a long black automobile arrived, inching its way through the crowd from the main gate. It was the first car Pei had ever seen up that close. She had seen a few in Canton, their large metal bodies parked along the crowded streets, but cars were rare in Yung Kee. Pei was fascinated to see it move along without the aid of human strength, powered by an engine beneath its shiny hood. It moved slowly yet defiantly through the crowd, and when it came to a stop, the black doors opened and Chung emerged.

The crowd regained its momentum upon seeing Chung, who cleared his throat and spat on the ground. "What is the meaning of this?" he shouted at them.

Chung was accompanied by several men who carried their

firearms prominently. They stood behind Chung, straight and menacing. Pei felt Lin shift closer to her at the sight of the guns, but the crowd seemed unaffected by their open display.

Chen Ling stepped forward and with a wave of her arm the voices quieted. Not flinching at the sight of Chung or his armed men, Chen Ling handed him the list of their grievances. Chung stared hard at Chen Ling, barely glancing at the list he held in his hands. Then, turning toward the crowd of women before him, Chung turned a deep shade of red and let out a long howl of laughter.

Chen Ling remained stoic, as if waiting for Chung to get over his fit of laughing and return to the business at hand. The women were silent and so were Chung's men, who now appeared more confused than dangerous.

When Chung's laughter died into the stillness of the air, he turned back toward Chen Ling and said in a loud, angry voice, "Who do you think you are, after all I have done for you!"

Chen Ling stared back at him and, with equal anger, said: "What have you done for us? As far as I know, we've done everything for you!"

The crowd laughed and cheered as Chung's eyes narrowed and his anger grew. He motioned to the men standing behind him and they lifted their guns, pointing them upward, toward the sky. Then, at a nod of Chung's head, they fired directly into the air. The sharp, explosive shots filled the air, followed by an eerie silence. Some of the women began to scatter as the stench of gunpowder drifted overhead, but Chen Ling raised her arms and called for them to remain.

Chung's smile disappeared when he saw that the silk workers couldn't be scared off so easily by the loud gunshots of his men. He eyed them curiously, then welcomed the challenge of his power. It was now time for him to teach them all a lesson.

"What is it you expect to get from all this?" Chung asked, lowering his voice with a little more diplomacy.

"It's all written out for you," Chen Ling answered, gesturing at the papers he held in his hand.

Chung glanced down to the papers and let them drop to the ground. His round face grew red. How dare a woman address him in that smug, emotionless tone? Chung's anger couldn't be contained. "Do you think you're indispensable to me? Well, you aren't. You're nothing but failures, female dogs who have just thrown away any luck you could have had in this life!"

"Shorter hours! We want shorter hours!" Chen Ling yelled, disregarding the little speech Chung had just made. The women took up the chant, speaking in perfect time with her.

"Shor-ter hours! Shor-ter hours! Shor-ter hours!"

Chung stood enraged, trying to make himself heard by the men who stood beside him. When one of the men would not do as he commanded, Chung pushed him back and took hold of the gun he carried. Chung pointed it upward and fired. The sharp, crackling sound rang through the air, but unlike the last time the women didn't scatter. They remained, chanting even faster and louder.

"Shor-ter hours! Shor-ter hours! Shor-ter hours!"

The women seemed to grow angrier with each breath; Pei could barely remain standing as the crowd pushed forward and the shouting became more frenzied. Lin's hand slipped away from Pei's, and suddenly Lin was no longer in sight, swallowed by the moving, pushing bodies of her sisters. Pei tried to move to the side but she was wedged in by the flow of bodies as they pushed wildly forward. Pei could faintly hear Chen Ling's voice rise above the noise telling them to remain calm.

Then it happened. The firecracker sounds of the guns going off rang through the air. The pushing stopped and so did the chanting, leaving an uncomfortable silence. The strong smell of gunpowder floated through the crowd as Pei strained to see what had happened. It seemed hopeless, since she'd been pushed far back in the mélée. Then nausea moved through Pei and she knew something had gone wrong. Her heart began pounding with fear. Where was Lin? She couldn't see Lin. She pushed forward with all her strength to see.

Shoving toward the front, Pei took no notice of Chung and his men standing silent with their eyes downcast. A small clearing had been made by the women, and when Pei finally squeezed through she saw two bodies half-lying on the ground. "Who?" she cried out in fear, but when she saw Lin kneeling and cradling one of the fallen bodies, Pei could barely remain standing.

Sui Ying lay lifeless in Lin's arms, a thin line of blood running down the corner of her mouth. Lin looked up and met Pei's stare with the same silent shock Pei felt. Pei knelt down beside Sui Ying and touched her face, still warm with life. The blood that flowed freely from Sui Ying's body stained the ground and Pei's trousers as she knelt in it. Chen Ling was helping the other wounded girl to her feet; she had simply been grazed in the arm by the same bullet that seemed fated for Sui Ying.

Chen Ling straightened herself and turned back to the crowd of women. In a voice choked with grief and determination Chen Ling began chanting, "Shor-ter hours! Shor-ter hours! Shor-ter hours!" until she had recaptured every voice there. As Chung and his men looked on in silence, the voices escalated into a deafening roar.

Chung refused to take responsibility for the death of Sui Ying. "They were getting out of hand," he told the authorities. "My men were just trying to protect me and themselves. No one wanted violence, but there was no reasoning with them!"

Chung was a man of wealth and considerable power in Yung Kee. Sui Ying's death was ruled an unfortunate accident, and no formal charges were brought against Chung or any of his men.

But as word of Sui Ying's death spread through Yung Kee, other silk workers followed suit and went on strike. Hundreds of women united against Chung and the other owners, shutting down most of the silk factories.

Chen Ling and Lin led the fight with strength and strategy, refusing to be strangled by Chung. His threats of starving them out before he would yield to their demands went unheeded. Chen Ling had learned from reading about the past failures of the strikes up north, and was prepared for a long fight. Before the strike, she had organized committees and had plenty of rice stocked up at each house. If all else should fail, Sui Ying's death remained a constant reminder of how much had already been sacrificed; less food on the table would make little difference.

For days Sui Ying's body remained unburied, waiting at the temple, her spirit roaming the afterlife for a place to rest. Kung Ma had immediately written to Sui Ying's husband, Lau Chen, sending the letter to an address in Hong Kong where he worked. That same night they all prayed to Kuan Yin so he would come soon for Sui Ying's body.

Sui Ying's death still seemed so unreal. All around the sisters' house there were bits and pieces of her life still unfinished. On the desk lay a half-written letter to her husband, Lau Chen, and in the reading room was a painting she had just begun. It didn't seem fair that there would be no end to these things, that they would always remain incomplete. Pei missed Sui Ying, but she knew right away that her feeling wasn't the same one she had had when Mei-li died. She missed Sui Ying, but in a sweeter, gentler way, like a fading song.

Each day Pei anxiously waited for the arrival of Lau Chen. Some nights she dreamed of Sui Ying's body rising up from the wooden box she lay in and returning to the sisters' house. Often, when it was very early in the morning, Pei would go out into the garden where the stale perfumes intermingled; there she could feel Sui Ying's presence most strongly. Pei sat and waited with her, hoping in some way to keep Sui Ying from being lonely until she could find her resting place.

Lau Chen arrived at the sisters' house three days later. He was a small wiry man, shorter than Pei had expected, dressed in the neutral white colors of a laborer. When he shook her hand, his rough, callused fingers wrapped around Pei's with surprising gentleness. Over the years Pei had heard so much about Lau Chen that it was almost as if she knew him, although he appeared not at all as she had envisioned. Pei remembered Sui Ying saying they were close in age, but his thinning hair and slight build made him appear older. He had a pleasant face and a mild, sweet manner. And though Lau Chen couldn't be considered a man of good looks, it was easy to see how Sui Ying might have fallen in love with his gentle nature.

Lau Chen sat quietly in a large chair listening to Chen Ling's words as she awkwardly tried to explain Sui Ying's death. His eyes revealed nothing as he stared blankly into her face. He showed no signs of anger toward Chung or any of them for encouraging Sui Ying to join in the strike. When Chen Ling had finished he simply asked, "Is my wife at a place near here?"

"Yes," Chen Ling said. "She lies awaiting you at the temple. I'll take you there."

"Would it be too much trouble if I ask that Pei take me there?" asked Lau Chen hesitantly.

"No, not at all," Chen Ling said. She shook her head and looked toward Pei, relieved to be replaced.

Outside the air was hot and heavy. Pei and Lau Chen walked slowly at first, as if becoming accustomed to the ground beneath them, which felt raw and uneven. Lau Chen looked at the ground as they walked, while Pei remained silent. She had walked this same road a hundred times, but never with a man. Pei couldn't help but feel the difference. People's stares didn't seem to linger as long as when she was with her sisters, yet she felt heavier, more obvious.

"I would have been here sooner," Lau Chen said suddenly. His lower lip trembled. "But there was some trouble at the border with my papers. They suspected I might be a Communist trying to return to Canton. So many of them are running now."

"Were you detained?" Pei asked. She realized Lau Chen was her first real contact with news outside of Yung Kee.

Lau Chen wrinkled his brow, and hesitated for a moment. "For a short while; then I was suddenly released. I thought for a moment I would never make it to Yung Kee. I've heard so many terrible stories of men and women tortured in the most brutal ways. I thought for sure it would be my fate."

"They just let you go?"

"It's hard to predict what will happen, isn't it?"

Lau Chen looked up at Pei, and his grief seemed to cover them.

"I never dreamed that I wouldn't see Sui Ying again. It doesn't seem possible," he said quietly.

"I'm so sorry," Pei said, her words sounding thin and empty.

"Sui Ying wrote to me about you. You kept her company while I was far away."

For a moment their silence was unbearable. Then Lau Chen cleared his throat and turned away from her.

The large, ornate temple stood on a busy open street filled with noise and people. The temple was often used as a temporary resting place because of its dark, cool interior, which protected the deceased from the heat. It was always a relief to Pei to step into its cool, incense-filled room. She and Lau Chen were greeted by a thin, shrunken old woman who seemed relieved to find out that Lau Chen had come to claim Sui Ying's body. Pei looked around the dark, high-ceilinged room. She wanted to ask

the old woman what happened to the bodies that went un-
claimed, but refrained. Did their spirits roam the unknown forever looking for a place to rest? Did the bodies eventually turn
to gray dust and simply blow away? While the old woman and
Lau Chen spoke in low, hushed tones, Pei watched them and
wondered.

Lau Chen was led into a room toward the back. He turned
around and his eyes asked Pei to wait for him. She sat down on
a bench. The fragrant room felt even cooler and darker as she
waited. Within it was a feeling of absolute stillness. It was as if
time had stopped.

When Lau Chen returned and they were outside again, it was
as if they had awakened from a long sleep. The sunlight was so
bright Pei squinted against it, and stood awkwardly in the noisy
street.

"Is everything all right?" Pei asked.

"Yes. I must go to make the arrangements for Sui Ying's body
to be taken back to her village for burial, if I can get past the
border guards. I want to thank you for all you did for Sui Ying."
Lau Chen's words of gratitude hung in the air and fell gently
against Pei.

"I did nothing," Pei answered.

"You gave her friendship." Slowly Lau Chen began to back
away. "If ever you come to Hong Kong, you must be sure to look
for me." He slipped a piece of paper into her hand. "You can find
me there," he said. He allowed his eyes to rest on Pei for just a
moment before looking away.

Pei watched Lau Chen turn to go. He appeared so old and
tired in the bright light. She didn't move as he made his way
slowly back toward the harbor. Pei waited, hoping for Lau Chen
to turn back, but he never did. He disappeared into a crowd of
people and rising dust, taking with him her last memory of Sui
Ying.

*   *   *

Within the week, Chung and the other owners called a meeting with all the factory leaders. Chen Ling and Lin were ecstatic, knowing the owners wanted to resolve some of their demands before more of their profits were lost.

The next day Chung remained stoic and unapologetic. He stood before them, slowly speaking of the concessions he would make, barely glancing up. Pei, standing beside Lin near the spot where Sui Ying had lost her life, couldn't bear to look up at Chung. The mere sound of his flat voice disgusted her.

"You will have ten-hour workdays from this day forward," Chung said, reading from an unfolded piece of paper. "Sometimes twelve-hour days, if there should be a large shipment due; you will be compensated for the extra work."

The cheers began before Chung could finish his sentence. He frowned, and waited impatiently for the voices to stop.

"You will have one day off every two weeks," Chung shouted, "provided it's worked out in a way that does not disturb production."

When Chen Ling came forward and confirmed the rest of the changes that would be taking place, the women cheered so loudly that she gave up and stepped back.

Pei tried to raise her voice along with them, but something caught in her throat. The strike was over, but Sui Ying was dead. It didn't seem like such a victory. Pei held back her tears. Lin took hold of her hand and squeezed it tightly, both of them silent as the voices rose steadily around them.

Chapter Twelve

1934

Auntie Yee

Auntie Yee was not well. It was just after the New Year that she began to slow. At first it struck Auntie Yee that the years were catching up with her, the unkindness of age had settled in. But the pain that gradually grew in her chest seemed to overtake her, leaving her without strength or breath. The simplest cleaning would tire her out. Sometimes she found herself having to sit so she wouldn't fall down. It was hard to believe that after all these years, her body had turned against her.

Auntie Yee hid her illness from everyone skillfully, disguising her tiredness as a cold and always keeping up her happy disposition. Most of the time the girls were so busy with their own lives that they paid little attention to how she looked, or if she'd lost some weight. Only Moi knew, though no words were ever spoken. She guarded Auntie Yee's secret as if it were her own. The rest of them were fooled until it was too late, until Auntie Yee was too weak to wear her frail disguise any longer.

One night Auntie Yee became very ill. Moi sent a girl to the sisters' house to get Chen Ling. The girl was frightened and trying to catch her breath, and they could barely understand her when she told them Auntie Yee was in great pain and coughing up blood.

When Chen Ling, Ming, Lin, and Pei arrived at the girls'
house, Auntie Yee lay in her bed, pallid and wasted. It was like
a bad dream. Auntie Yee appeared a different person to them,
her once-round face distorted from the pain. There was little
resemblance to the Auntie Yee they had known as girls. Pei and
Lin had seen her several weeks before, and she seemed to be
nursing a cold—nothing more, she had told them. Now they
stood to the side and stared at Auntie Yee wide-eyed as Chen
Ling and Ming fussed about her, their faces full of concern.

Chen Ling sent immediately for Chan, the herbalist. He came
quickly and spent a long time with Auntie Yee before mixing
together several different herbs to be given to her. After a few
days' rest, Auntie Yee was up and around again, but she no
longer hid the fact that she was very ill. She moved with slower,
more deliberate steps, and seemed to watch the faces of the girls
longer and harder, not missing a thing.

After Auntie Yee became ill, Chen Ling and Ming remained
at the girls' house. Chen Ling took time off at the factory to be
with her, but as soon as she was well enough, Auntie Yee pushed
Chen Ling back to work. The silk work had always been as
important to Auntie Yee as it was to the girls. Each evening she
questioned them about their day, and every once in a while,
when there was a problem at the factory, Chen Ling would
come to her. Auntie Yee would then retreat into herself, pacing
the floor, until suddenly she would look up with an answer. In
the twenty-eight years since she had scrimped and scraped to
begin the girls' house, Auntie Yee had never gone back to the
silk factory. She preferred to take charge of her girls spiritually
and personally, leaving the talk of cocoons and reeling to Chen
Ling and Lin. During the strike, Auntie Yee kept silent in her
concern and sorrow. But it was widely known throughout the
village of Yung Kee that no one knew more about the silk work
than Auntie Yee.

The news of her illness spread quickly. Most of the girls knew her or knew of her. Many of them had grown up at the girls' house, while others knew her as the mother of Chen Ling. Everyone who had lived at the girls' house saw Auntie Yee as her mother. In many ways, she was better to them than their real mothers had been, and through the years she'd kept their devotion. Those who had left often returned to visit Auntie Yee. Sometimes she would forget a name, but never a face. Her influence would always remain a vital part of their lives, even if they didn't choose the sisterhood. Auntie Yee knew there wasn't any deep, dark secret to their devotion. It was simply because she had to work harder to reach them when they had lost their first mothers. And once she won the battle of becoming their second mother, there was no letting go.

The girls' house had been the one reward in her life that made it possible for her to bear all the sorrows of her daughters. Auntie Yee refused to become paralyzed by life. She seemed to move out of some kind of invisible necessity, knowing that if she stopped, it would be for good. She talked, laughed, and loved the girls out of their lonely and bruised lives, pointing them in a new direction.

"Nothing ever stands still," she told them. "And neither should you."

Moi answered the door for every one of Auntie Yee's visitors. Some she suspiciously ushered in, in her abrupt, careless way, while others, like Lin and Pei, were given appreciative nods. The rooms in the girls' house now seemed small, still bare and immaculate. And everywhere was the thick, sweet smell of burning incense.

When Auntie Yee felt well enough, she greeted her visitors in the reading room, where she always felt the greatest sense of calm. She was no longer strong enough to see all the girls who came to visit, but on occasional evenings she felt happy to be up. She knew these times were numbered. As the ache of this thought rushed through her, Auntie Yee washed it from her mind. The smell of incense was even sharper and more over-powering; Moi burned a forest of thin incense sticks in front of the shiny statue of Kuan Yin. Moi lingered like a shadow in the reading room, and stayed with Auntie Yee to tend to her needs. Her eyes darted quickly over at Auntie Yee before she moved across the room to light another stick of incense.

When Moi returned, carrying a bowl of dried plums, she sat down in the chair across from Auntie Yee. Moi sitting down was a rarity, and try as she might, Auntie Yee couldn't remember ever seeing Moi sit anywhere other than the high wooden stool she kept in the kitchen. The kitchen had always been the only place Moi really looked comfortable. It never took long for a new girl to understand that she was never to touch anything in the kitchen without asking Moi's permission. Auntie Yee once told them all, "Moi guards her pots and pans as others guard their money."

Moi looked over at Auntie Yee and suddenly asked, "Are you hungry?"

Auntie Yee shook her head, conserving her energy. "You can go," she finally said. "I'll be fine here."

Moi started to rise, then sat back down in silence.

"So when all this nonsense is over, will you take a room upstairs? It will be more comfortable."

"What do I need with a room?" Moi returned. "I would have nothing to put in it."

Auntie Yee smiled at their ongoing argument. Moi's room had always been a flat gray cot at the far end of the kitchen. The few clothes she had were stacked neatly in a basket, or sometimes hung across a thick rope that held the blanket separating her space from the rest of the kitchen. Wherever Moi went, the stale smell of cooking was always embedded in every article of clothing she wore. For years Auntie Yee had been trying to get Moi to take a room upstairs, but she refused to leave her corner in the kitchen.

"I want you to have my room," Auntie Yee said, adding a new element to their old argument. She knew it was unfair, but said it anyway.

Moi glanced up surprised, a look that had rarely crossed her face in all the years they'd been together. Then she looked away from Auntie Yee, down at her own rough, overworked hands. When she was ready to speak, Moi lifted the bowl of plums towards Auntie Yee. "I make no promise to sleep in it," she finally said.

Auntie Yee smiled and nodded. She knew Moi had never been close to anyone except for her. In their mumbling, argumentative way, they'd been a family to each other for many years. And it was Moi she worried about most when it would be time for her to go into the other world. These thoughts ran through her head now as they sat in a comfortable silence. Upstairs, she could hear the quick movements of Chen Ling and Ming cleaning her room and making up a fresh bed. When Auntie Yee looked back over at Moi, she could see her lips moving silently as if in prayer.

Auntie Yee dreamed that night of her brother, Chan. She was so happy to see him again as he lifted her into his arms. He appeared just as she remembered him, so young and strong, but she couldn't help thinking how old and worn she must look. She opened her mouth to say something, but Chan put up his hand to stop her. Ahead of them was the house of their childhood, a white light shining. Chan smiled calmly and held her hand. There was no more pain or struggle; Auntie Yee remained silent, comforted.

Pei

The evening Auntie Yee died, Pei and Lin were still working at the silk factory. It was Ming who came to tell them. Pei knew immediately that Auntie Yee was gone from the look on Ming's face, an expression caught somewhere between sorrow and relief. From a distance it looked almost like a frown. Ming walked slowly toward them and whispered some words to Lin, who then looked over toward Pei and nodded her head slowly.

They went directly from the factory to the girls' house. As soon as Pei turned the corner she felt what she'd been dreading. The girls' house she had once known so well had lost its spirit, standing grave and silent against the darkening sky. The pale glow of the oil lamps burned low in the courtyard. Already mourners, both young and old, waited outside in scattered groups for their turn to pay their respects. Moi answered the door and ushered Pei and Lin in. She wore the dark clothing of mourning and kept her eyes downcast. Pei looked hard around the familiar rooms for any difference, any hard evidence that Auntie Yee was no longer alive and well. She glanced toward the stairs, still waiting anxiously for Auntie Yee to come down them.

Then Moi suddenly stopped, turning toward them. Her eyes were cloudy and faraway. She leaned forward as if to convey a secret to Pei and Lin. "I knew all along it was a bad sickness. The old woman could not fool me. Aii-ya, did she think she could fool me? When you have lived together as long as we have in the same house, you know these things."

"Why didn't you say something earlier?" Pei asked gently.

Moi looked down and rubbed her bad leg. "What was there to say? If Yee wanted you to know, you would have known. I did what I could, brewing her strong teas and slipping very hard to find herbs into her soup. For a while she was better, then all of a sudden it came back stronger to take hold of her again." Moi shook her head sadly. "I did everything I could."

"We know you did," Lin said, letting her hand gently touch Moi's arm.

Moi was silent again, having said what she needed to. For the first time she appeared old and lost. Pei knew how helpless she must feel, and how hard it would be for her now that Auntie Yee was gone. She wanted to say something comforting, but Moi turned quickly around and led them upstairs to Auntie Yee's room.

There was a strange feeling in Pei's stomach as they made their way upstairs. It felt like the first time she walked up the stairs with Auntie Yee as a child, a knot of anxiety growing inside her with each step they took. It had been as if Pei knew her father was leaving her that day; now that same tiny whisper moved through her, only this time it was Auntie Yee who had left.

The room was dark, illuminated by a single lamp in the far corner. Incense burned in thin, shadowy streams beside the bed on which Auntie Yee lay. Her eyes were closed, as if in sleep. Chen Ling was kneeling on one side of Auntie Yee's body, softly chanting in prayer. Ming touched her on the shoulder to let her know they had come.

Chen Ling rose and whispered, "She's at peace."

Auntie Yee's body had been bathed by Moi and Chen Ling, then dressed in the white silk tunic and pants she had worn so many years ago at her own hairdressing ceremony. On one of Lin's and Pei's last visits, Auntie Yee had shown them the tunic. She had proudly displayed the superior quality of the silk and pointed to the intricate weaving, as her swollen fingers moved lovingly over it. "When you die," Auntie Yee had said, "and the fates are kind, you have the time to prepare."

But seeing Auntie Yee dressed in the tunic now was something entirely different. With her hair neatly coiled on top of her head, Auntie Yee appeared serene and very beautiful. Suddenly Pei was filled with the desire to tell Auntie Yee how beautiful she was, but it was too late. Auntie Yee was dead. She would no longer self-consciously dismiss, with a high shrill laugh or a quick wave of her hand, anything Pei said or asked.

Pei turned to Lin, who seemed deep in her own memories. Her eyelids were lowered, almost closed, and Pei suddenly felt helpless amid the silence and the thick waves of incense that stung her eyes.

The funeral was held two days later. The morning after her death, Auntie Yee was placed in a silk-lined coffin of thick hardwood polished a shiny brown. It sat like an unwelcome intrusion in the reading room, with Auntie Yee filling three fourths of its length. Incense burned on a table at the head of the coffin. At her feet and all around her body were heavy silk quilts, which held her body firmly in place, and between her lips Chen Ling had placed a white pearl in case she would need to buy her way into heaven.

Auntie Yee was to be buried in a small cemetery, just outside Yung Kee, which was the resting place for many of the sisters who had gone on into the other world. It was the kind of day Auntie Yee would have loved, cool and crisp. The sun was shining weakly as they gathered in front of the girls' house. Mourners from all the different girls' and sisters' houses in the area came to pay their final respects to Auntie Yee, wearing coarse muslin burial outfits over their own clothes, with two lengths of muslin draped over their heads. Slowly the funeral procession made its way down the dusty street, following the coffin bearers like a flock of birds. Chen Ling, Ming, and Moi led the mourners past the countless staring eyes of the Yung Kee citizens.

When they finally reached the cemetery, Chen Ling spoke briefly to the man attending the gate before they continued along a dirt path, leading to the site Auntie Yee had chosen. It was on a slight hill, with two large trees on each side to shade her from the sun. Pei moved forward and let her hand touch the place on the box where she imagined Auntie Yee's hands were, folded gently across her chest. Pei's hand remained there for several minutes, pressing harder and harder against the shiny, slippery wood.

The ceremony was short and simple. After a few words spoken by Chen Ling on the occasion of the acceptance of Auntie Yee into the land of her ancestors, the young men hired to carry the coffin slowly lowered it into the ground. Following Chen Ling and Ming, Pei and Lin walked toward the grave and kowtowed three times before Auntie Yee. They each picked up a handful of dirt and threw it into the grave. Then Chen Ling lighted a match and burned the paper money, paper servants, and paper clothes that would accompany Auntie Yee into her next life. Very carefully Pei, Lin, and the other mourners removed the muslin outergarments they wore. One by one these clothes would also be burned, so that no remnants of death would be taken back into their daily lives.

That evening, Pei and Lin returned to the girls' house for a simple meal of vegetables, prepared by Moi. They ate little and exchanged few words. Not until much later, when they returned to the emptiness of the sisters' house, did Pei weep for her great loss.

The Ghosts' Feast

Moi rolled out the sticky rice-flour dough in small jerking movements. Every so often she sprinkled water and more flour onto her dough until it reached the right consistency. On the table next to her was a bowl filled with several different kinds of chopped vegetables. Moi had spent a good part of the previous evening chopping and mincing, preparing to make the dumplings that she would steam or cook in broth.

The Ghosts' Feast occurred once a year, when they prepared food and went to the cemetery to eat and to worship their family and sisters who had gone into the other world. It was the first Ghosts' Feast since Auntie Yee's death, and Moi was determined to make it a memorable one. Since the death, Chen Ling and Ming had moved back to run the girls' house. They'd left early to buy the incense and paper money necessary for the celebration at the cemetery.

Moi stopped and looked toward the door that led outside to the well. It had become a habit since Auntie Yee's death to suddenly stop whatever she was doing and look toward a door, any door leading elsewhere. Most of the time Auntie Yee came to her through the back door, keeping Moi company while she prepared the evening meal or when she scrubbed the wash. Auntie Yee had made Moi promise that she would tell no one of these visits.

The first time Auntie Yee appeared, Moi almost sliced off part of her finger. It was less than a week after Auntie Yee had died, and Moi was suffering terribly from the loneliness. Auntie Yee had been her only source of companionship, even if it was sometimes harsh. Without her, Moi lived in a void. She moved through her daily routine unhappily and said almost nothing to others.

But one evening, Auntie Yee had entered right through the back door, dressed in the same white tunic she was buried in. In her hand she carried the pearl that had been placed between her lips.

"Who are you?" Moi hissed, lifting the cleaver up as the blood dripped from her cut finger onto the floor.

Auntie Yee kept walking toward her. When she reached the table Auntie Yee sat down in the chair across from Moi, as she had often done when she was alive. When Auntie Yee smiled, exposing her crooked teeth, Moi knew that she had really come back to her.

"Have I also entered the life after?" Moi wondered aloud, calm at the thought.

Auntie Yee laughed and pointed to Moi's finger. "By the looks of that, you're very much alive," she answered, assuring Moi that life remained with her.

Moi lowered the cleaver and felt the sudden throbbing of her bleeding finger.

After that first night, Auntie Yee often came to visit. They spoke in low tones in the kitchen while Moi cooked, before the girls came back from the factory. For the most part Auntie Yee was happy where she was, though she spoke little of the life after. Most of their conversation dealt with the running of the girls' house now that Chen Ling had taken over. Moi asked little of Auntie Yee, only too grateful for the company.

Moi put a spoonful of vegetable mixture into the middle of a small circle of her rolled-out dough. With her fingers she quickly pinched the edges together in the shape of a half-moon and added the dumpling to her growing collection. When Moi felt there were enough, she dropped half of her dumplings into a large pot of boiling soup. The other half she steamed in bamboo baskets, one stacked on top of the other.

At any moment Chen Ling and Ming would return with the soy-sauce chicken and some incense. Moi wrapped the last of the dumplings and waited. They were already late and would have to hurry off to the cemetery, where Lin, Pei, and the others would be waiting for them with the roast pig. When Moi heard a noise, she quickly looked up, hoping it might be Auntie Yee, but it was only a stray dog scratching at the back door.

*   *   *

The morning air was still fresh when they arrived at the cemetery. Chen Ling had spared no expense in erecting a suitable memorial for Auntie Yee. The white marble headstone stood upwards of six feet tall; it was flanked by two angels on either side, especially carved and brought back from Canton. On the headstone was an inlaid photo of Auntie Yee, taken when she was still a young woman, and underneath it were a few words describing her life. The inscription ended with a large gold engraving:

"BELOVED MOTHER OF MANY."

Lin and Pei were already waiting. A makeshift table held an entire roast pig and the sweet cakes Auntie Yee loved. Moi placed the dim sum and chicken next to them, then looked around to see if Auntie Yee might be waiting for them. When she saw that Auntie Yee was nowhere in sight, Moi took a bowl and filled it with choice pieces of pork and chicken. In another bowl she put the dumplings and cakes, along with a pair of chopsticks, and placed them next to Auntie Yee's headstone. One by one, Chen Ling and the rest joined Moi around the headstone, respectfully kowtowing to Auntie Yee. Thin, dark strips of smoke drifted into the air as they burned the incense and the gold, silver, and white paper money that would go to Auntie Yee in the next life.

Afterward, when they all sat down to eat, Moi stood aside. Even at Chen Ling and Ming's urging, Moi could not bring herself to join them. She was too accustomed to eating alone in her kitchen, and stubbornly refused to break her habit now.

Then something made Moi turn around quickly. She almost cried out in happiness when she saw Auntie Yee sitting at her gravestone. Very slowly, Auntie Yee picked up the food that had been left for her and, without saying a word, lifted her hand and gestured toward the others. Moi remained silent and smiled, then obediently made her way back to eat with the others.

Chapter Thirteen

―――

1936

Pei

The music blared harsh and scratchy from the machine called a phonograph. The phonograph and records were a gift from Lin's younger brother, Ho Yung. They came all the way from Canton and had been hand-delivered to the sisters' house so that nothing would be broken. Chen Ling, Ming, and even the reclusive Moi came over in the evening, curious to hear what miracles the machine could create. The first time Lin wound the handle and placed the needle on the record, the music erupted like a scream from the phonograph's long sprouting horn. The sudden wail frightened them and sent several for cover. Moi shook her head and mumbled, "Who would send such a thing, filled with spirits trying to get out!"

In a note accompanying the gift, Ho Yung wrote to them about different dances, each step vividly described. He had written regularly since their visit to Canton and was now working in the trade business, having defied his mother's wishes for him to follow his brother into a government position. "Somebody has to support the family when the government collapses!" Ho Yung wrote. He traveled regularly from Canton to Hong Kong, and sometimes even to London and Paris, and other places Pei could only dream about. Often he sent them gifts and vivid descriptions of the cities and people. Lin read his letters aloud, proud of her younger brother. They had much in common now, both of them defying their mother and choosing their own paths. Pei knew Ho Yung's letters and gifts brought Lin great happiness, filling a void left by her mother. Pei began to gain something too, a new sight of a world she longed to see.

The girls giggled when the first foreign sounds entered the room, then fell silent and curious as the music continued. The song, which played in distinct beats, was something called a tango.

A moment later, Lin stood up. "Let's try this tango. Just follow me," she said, taking Pei's hand and slipping her arm around Pei's waist. In the next moment Lin was following Ho Yung's instructions, and gliding with Pei down the length of the room to the beat of the music. Pei concentrated so hard it took her a few minutes to realize the rest of the girls in the room were laughing at them.

Kung Ma, who usually just smiled at their antics, was laughing so hard she fell back into a chair. Not long ago they had gone to see a moving-picture show, the first in Yung Kee. It showed tall, splendid white devils dancing across a shiny dance floor, dressed in a glitter of finery such as Pei had never seen before. This was what Pei saw again in her mind as Lin moved her across the floor. Slowly the others stopped laughing, and gradually tried to join them, following the moves Lin tried so carefully to imitate.

"Now turn!" Lin shouted. They switched hands and turned their bodies awkwardly in the opposite direction. The others clumsily followed, knocking into each other.

"No, no, not that way!" said Kung Ma suddenly, jumping onto her feet. "The change of hands must be sharper, like this." She took Pei's hand and led her back across the room, only this time there was no hesitation. Kung Ma turned Pei with a pronounced yet graceful change and led her back to Lin.

"Where did you learn to dance?" Lin asked, as surprised as the rest of them.

"I wasn't always a silk worker." Kung Ma laughed. She waved her hand in the air and took a quick spin, her thickening body still light and fluid. "A girl from Hong Kong taught me," she finally admitted. "Just before she left our girls' house to be married. Her mother was once a professional dancer in Hong Kong. When her mother became ill, the daughter was sent here to do silk work. Shortly after, she was called back to Hong Kong to be married. It must be almost twenty years ago now. Well, until she left, she would teach us a few steps each evening."

"Will you teach us?" Pei asked.

Kung Ma blushed. "It was so long ago. I hardly remember anything."

"You know more than any of us," Pei said pleadingly.

Lin walked over to the phonograph and lifted the needle. Instantly the room was silent.

"All right," King Ma finally agreed. "Start the record over. Let's begin with the tango!"

For the rest of the evening, the room was filled with laughter, childlike and contagious. Even Moi participated in their dance class by changing the records, once she had been convinced that no spirits lived inside the phonograph. It seemed like such a long time since they had had so much fun. The slow spread of Japanese threats seemed far away, lost in the tango and another dance Kung Ma had learned, called a waltz. Kung Ma was like a different person, someone Pei had never known, so young and carefree. They all were. The music moved through the air around them, filling the room.

The Year of the Rat was almost upon them. Only during the New Year were they given a week off and allowed the luxury of some free time. The silk factory closed down and they were left to their own wanderings—but only after their New Year's preparations were done.

Nothing was taken for granted in order to start the New Year in purity. Pei and Lin immediately began cleaning the sisters' house and washing their clothes for the New Year. Each year they all scrubbed behind doors and under beds till their hands were raw and the floors rediscovered their natural color.

It was a relief when Kung Ma asked Pei and Lin to pick up some nien kao at the bakery. Nien kao was the sticky sweet cake that Pei loved best about welcoming in the year. Few shops stayed open during the week, except for the market stalls and those that prepared nien kao.

"I love this time of year," Lin said happily as they walked through the streets filled with people. Red-and-gold banners, for felicity and prosperity, hung from windows and doorways. "It's the one time that all of China celebrates together!"

"Even with the war?" Pei asked Lin.

"Especially because of the war," she answered.

And even if Pei wasn't so sure this was true up north, she kept silent. Pei knew China was struggling. What little information they received came from Ho Yung's letters and from the merchants and peddlers who made their way to the sisters' house, selling their wares and dispersing the bits of information they gathered along the way. Pei and Lin listened, drinking it all in with a great thirst.

"It does not look good, Missy," the last peddler had said. "China is surely to fall under the weight of the Japanese devils, if not by the hands of her own people."

There was definitely something in the air, voices echoing with a quiet threat, thinly disguised underneath all the celebration. It left Pei feeling cold inside, but by the time they reached the bakery, the rich, sweet aromas helped to erase her fears.

It was still early, but the bakery was already crowded with customers trying to buy nien kao and the little red mountains of

bread neatly lined in their wooden boxes. Pei felt like a child
again as she ran ahead of Lin to wait in line. She turned around
to wave for Lin to join her, when a face caught her eye. A shiver
moved through her as she opened her mouth, then closed it
again in silence. Standing with a group of young men waiting in
front of the bakery was Su-lung's brother, Hong.

"What is it?" she could hear Lin ask.

Pei couldn't answer, even when she knew that Lin's gaze was
heavy upon her. It was Mei-li's presence she could feel beside
her, the salty smell of her river death still upon her.

"Over there," Pei finally whispered.

"Where?" Lin asked.

"Hong, Su-lung's brother."

Lin's gaze left her instantly. Pei didn't know if Lin had caught
sight of the tall, thin, serious-looking Hong before he disappeared behind some others. Pei thought the years would have
softened the shock and the blame she felt for having kept Mei-
li's secret, but the pain of Mei-li's death returned like a freshly
opened wound.

"Let's go," Lin said to her.

"But the nien kao?"

"We can get it later."

"No," Pei insisted.

Before anything else could be said, another event left them
standing speechless in the same place. Not thirty feet from
where they stood, a man was screaming while being dragged
away by several men. One of the men gathered a handkerchief
from his pocket and stuffed it roughly into the screaming man's
mouth. "The son of a bitch is a traitor!" they shouted. "He would
sell his family to those Japanese devils!"

In the suffocating crowd that had gathered, Pei and Lin
watched as the man was dragged down the street. In the past few
months, more and more hysterical accusations were being made,
singling out those who were said to be traitors or spies. Fear of

the Japanese was so great that such accusations could happen anytime, and for any reason. The traitors were usually taken care of in one swift motion, before the authorities could intervene. Sometimes the accused were left hanging from a tree; or their bodies were found slumped over in a pool of blood, their throats slit from ear to ear.

"Where are they taking him?" Pei asked.

Lin said, "They've found him guilty."

"But how can they be sure? How can we just stand here doing nothing! What if he's innocent?"

"Fear seems to be the ruling judge."

"Then we're all guilty."

"Pretending to be innocent," Lin said, shaking her head in apology.

"What's going to happen to us?"

Lin thought, then answered: "I'm afraid we won't have much choice. We'll do what we have to do to survive this terror."

When the crowd dispersed, Pei turned around to find that Hong was no longer to be found. They waited in line for the nien kao, then went quickly back to the sisters' house, saying nothing of what had happened.

For days after, the shock and then the dull grief of that morning hung on. Pei tried hard to shake it off. She knew it would be bad luck to carry it into the New Year.

A few days after the New Year, Lin said, "I think we should take a short trip."

Pei had remained quiet and preoccupied since the morning they saw Hong. Even the opera performance they were returning from did nothing to lift her spirits. The music, made up of cymbals, drums, and the high whining voices of the actors, only proved to be irritating.

"Where?" Pei asked, surprised.

"I've never seen much of the countryside. We could take a

boat part of the way, then hire a sedan chair to take us out to some of the temples," Lin said, watching Pei closely.

"Is it safe to travel?"

"The Japanese are still far up north. There's no telling when they'll ever make it this far south."

Pei hesitated, then smiled. "It would be a nice change."

Lin smiled and appeared encouraged. With her fingers she brushed a wisp of hair away from her smooth forehead. Even in the waning light Pei could see the curve of Lin's fingers and the face that grew more beautiful with age. Pei knew what she had always known: She would have died if Lin hadn't saved her.

"And we could visit your village and family if you would like," Lin said softly. "It's your decision."

Pei couldn't answer right away. The thought was so new to her. She let the words move through her mind, slow and even. Lin and her sisters at the factory had been her family for so long, Pei found it easier to bury the fact that she came from others. After all these years, her parents' silence gave her the strength to move forward, no longer looking back. Still, the questions lingered. Would her family still be there? And what of her sisters, Li and Yu-ling? She took a deep breath. The night air was so sweet, it suddenly filled her with such sorrow Pei wanted to cry.

The Guest People

Pao Chung quickly pushed the wire net closer and closer to the side of the pond, even as it grew heavier with his catch. He had been doing this for so many years that the weight of the load made no difference to the speed at which he worked. He could have done it just as easily blindfolded. Once the load of fish had been pushed as far as possible to one side of the pond, Pao would scoop the struggling fish up in baskets and ready them for market.

The fish never ceased to amaze Pao in their gasping struggle for life. Like silver and orange flashes of light, they jumped in the air, trying to find their way back into the water. This would sometimes continue for as long as fifteen minutes after they had been taken from the pond. The strongest survived longer, wheezing and bloating in their final moments of life. As a boy Pao had sympathized with the fish. As a man he could think of more miserable ways to die.

Most of the time Yu-sung helped with loading the fish into the baskets. They had worked side by side like this for almost twenty-five years, except for the month she stayed in after each birth. But lately Yu-sung had not been feeling well and had become bone-thin. Pao forbade her to do any more hard work. Still, he knew she might be inside scrubbing the floors or doing some other taxing job. It was her nature, and though Pao would never say it aloud he was worried about Yu-sung.

Pao Chung was no longer a young man, though his lean, hard body and tall, straight stance made him appear so. The only telltale sign of his age was the tiny wrinkles that textured his leathery face. Unlike Yu-sung's hair, which had turned gray, Pao's was thick and black; not one gray hair emerged from his head.

Every day of his life was spent tending to the ponds and the mulberry groves. Even in the hard times when there was little work to be done in the fishless ponds and empty groves, Pao stood among them, waiting. The work was what had always kept Pao Chung alive, ever since he was a boy working alongside his Hakka father from morning until night. He was at home on the land as he had never been among people. In front of others, Pao always felt too tall and awkward. He would always be a Hakka among them. Only when his muscles ached and his hands were bloody and raw from bringing in the fish did Pao feel at his best.

* * *

Pao unloaded the last of his empty baskets from the boat and stacked them among the rest. It had been a good day at the market and he was able to return home in good time. It was dark, with only a thin moon giving off light, but Pao felt content in knowing he had gotten a very good price for the fish. At first, Pao had hesitated to leave Yu-sung alone. She seemed to grow weaker by the day. He couldn't give her illness a name, but he knew it was growing, dark and dangerous. Pao felt his pocket for the herbs he had bought at the market hoping they would give Yu-sung back her strength.

Lately, Pao noticed, Yu-sung's grief could no longer be silenced by hard work. It had taken on a new form, something hard and concrete that Pao couldn't penetrate. She lay motionless in their bed at night and took little notice of him when he walked in. It was as if she was simply tired of her life. On her better days, Yu-sung would be sitting at the table waiting with his dinner, exchanging a few words with him. Pao relished the simple gift of her voice.

Seeing Yu-sung in this state, Pao began to grieve along with her. He found himself haunted by the deaths of his children and the absence of his daughter Pei, whom he had been forced to give away. Sometimes he saw Pei in his dreams, as he had seen her that day he left her at the top of the steps at the girls' house. Whenever Pei came to him it was always with the same anxious smile she had worn the day he left her. Only, in Pao's dream, Pei would lift her hand and point her finger at him accusingly, the tears of abandonment staining her cheeks. Pao never sought forgiveness; he had had no other choice. He could only hope that Pei would someday grow to realize how much the money she made meant for their survival. The years after she went to work at the silk factory were hard ones for them. It took three seasons for the fish to be restored to the ponds and even longer for the mulberry leaves to flourish again.

It was completely dark by the time Pao reached the house. There was no light on from inside to tell him what to expect. Instantly his hands became sweaty and his heart began throbbing as if it would jump out of his throat. Yu-sung always left a candle lit for him, no matter how late it was. His hand gripped the latch on the door and paused for a moment before pushing it open. The familiar smell of her cooking reached him first and immediately put him at ease. Yu-sung had cooked for him, she must be all right. Pao walked in slowly. Even in the dark he knew every square inch of the house he built. For months now the fear of losing Yu-sung had slowed him, turned him into an old man. Now it wasn't so much the dark that worried him as it was the quiet.

Pao fumbled to light a candle. It flickered twice before filling the room with its glow. The food Yu-sung had prepared waited for him on the table. He walked to the thick curtain that hid their bed and lifted it. Yu-sung was in their bed, lying on her side with her back to him. Pao listened hard until he caught the slight sound of her breathing. He took a deep breath and returned to his food.

He had seen her bedridden only once before. It was a year after Pei left and the quiet baby Yu-ling had come down with a sickness. In a matter of days Yu-ling was gone. Yu-sung had said nothing. She lay in bed with fever, as white as a ghost, grabbing at air in delirium for the death that stole her daughters. Li was still with them then, taking care of her mother as if she were a much older person. But Li had been gone for years, with a husband and children of her own. It was Pao who would take care of Yu-sung now.

Pao undressed quietly in the dark and let his fallen clothes lie where he stood. Once he had lifted the thick curtain he breathed in the same sticky air Yu-sung did. Very carefully he slid in beside her. Her rhythmic breathing tensed into one long sigh.

Pao lay frozen until her breathing became steady and he was sure she was asleep.

Yu-sung had always been such a light sleeper. The first month of their marriage Pao was sure she hardly slept, pretending to be asleep every time he came near her. He had wanted her so badly he didn't care if she was asleep or not. He pressed his body on top of hers and entered her roughly, even when he knew he was hurting her. He couldn't help himself. Once Pao watched her face when he was inside her. Yu-sung squeezed her eyes shut in pain and bit her lip rather than cry out. Seeing her like that, he became soft and quickly rolled off her with a low grunt. He had never been more ashamed of himself.

Then the babies came, one by one, and Yu-sung slept lighter than ever, always listening for their cries. Even after the dead ones were buried she seem to be listening for them. She would bolt right up in the night hearing these phantom cries, then sometimes cry herself. Pao wanted to say something but he didn't know what or how.

Pao turned towards Yu-sung and saw the smooth curve of her back. Very slowly he pushed his body across the space that divided them, until he could feel the warmth of her body next to his. He carefully shaped his body against hers so that his face touched her hair and he could smell the oily remnants of cooking in it. Pao moved still closer and let his hand hover over the sharp curve of her hip, then let it fall, as light as a feather.

Chapter Fourteen

1936

Pei

It felt like stepping back in time to be so close to the earth again. At first the immediate thoughts of her childhood stung, but the raw beauty of the land was somehow calming. The brownish-orange soil, like rich mahogany, looked brilliant in the warm sun.

"Please stop here," Pei suddenly told the sedan carriers. Once they did, she jumped out of the sedan chair and ran toward the edge of the road.

In the near distance a maze of fish ponds stood surrounded by thick, healthy mulberry groves. Pei stopped to listen to the soft rustling of their leaves in the wind. It was hard to understand how something so beautiful could bring back such sadness.

The sky seemed endless. It was an inviting blue, cleaner and clearer than the sky over Yung Kee, which was often filled with billows of dark smoke coming from the various factories. Everything around them seemed so much more brilliant in this pure light of day. Even the air was lighter and fresher, with a slightly sweet aroma that couldn't help but invite memories of Pei's childhood.

"Would you like to walk for a while?" Lin asked, her voice filling the air.

Pei turned around to see Lin still sitting in the sedan chair, watching her intently. The sedan carriers observed them without concern. They had readily accepted Lin's offer of a good price to take them out to the countryside.

Pei ground her foot into the rich soil, and knew immediately it was ridiculous to be riding in a chair and not feeling the land beneath their feet.

"Yes, if it's all right with you," Pei answered.

Lin climbed down from the chair and walked toward Pei, directing the carriers to follow them. The two lean, shirtless men picked up the lightened sedan chair and followed without question.

They walked slowly at first, the mild wind pushing against them, while the dust from the road left a thin reddish film on their shoes. Pei remained quiet as Lin walked beside her. Pei knew that just over the hill was where her village had once stood, and she now moved toward it with a mixture of feelings that moved from curiosity to extreme fear.

"What's that growing over there?" Lin asked after a while, her voice a gentle intrusion.

Pei turned. "Most of those are mulberry groves," she answered. "And there's some sugarcane. Much of it is grown around fish ponds to help nourish the groves."

Lin pointed west, toward fields sprouting thinner, shorter shoots that didn't resemble the others. "What's that grown over there?"

"That's rice. A great deal of it is grown in the area around here. After it's harvested, the earth is turned over and another crop is planted so that the process never ends."

As Pei spoke, she remembered one of the rare times when her father told Li and her about the land. There was a light in his eyes as he spoke. For the first time she felt the strength of the earth and fully realized the tenderness her father felt for its great, fertile body.

"It must have been wonderful growing up here."

Pei smiled. "I never had anything else to compare it with. I never realized that there was anything beyond mulberry groves and fish ponds, and our occasional trips to the village."

Lin laughed. "That doesn't sound so bad. Growing up in a large city can be suffocating. Here, you can see as far as the eye can take you!" She swept her arm through the air and let it float back down to her side.

"As much as the land gives, it can take away too," Pei remembered, thinking of the intoxicating spell the land had woven in the lives of her parents and of so many others before them. How simply lives were ended, and the fates of children determined, by the land they worked. As she looked upon it now, so harmless in its calm beauty, the cruelty it could also yield made her shiver. For the first time, she realized that the price of this land was sometimes paid in blood. It didn't make the hurt she felt at being abandoned disappear, but it did help to soothe the wounds.

"Did you live near here?" Lin asked hesitantly.

"Beyond that hill." She pointed toward the small hill in the far distance.

"Where would you like to go first?" Lin asked, brushing away the dust that had begun to settle on her white trousers.

"If we continue down this road we should come to my village," Pei answered.

"I'd like to see it, if you don't mind."

Pei looked at her and said softly, "Of course."

She couldn't bring herself to tell Lin that she was afraid her village might no longer exist. She imagined a great expanse of empty land where the makeshift buildings had once stood. The voices of the villagers, and the cries of the animals, which once echoed through the air as they were bought and sold at the weekly market, would be silent. There would no longer be any signs of life, no sign of her childhood. And beyond the village, only more emptiness.

But as soon as they descended the hill, the village came into sight. Pei felt like a child again, moving excitedly along the road towards the village. Lin kept up with her, while the sedan carriers moved at their own pace, falling farther and farther behind them.

At the edge of the village, Pei slowed down. It had grown—a few more buildings lined the dusty road—but it felt smaller and much more colorless than she remembered. When she was a child, a journey to the village had meant an occasional sugar candy and the excitement of mixing with people other than her own family. Now Pei saw it for what it really was, a dusty village with its dilapidated buildings that depended on the trade of the poor farmers surrounding it. Dogs and livestock wandered aimlessly, leaving soiled spots on the earth. When Pei turned to Lin, her face was flushed with embarrassment.

"It isn't very much, is it?" she said.

"I'm sure they make do." said Lin, reassuringly.

Pei thought of how different her life had once been before Yung Kee and the silk factory.

The village people eyed them with restraint and curiosity. Their conversations turned into low whispers as she and Lin walked by them. Pei couldn't help but look hard into each face, thinking one of them might be Li, or her mother, or even her father. She smiled, thinking what a sight they must be marching down the road, dressed identically in white, being slowly followed by two coolies carrying a sedan chair.

"Would you like to see the temple?" she asked Lin, relaxing into remembering the one nice building the village held.

"I'd love to see the temple," Lin answered, her body straightening.

Pei led Lin toward the temple, which stood at the far end of the village. After so many years, it still appeared a grand building with its ornately painted red-and-gold doors and its tall, thick columns.

"It was built by the villagers and farmers," Pei explained.

"It's beautiful," Lin said.

"I've only been inside once, and even then I wasn't supposed to be. My parents were very angry at me for wandering away."

Lin laughed. "You must have been a handful."

"I was determined to see what it was like inside."

"And did you?"

"Not without consequences, but it was worth it." Pei laughed. "My chores were endless, and I wasn't able to sit for a week after."

For the first time Pei felt proud. She directed the sedan-chair carriers to wait for them outside. As they pushed open the heavy doors of the temple, a cool wave of air and incense surrounded them. She felt her heart beating quickly as they entered the hollow room with its high altar; the temple resembled many others she'd since seen. Yet Pei felt something different here, and all of a sudden the dark mystery, the sharp excitement of her childhood returned.

As they emerged into the bright sunlight from the darkened interior of the temple, Pei blinked herself awake. She had said nothing about visiting her family, though she knew Lin wondered if they would. Pei turned to Lin and was about to say something but stopped, her lips slightly parting as her tongue appeared to moisten them.

"What would you like to see next?" Pei finally asked.

"Where you grew up," Lin answered.

Pei hesitated. She shifted her weight from side to side before answering, "It's quite a distance."

Lin pointed toward the sedan chair. The two carriers sat in its shade, drinking from tin cups.

"That's why we hired them."

Pei was quiet again, trying to weigh the possibilities that lay before her. She knew Lin wouldn't push her if she chose to return to the boat. For the past few years Pei had chosen to say little about her family, even though the pain and curiosity burned inside of her.

"You don't have to make up your mind right away; let's get something to drink," Lin finally said. "We can decide where to go afterward."

They turned around and began walking back toward a small teahouse they had passed. A small crowd of villagers sat outside the teahouse, their conversation ending abruptly with Pei and Lin's appearance. In the thick silence, Pei could feel curious eyes following them as they walked quickly by. Instead of turning away, Pei stared back at the weather-beaten faces, their squinty glares burning right through her.

The teahouse was small and crowded. They sat on wooden crates, which creaked under their weight. The long wooden table where they sat was one of three that filled the room. The teahouse patrons stared and whispered. The air smelled faintly of jasmine tea, intermingled with smoke. A small, accommodating man nodded and poured them two cups of tea. Then, carrying his large silver pot, he refilled other cups with the steaming liquid. Lin ordered a plate of shrimp dumplings, and then another of sweet cakes. Pei sipped her tea slowly.

"Would you like to return to the boat?" Lin finally asked. "Or go to another temple?"

Pei didn't answer right away. They had come this far; she knew it would be foolish for them to turn back. She picked up a dumpling and ate it slowly. Each bite brought her closer to an answer she'd known since she first felt the red earth beneath her feet again. When she looked up at Lin, she had come to a decision.

"I'd like to show you where I grew up," Pei said, lifting her cup to have it refilled.

* * *

The road curved just as Pei remembered it. The sedan bearers moved swiftly through the sleeping land. Pei was amazed at the fact that this same great expanse of land that surrounded her as a child meant so much more to her now, even after all the years that had separated them.

"When I was young, I paid little attention to the land. It was simply filled with the cracks and crevices that Li and I discovered and played in," Pei said.

"Is your farm much farther?" Lin asked.

"We're very close now."

"We can still turn back if you want."

Pei shook her head. "I'm fine. Would you mind if we get down and walk the rest of the way?"

"No, of course not."

Pei immediately told the carriers to stop. They lowered the sedan chair as she and Lin stepped out. The women instructed the carriers to wait for them under the shade of a tree to the side of the road. They then continued on foot.

It was only a short walk before they approached a slope, which descended to her father's farm. Pei felt frightened. It was the same feeling of being lost she'd had when she first arrived at the girls' house. She felt Lin take hold of her arm. "What if they're no longer there?" Pei whispered. "What if they no longer recognize me?" These questions moved from her lips one after the other, but she didn't wait for Lin to answer.

Instead, Pei turned away and stared hard at the maze of water and land down below. Her eyes suddenly focused on a lone, dark figure in the distance. Quickly she turned back to Lin and pointed him out. She felt the blood rush to her head. "It's my father," she said.

"I'll wait here."

"No, I want you to come with me, please."

"Are you sure?"

Pei nodded.

Neither of them said a word as they descended the dirt road. They walked towards the largest pond, where Pei's father was working. He seemed to take no notice of them, swinging his body and steadily spreading handfuls of something into the dark water. Pei felt Lin watching her, but she couldn't respond. It was as if she were seeing a ghost. She couldn't take her eyes away from the tall, slender figure of her father.

To Embrace the Earth

From the corner of his eye he could see them approaching. When Pao Chung first noticed them, he thought he was dreaming to see such an unusual sight. Then he turned his head just enough to see the two young women dressed in white coming toward him. For a moment he thought his time had come, that the two were sent to lead him into the other world. "What of Yu-sung?" he mumbled to himself, his heart beating faster. But as he drove his fist deeper into the bucket of fish food, scraping the bottom of it, he knew he was still very much alive.

Most of the time, weeks would go by without his seeing anyone other than Yu-sung. The silence would be broken only by his trips to the market, where he would try to complete his business as fast as possible, then boat along the narrow canals home. The village people with all their needless talk made him uncomfortable. He had always preferred the solitude of his ponds and groves.

But as the two females approached where he stood by the pond, Pao Chung had no choice but to straighten up and turn to face them. It took a few moments before he allowed his eyes to meet theirs, and when he finally did, he knew immediately it was his third daughter, Pei, who was standing before him. She had grown tall and quite beautiful. Her cheekbones and mouth were definitely his, but her eyes were Yu-sung's. After so many years, she had found her way home. Pao Chung stood at the edge of the pond watching her, suddenly embarrassed at how he must look to her: a tired old man.

But what surprised Pao Chung even more was to hear the sound of his own voice speaking first. "Pei?" he asked.

"Yes, Ba Ba."

"You have returned home?"

"Just to visit, to see you and Ma Ma."

Pei's voice quivered as she said this. He watched her look toward the groves, searching among the lush leaves for any sign of Yu-sung.

"Your mother will be happy to see you again."

"Where is she?" Pei asked, turning back to him.

"She has not been well." Pao Chung put down the bucket he was carrying and wiped his dirty hands on his trousers. "She is inside."

"And Li?"

"She has a family of her own now," he said quickly.

He looked away from Pei, toward the house. When his gaze returned, it rested on the young woman who stood beside his daughter. Her fair skin and even features made it obvious she was not a farmer's daughter.

"This is Lin," Pei then said. "She's my friend from the silk factory."

Lin bowed her head slightly and said, "I'm very honored to meet you."

Pao Chung paused uncomfortably, then nodded awkwardly toward Lin.

He quickly turned away from them and, picking up his half-filled bucket, he flung the rest of the fish food out into the water.

"Come," he said, leading them back up to the house.

* * *

When Pao pushed open the door to the house he had built, he suddenly felt ashamed of the small, crude space in which they lived. As the warm stale air greeted them, he stepped in and let his eyes adjust to the darkness of the room. Already something had changed as they entered; his life, which had dulled over the years, seemed to stir again. He turned back to make sure Pei and Lin were really there, only to see Pei's eyes move slowly around the room of her childhood. Her gaze stopped at the bed in the far corner of the room where she and Li had once slept. She said nothing.

He moved to the table and lit a lamp. Yu-sung was nowhere to be seen. She was not standing by the fire, cooking or staring blankly into its flames as he often found her. Pao Chung hoped Yu-sung would be up and in better spirits to welcome their daughter home. But even more he hoped that seeing Pei again might give Yu-sung back her strength.

"Your ma ma must be resting," he said, a moment of panic moving through him. But before he could say anything else, there was movement from the other room, and Yu-sung suddenly stepped out from behind the blanket.

Pao Chung remained silent. It was Pei's voice that said softly, "Ma Ma."

Pao Chung turned back toward Yu-sung. At first her eyes grew wide, as if she had seen a ghost; then, slowly, he saw the familiar glow of spirit return. For years he had watched her once-young heart die slowly, along with three of their children. He had given up hope of ever seeing her happy again—until now.

As Yu-sung moved slowly toward Pei and Lin, Pao stepped back out of her way.

"Pei?" Yu-sung whispered. "Is it really you?"

"Yes, Ma Ma."

"You are still alive, Pei?"

Pei laughed. "Yes, Ma Ma, I'm very much alive."

Without any hesitation, Pei wrapped her arms around her mother's frail body, stroking her gray hair.

"I prayed to the gods that you would still be alive. After a while, I didn't believe your father when he said you were happy with your new life, but it was too late, we had given you to the silk work. I prayed for the day when you would return and forgive us."

"I have, Ma Ma."

Yu-sung stepped back and looked long and hard at her daughter. "I knew you would be a tall one," she said, her voice breaking as she took Pei's hand. "Even as a young girl you were taller than the others."

Pao Chung stood silent, watching his wife and third daughter. How small Yu-sung looked next to Pei. And how old she had become. He wanted to wrap his arms around both of them, but he didn't know how. When he felt the tears burning in his eyes, he quietly left the house and returned to his ponds.

Chapter Fifteen

Yu-sung

At first, Yu-sung thought she was still asleep and dreaming. She hugged Pei again, and held on to her for a long time. When she finally let go of her tall daughter, something almost painful moved through her fragile body. The years of stagnation felt heavy. Yu-sung had always wondered if she would ever see her third daughter again. Pei had been the child of guilt: Not seized by death or marriage, she had been given away, sold, in order to save the farm.

In the past year, with her health failing, Yu-sung had sought forgiveness. She feared dying and going into the other world, not knowing if Pei would always hate her. She never dared to dream there could still be tenderness between them. It was something they had never known.

When Yu-sung finally pulled away, it was with embarrassment. She blushed and pushed back a fallen strand of her gray hair. Then, unconsciously, her hand moved to smooth the wrinkles from her coarse clothing.

"Ma Ma, I want you to meet my friend, Lin," Pei said, filling the quiet room with the music of her voice.

Yu-sung turned, and for the first time realized that another person stood near her. Her eyes came to rest on a shorter, fairer

young woman with a face so smooth and lovely, Yu-sung immediately bowed and welcomed her.

"I'm so happy to meet you," said Lin, moving closer.

Yu-sung stepped back and turned shyly away from the two
young women. She moved quickly to the barrel where the water
was kept, ladling some into the kettle used for tea, then putting
it on the fire. At once she felt the comfort of doing something
that was simple habit. From a jar she took out the dry tea leaves
and sprinkled them into a pot. It took a few moments for her to
swallow all that was happening. After she had stoked the fire,
Yu-sung turned back to take another good look at her third
daughter. Pei had grown up to be very different from what she
had imagined. She still appeared so much like her father, but
Yu-sung could also see herself around the eyes. And Pei had
grown so tall and confident, obviously well taken care of during
all the years that separated them. Could Pao have been right
after all, that Pei was better off at the silk village? The thought
had tormented her every night since the morning Pei had left so
many years ago. When Yu-sung had closed her eyes, she saw her
curious child, Pei, and every night it felt as if her heart would
burst.

Yu-sung opened her mouth, but there seemed to be something heavy and solid caught in her throat, stealing away her
voice. She felt a burning sensation in her eyes, but there were
no tears. Yu-sung's hands moved instantly to cover her face.
When she felt the comfort of her daughter's arms around her,
Yu-sung weakened, and let her body relax against Pei's warmth.
It was not a dream; the gods had not abandoned her after all. Pei
had really come home to forgive her.

"Sit, sit, the tea will be ready soon," Yu-sung said, pulling away
from Pei and smiling shyly at Lin.

"Please, don't go to any trouble," said Lin, taking a seat on the
rough bench.

Yu-sung poured the hot water into the jar with the tea leaves and let it sit. She reached up and found the tin of dry biscuits she purchased in the village, and placed them on a plate. With a thin wooden stick, she stirred the tea and divided it into three clay cups. It was only then that she felt more at ease with Pei and Lin. She carried their tea to the table and sat down across from them. Yu-sung wrapped her hands around a hot teacup and inhaled slowly, letting out a small sigh of contentment.

"Have you and Ba Ba been well?" Pei asked, breaking the silence.

Yu-sung was amazed at how smooth and calm her daughter's voice was. "As well as can be expected," she answered slowly. "We are getting old."

Pei shook her head and smiled.

"If you hadn't come now, I might not have been here for much longer."

"I always wondered why you never came . . . " Pei began.

"Your ba ba has always been busy with his ponds, and I have kept busy. There has been time for little else," Yu-sung said before her daughter finished her sentence.

Pei sipped her tea. She looked around the bare, unfinished room. Yu-sung knew that, in all Pei's years away, nothing in the room had changed.

Then in a voice filled with concern and curiosity, Pei looked at her and asked, "Ma Ma, where is Li?"

Yu-sung's eyes never left her daughter, as they might have when she was young and asking too many questions. "She is married to a farmer on the other side of the hill."

"Is she happy?"

Yu-sung's eyes wandered away from Pei. She took a sip of her tea and stared at nothing. "She has a husband and his family to care for," she said absently. "She can at least be happy for a roof over her head."

"How long ago did Li marry?" Pei continued, hungry for details about her sister.

"A long time ago, just past her fifteenth birthday."

Yu-sung saw the stunned look on Pei's face. She saw Pei's lips tremble at the news that her sister had been married for more than ten years.

"Does she have any children?" Pei asked, her voice strained.

Yu-sung shook her head. "We have not heard from her in a very long time. The farmer had children of his own when his wife died in childbirth. He had seen Li in the village and sent the matchmaker over to speak to your father, wanting Li for his wife."

"And Ba Ba just let this farmer have Li?" Pei said quickly, hard with a sudden anger. Lin reached over and touched her shoulder.

"It isn't what you think," Yu-sung replied sharply. "Your father spoke with Li, and allowed her to make up her own mind. She chose to be the wife of the farmer. It was her decision to go!"

Pei swallowed hard and said nothing. Yu-sung knew Li had had more of a choice than Pei was given. She glanced over at Lin, who sat quietly staring down at the table. Yu-sung paused, but she didn't stop there. She would never keep her words from Pei again. In an even tone, she told Pei of Li's customary return home after three days of marriage. It was the last time Yu-sung had seen her.

"On the first morning of your sister's return home, your father had left very early to work at his ponds. I got up to find Li still asleep. I moved very quietly, so I wouldn't wake her. Li must have been exhausted, having walked all the way back here, because she never flinched, even when I moved toward the bed and watched her sleep. It was then that something caught my eye, and still I don't know what possessed me to pull her blanket back, just enough to see the strange marks on her arms. Li moved, but she didn't wake. Slowly I pulled the blanket back, and the lower my eyes traveled, the more discolored bruises and deep scratches I found on her calves and thighs. Even asleep, Li seemed to have aged right before my eyes. I wanted to wake her, and soothe her in my arms, but it was as if I were frozen. You know how much Li is like your father in that way; she keeps things to herself."

Yu-sung stopped and took several deep breaths. When she looked up at Pei, her eyes were red and moist. Pei opened her mouth slightly, but said nothing.

It was Yu-sung's voice that filled the silence again.

"Li did not wake. She could have been dead, if not for her slight breathing. I stood there watching my eldest daughter, her body beaten black and blue, wishing she had died like my other children, rather than have to return to that devil farmer. I carefully covered up Li and returned to my work. When she woke, Li quickly dressed and went about her chores as if she had never left."

"You didn't say anything?" Pei asked, her eyes avoiding Yu-sung's.

Yu-sung waited for Pei to look back at her. Only when Pei did, did she continue. "Neither of us said a word. When your sister prepared to return to her husband a few days later, I told her it wasn't too late. If she should decide not to return, it would bring no shame to us. But she shook her head and said, 'No, I have made my choice.' I wanted to say something else, but what was the use? Her life was with her husband, no matter how hard it would be, just as mine was with my husband."

"But how could you let her go back, knowing..." Pei stopped when she felt Lin move closer.

"What choice did she have—either return to her husband, or stay here and bring shame to her family," Yu-sung said quietly. She coughed, and a dry, harsh sound filled the room. Slowly she lifted her body up, her hands pushing against the splintered table. When Pei tried to help her, she motioned for her to sit back down and steadied herself.

"Pour your friend more tea, I will be right back," Yu-sung said. Moving slowly, she disappeared behind the other side of the hanging blanket.

Pei and Lin sat in silence.

When Yu-sung returned, she carried a rolled-up scroll. She placed it on the table in front of Pei and sat down again.

"I've been waiting to give this painting to you. I've always remembered how you liked to look at it when you were a girl," Yu-sung said, clearing her throat.

"I don't have anything for you," Pei said quietly.

Yu-sung saw Pei's eyes instinctively move toward the empty wall where the painting had once hung. Only its faint outline still marked the wall. Pei's fingers slowly stroked the smooth edge of the rolled-up painting. With no words, Yu-sung reached over and placed her hand on Pei's cheek, wiping away her tears.

A Clear Light

"Go now, before it becomes too dark," her mother said, pulling away from Pei's tight embrace; then she turned and touched Lin's sleeve, but said nothing. Lin accepted the gesture and returned it with a shy smile.

The sun had fallen, but still glared hot and bright across the glassy ponds below. Pei stepped back and looked toward the faded house and the surrounding land that had been the entirety of her childhood. It had changed so little with time that she imagined at any moment the young Li of her memory would come running up from the incline. When she felt her mother's hand on her arm, Pei turned back toward her. There was a serene smile on Yu-sung's face, no hint of her earlier embarrassment. She held on to Pei's arm for a moment longer, then let go.

After so many years, Pei would have known her parents anywhere, though they were older and slower than she had imagined. Her father's distance had seemed well established before she was born; Pei knew her mother was different. She felt it every time her mother deliberately separated herself from the children with her stern words. What Pei saw now was the yearning she could never name, a craving that must have ached in her mother's bones. So it was without hesitation that Pei had gone to her, finally wrapping her arms around her mother's thin body as she had always wanted to do. Pei might have never let go if her mother had not gently pulled away from her. Only then had she seen how her mother had aged, how her once beautiful black hair had gone white, matching the wrinkled pallor of her skin.

Pei had always wanted nothing more than to please her mother. As a child, she was never able to. That gift had been reserved for Li, who did naturally what Pei strived for. Li only needed the simplicity of routine to keep her spirit satisfied. Pei was always the stronger and more restless of the two. And though she tried, she was always less than obedient. She had thought for the longest time that that was why she was given to the silk work. She always wanted much more than her parents could give her. Pei only realized now that it had been her fate to be chosen. Her parents had had no more choice than she. Li would have shrunk away; she had survived.

In the bright light, Pei searched for her father down by the ponds for one last time, but saw no one. The heavy, dank smell filled her head. He had not returned to see them off, and she somehow knew he needed to stay hidden among his ponds. Still, she would never forget the expression on her father's face when he first recognized her. He had squinted toward the light, but even then she saw the first glimmer of recognition. There were no words at first, but his eyes opened wider, and he might have gasped in surprise if he were someone else. Instead, he had looked hard at Pei and said her name as if she had just come in from the next room. Her words were as restrained as his, though she wanted to say "Yes, Ba Ba, I'm your daughter Pei and I've finally come home." But after so many years she stood before her father, just as she'd always dreamed, only to find him not half as tall as she remembered.

"Will you say good-bye to Ba Ba?" Pei asked.

Her mother nodded. "He won't leave his ponds," she then whispered to Lin in a tired voice.

"It's okay, Ma Ma," Pei told her mother. "I'll be back again."

Yu-sung inhaled and let out a sigh. "Go, go now."

"Take care of yourself, I'll be back soon."

Yu-sung nodded and waved as they made their way back up the dirt slope. Pei turned around and caught a last glimpse of her mother, dressed in her coarse cotton clothing that now seemed too large for her thin, withered body. As Pei moved farther and farther away, her mother remained. She stood perfectly still, slowly fading from sight.

Yu-sung finally turned around, long after Pei and Lin had disappeared up the hill. If she hadn't been certain she was awake and standing, she might have thought it was all the tricks of an old woman's imagination. Pei had returned and forgiven her. For the first time in her life Yu-sung stood helpless, not knowing what to do next. Then sudden fear grabbed her and pushed her back against the closed door. There had never been a moment in her life when she felt such an emptiness.

Yu-sung took a small step forward. She glanced down toward the ponds, knowing Pao was probably down there among the mulberries, watching her. He had been watching her closely for the past year, as if she couldn't stand alone and might fall at any moment. How could she tell Pao that she needed to be alone, that she deserved no more than filling her days with work? It was the only way she could stand the fact that the gods had taken away her children, and that she was partly to blame. She could offer Pao very little, and expected even less from him, but lately he seemed as persistent with her as with his land.

Yu-sung took several deep breaths and looked down again toward the groves. For a moment, she thought she saw some movement of the leaves on an otherwise windless day. She straightened, smoothed back her hair, and slowly began walking down to the groves.

Chapter Sixteen

———

1936

Pei

Pei lived with the last glimpse of her mother for weeks after they returned from visiting her parents. She spoke continually of their next visit, and of finding Li.

"Li can't be far from my parents," she said. "My mother said the farm was just over the hill."

Pei was sitting in Lin's small, windowless office at the silk factory. For the first time in months they were busy again with a large order. The steady cranking sound of the machines filled the air. The factory had seen some very hard times for the past few years. There'd been a steady decline since the depression, forcing other factories to close down. Many of their sisters were retiring early to spinsters' houses, or finding employment elsewhere as servants in Canton or Hong Kong. The owner, Chung, held on, but it was just a matter of time before they might have to look elsewhere for work.

Outside, the commanding voice of Chen Ling could be heard above the loud machinery. "Those over there, yes, yes, be careful!" she said, giving orders to the men from the manufacturers who came to pick up the racks of spun silk.

When Pei rose to close the door, the small moment of quiet was like a gift. She waited for some kind of response from Lin.

"Is everything all right?" Pei finally asked.

"Everything's fine, for now," Lin answered. "We just have so much to do in the next week, and then afterward I'm not sure we'll even be here if things don't get better." She looked up helplessly at Pei.

"We'll be all right," Pei said gently. "We can always go to Canton or Hong Kong like the others. Besides, everything's changing so quickly, who knows what's going to happen tomorrow."

Lin tried to smile. She nodded her head absentmindedly. Pei knew Lin had been worried about more than just the demise of their silk factory. The internal struggles of the country were no longer something distant, and the Japanese devils were making their way toward them at an alarming rate. They watched and waited, certain that they would have to leave Yung Kee anyway in a matter of months, regardless of anything else.

Still, Pei knew there was something else bothering Lin.

"What's really wrong?" she asked.

"I don't know why I'm acting so foolish," Lin answered. "I don't know what's got into me, it's just the work and the Japanese."

"I know I haven't been much help. I've been so preoccupied with my family that I haven't been able to see or hear anything else," Pei apologized. She watched Lin, waiting. "What is it?" she finally asked. "I know there's something else."

"There *is* something else," Lin said, trying to shake off her uneasiness. "Chen Ling spoke to me this morning about Moi. She may have to let her go. It seems that Moi is frightening the girls. It's gone beyond her talking to the air; now she won't let anyone into the kitchen, and screams murder if anyone should go near Auntie Yee's room."

"Where would she go?" asked Pei. "The girls' house is the only home she knows!"

"Chen Ling knows that. That's why she wants me to speak to

Moi, in hopes that something can be worked out. It goes without saying that Moi will always be taken care of."

"She can't possibly live anywhere else after all her years at the girls' house!"

Pei began to pace back and forth. Moi had been an integral part of the girls' house, just as Auntie Yee had. Without her, the house would lose its last hold on the past.

"Don't worry, we'll go see Moi this evening," Lin said soothingly. "We'll work something out. Now go, we have an order to fill!"

"You'll think of something," Pei said.

Lin smiled wearily.

Pei opened the door and hesitated. She wanted to turn back and say something to ease Lin's mind, but the harsh sound of machinery entered, making the room vibrate with a life of its own.

Gathering

Moi dragged her bad leg quickly across the kitchen and filled a clay jar with a handful of rice. In a few days the jar would be full and no one would know that any rice had been missing from each evening's meal. She did this with equal vigor when it came to tea and flour, though she knew this siphoning off of food would soon have to end. It was getting much too difficult to get enough food for each meal, much less to save some. The roads and harbor were heavily guarded by Chiang Kai-shek's troops, watching for the Communist infiltrators who stole much of the incoming food supply for their own stomachs.

Moi jerked forward and looked up when she heard a noise from outside. She listened carefully, and when she was satisfied that it was only the night rumblings of the neighboring cats, she returned to her work. When she looked up again, Moi smiled to see Auntie Yee sitting in a chair across the room, watching her work.

"Another jar is almost filled," Moi said, proudly holding up the jar to show Auntie Yee.

"Have you hidden them?" asked Auntie Yee.

"Just as you told me." Moi laughed. "No one dares to enter your room."

Auntie Yee nodded her approval and watched silently as Moi filled two other jars with the dry food. When she was through, Moi closed the jars tightly and carried them to her hiding place, underneath her bed. She guarded them with the tenacity of a mother for her child, and no one could enter the kitchen without her permission, including Chen Ling. When the jars were filled, Moi would sneak them upstairs to Auntie Yee's room.

When Moi returned to the table, Auntie Yee was standing and inspecting Moi's evening meal.

"The girls are getting enough to eat?" Auntie Yee asked.

"Oh, yes, I never take more than we can afford."

Auntie Yee smiled. "Good, good."

Moi hesitated, then said, "I think Chen Ling is becoming suspicious."

"Ah, Chen Ling can never leave well enough alone, even if it's for her own good!"

"What should I do?"

Auntie Yee moved back and began pacing across the kitchen, her feet floating above the floor. "Continue as you are, but if Chen Ling persists, then stop gathering the food until it is safe again."

"Can't we just tell her?"

Auntie Yee shook her head and rolled her eyes upward. "Who would believe you? Not Chen Ling, especially if you tell her that I was the one who told you to gather food for the difficult times ahead. To her I am dead and buried. They would all think you've gone mad—they already do!"

Moi silently bowed her head. Knowing that Auntie Yee was right, she could think of nothing else to say. She was only too grateful to have Auntie Yee back at the girls' house keeping her company. Moi didn't want to disturb her spirit and possibly lose her forever. Instead of arguing with Auntie Yee, Moi looked up and nodded her head obediently at her oldest friend.

That evening, when Moi answered the door, she was surprised to see Lin and Pei waiting to enter. It had been months since she had last seen the two, and unlike with other girls who came and went, Moi was genuinely happy to see them.

"You have come to see Chen Ling?" Moi asked expectantly.

"No, we wanted to see you," said Lin, who had always been Moi's favorite among all the others.

"Me?" Moi laughed bashfully.

She stepped back and let the two young women in, leading them to the dining room. When they were seated Moi went to the kitchen and returned carrying tea.

"What is it that you want to speak to me about?" Moi finally asked, standing beside them.

"Sit down, Moi," said Pei, pulling out a chair for her.

Moi hesitated at first, then sat uncomfortably beside them.

Lin then cleared her throat and said, "Some of the girls wanted us to talk with you. It's about the way you've been acting—"

"Who?" Moi demanded.

"It doesn't matter who," continued Lin. "It's just that you've been frightening some of them when you scream at them to stay away from the kitchen."

Moi half stood up from her chair, her hands gesticulating in the air. "Isn't it Moi who cooks for them every night and cleans up after them! They can have every other room in the house, but the kitchen belongs to Moi. You knew that when you were here!"

"What about Auntie Yee's room?" asked Pei.

Moi looked stubbornly at the two of them and defended her position, as all her years battling with Auntie Yee had taught her. "The room is mine. Yee left it for me to use as I wish. I don't want her spirit disturbed. Besides, if they just stayed where they belonged there would be no trouble!" Moi said, mumbling the rest of her thoughts to herself.

"Can't we find a simple way to settle this problem?" Lin pleaded.

Moi straightened and said angrily, "There is only one way to solve the problem: Tell them to stay away from my kitchen once and for all!"

Then Moi pushed back the chair and quickly went into the safe haven of her kitchen. She sat rigid on her bed in the darkness, not answering the pleas of Lin and Pei to come out and talk to them. Still, neither of them dared to enter her kitchen, which brought an immediate smile of victory to Moi's face. Moi waited until she was sure they had given up and left, listening for the final click of the front door. Then, very carefully, her hand felt underneath the bed until she had counted by touch the three hidden jars of stored food. Once assured of their safety, Moi let her body relax onto the bed and closed her eyes.

Chapter Seventeen

1938

Pei

Everything moved swiftly in the years following Pei's visit to her parents. All the echoes of war she had suppressed came rising up, filling their lives with growing fear. Even though the war had been raging within China for so many years, Yung Kee had existed untarnished and unaffected by much of it. The little bits of information they heard filtered down to them through those who came and went from Canton and other large cities. Pei lay sleeping within her own dreams, only to be awakened now that the storm was finally reaching them. And like all gathering storms, it had grown to full strength as it headed toward their enclosed world.

What had been such a simple trip to the outlying villages was now a series of hardships. Several checkpoints were set up to guard against agitators and keep a watchful eye on the Japanese. With the fighting in the south escalating, fewer and fewer people were allowed easy movement from one place to another. Pei tried in vain to find out more information about her sister Li, but her mother wrote letters slowly if at all. Pei received only a few letters from her mother, then heard nothing more. In large, shaky characters, her mother wrote very little of what Pei craved, any information about Li. Her mother said only that too many years had passed, that she couldn't be certain where Li was. Her father knew even less. Yet, even if it was a slow, frustrating process, Pei knew she wouldn't give up until she found Li again. She could only hope that her family would remain safe in all the uncertainty that surrounded them.

Each night, Chen Ling began gathering those of the girls left at the factory for nightly meetings. With the ongoing war, the production of silk had slowed to the point that only a handful of girls remained. Only one of the factory's three buildings remained in operation. Chen Ling took on the responsibility of preparing them for the time when they would have to leave the factory. As usual, this came to Chen Ling naturally, and Pei always marveled at her talent in bringing even the most demure to their feet.

"We are the last ones," Chen Ling said. "And our days are numbered. Now we must prepare for our safe futures, as many of our sisters have done. If you haven't already, then you must begin to think of your lives and in what direction you will journey."

As always, they listened to what Chen Ling had to say and obeyed.

At one meeting, it was agreed that the women would all stay at the factory until its closing. Pei and Lin knew this would be in only a matter of weeks, yet they needed the time to slowly feel their way into what appeared a very hostile world. Kung Ma, who had always said very little throughout their meetings, was slowly preparing to retire to a spinsters' house. Chen Ling and Ming spoke of vegetarian halls in the countryside, where many unmarried sisters could go and give themselves to the Buddhist faith. Lin began to speak of their going to Hong Kong, knowing that if the Japanese should invade, Canton would quickly be taken as a vital port. Lin wrote to her family and anxiously awaited news from them. Still, all the women held on to the hope that things weren't as bad as they appeared.

Much to Pei's relief, Moi had stayed on at the girls' house, serving them tea at each meeting and remaining in full command of her kitchen. She still allowed no one to enter her kitchen or Auntie Yee's room. Chen Ling had given up, allowing Moi to do as she pleased. "She's old, and has her strange ways," Chen Ling said, surrendering. "Let her do as she wishes." So Moi moved through the house as unapproachable as ever, keeping her secrets and avoiding any direct contact with them.

One evening, when Pei and Lin returned from a meeting at the girls' house, Pei was given a stained envelope that had come for her that afternoon. She took possession of the letter, hoping it would contain some news about her sister Li. But Pei immediately saw it wasn't in the shaky writing of her mother. She quickly tore open the letter and read the brief note, feeling a knot of disbelief growing in her stomach. On the paper was the awkward, scribbled writing of a stranger. In a few crude lines, it told Pei that her mother had died in her sleep, and that her father had buried her among his ancestors. Pei read the letter over and over, trying to rearrange the words so they would tell her something else. She imagined the unconcerned letter-writer from the village whom her father had paid to write the words, and they stung her heart even more. Pei couldn't move, caught in a tearless daze until Lin found her, the wrinkled piece of paper lying innocently on her lap. Lin read the letter, and then, whispering "I'm sorry," led Pei upstairs to her bed.

That night, Pei's disturbed sleep was filled with shadows and spirits, which seemed to stay just out of sight so she couldn't see the faces of those who haunted her dreams. Pei dozed and woke several times in the night, the darkness of the room leading her back into the hazy stupor of sleep. Then, it was clearly her mother who came to her in a dream, once again silent, and as beautiful as in her youth. Her mother hovered over her and whispered just once how much she loved Pei, and how happy she was to be reunited with her dead children. The rest Yu-sung said with her eyes, the years of work and restraint slowly disappearing into a clear, peaceful gaze. When Pei tried to reach up and touch her mother one last time, she jerked forward and woke, only to find the dawn's muted light seeping in and her mother gone.

Pei felt nothing. The emptiness seemed to swallow her whole. She heard Lin's slight breathing from the bed next to hers, yet it gave her no comfort. Pei sat up and wrapped her arms around her knees. She needed to be holding on to something. Slowly the cold permeated her body, followed by an uncontrollable trembling. It was her inability to stop trembling that first brought her tears. Then Pei began to cry, at first quietly so she wouldn't wake Lin, then without care.

Pei couldn't tell how long it was before she realized the oil lamp was burning brightly beside her. She lay curled up in one corner of her bed. Then she heard Lin's soothing voice calling her back to reality, and felt Lin's arms wrap tightly around her. Only then did her tears calm.

After her mother's death, Pei's sleep continued to be restless with fears she couldn't name. Stories of the war and of violence filled the air. Tales of Japanese executions spread into the most remote parts. Men, women, and children who by fate's hand had escaped the Japanese invasions of Shanghai and Nanking made a desperate run south. Many of those who had not starved to death along the way lived to tell the tales of those they saw slaughtered. The Japanese had raped and murdered hundreds of thousands at will, creating mass graves on the city streets. Bodies were left to rot, producing an unbearable stink of death until they were buried in mass graves.

Each day Pei tried to find a way to reach her father. She'd written several times, hoping he would go to the village letter-writer and send her a more detailed account of her mother's death or some clue to her sister Li's whereabouts, but the days only brought his familiar silence.

It wasn't a surprise to any of them when their long-held fears about the silk factory came true. It was a windy, dry afternoon when Chung came to the factory in his large black car. There was only a small group of girls left; the others had scattered to spinsters' houses and other jobs overseas. They were called outside to listen to what Chung had come to say, knowing full well it was about closing the silk factory. Chen Ling and Lin led the handful of women out to the open courtyard, just as they had several years ago to the sad victory that had cost Sui Ying her life.

Seeing Chung again, defeated and so much older, still didn't diminish the hatred Pei felt for him. He stood alone this time, without his bodyguards or their weapons, wiping off the dust and sweat that had collected on his forehead.

"You must know," Chung began, "that the past few years have been difficult. And so, even though I've done all in my power to keep this factory running, it's no longer a wise course, and I regret to say we have come to the end of the road. I just want you all to know that I hold no bad feelings toward any of you over our past grievances."

When Chung stopped, they were completely silent. Not even the faintest breath could be heard in the stillness. Chung stood waiting for any response. He looked anxiously toward Chen Ling to join him up front, wiping his brow over and over again. No one moved. They stared at him placidly, knowing that within their silence was all the hatred the years had stored up. Chung waited a few moments longer before their silence became too obvious. His eyes grew angry, but he said nothing more, simply throwing down his handkerchief and quickly walking back to his car. Only when the dust had cleared and his car was well out of sight did they raise their arms and rejoice at their one last victory.

* * *

Not long after, Lin received word from her brother Ho Chee telling them to come to Canton as soon as they possibly could. He had friends who would help them find a way to Hong Kong.

Lin had chosen to stay behind at the silk factory a few weeks more, only because Chung had promised to pay her and Chen Ling for another month's work of cleaning up and closing the account books. At first, Pei was apprehensive and wanted to leave for Hong Kong as soon as possible, but Lin was more prudent.

"We'll need the extra money until we can find work in Hong Kong," Lin said. "Besides, Chung's managers don't know enough about the overall operation."

"But Chen Ling can take care of everything," Pei said.

"I can't leave it all for Chen Ling."

"But the Japanese are getting close to Canton!"

"I know they are, but there's still time. I just want to make sure things are settled here first."

Pei reluctantly agreed. She knew it was far more difficult for Lin to leave than it was for her. For the past eighteen years Yung Kee had been Lin's home, and leaving its dusty streets and crowded marketplace seemed to leave her shaken. But slowly Lin began to rid herself of everything accumulated over the years, keeping only what was necessary for their journey.

For Pei it was entirely different. She anxiously waited to see Hong Kong. She'd read a great deal about the large, brilliant city, where foreigners from all over the world did business. But slowly, a quiet fear began to mix with her anxiousness. She tried hard not to show it. The Japanese moved like locusts, devouring cities in rapid succession. She knew that the longer they waited to leave, the more difficult it would become. Each day, more and more people were leaving the area in hopes of going to Hong Kong or overseas. Ho Chee would leave first to take his mother and his wife to Hong Kong, while Ho Yung waited for them in Canton.

The first day Lin and Chen Ling returned from work after the factory closing, they looked tired and pale.

"How was your day?" Pei asked.

"The factory seemed filled with ghosts," Lin replied in an even tone. "It was strange to have the machines so quiet and still. Chen Ling and I chose to work on the books in my office, and every once in a while we could swear we heard the humming sound of the machines spinning, only to realize it was just our imaginations playing tricks. I can't explain it, but it felt as if someone or something was waiting in the shadows."

Pei laughed and said, "Now whose imagination is going wild?" Then, in a more serious tone, she asked, "Why don't we just leave here?"

Lin nodded slowly and said, "In a short time, we'll be far away from Yung Kee and those Japanese devils."

Yet the fear inside Pei continued to grow with each passing day, though it had no face and carried no name.

Gradually, many of their older sisters left the house, finding ways to sit out the war in religious or spinsters' houses. Each night before one of them left, they celebrated with what meager food they could find at the market. If they were lucky enough to buy a chicken or a piece of pork, then there would be salted chicken with oyster sauce, or pork strips fried with vegetables; if not, then rice and vegetables would do.

The day Kung Ma left for a spinsters' house was a sad one. Pei and Lin stood outside as Kung Ma packed her scant belongings into a sedan chair. In her hand, she grasped a red-and-black book and a small white box.

"What do you have there?" asked Pei. She had never seen either of the possessions Kung Ma carried in all her years at the sisters' house.

Kung Ma blushed. "It's part of my history," she said, clutching the objects tighter to her breast.

"We're going to miss you," Lin said.

Pei smiled sadly, and couldn't say anything. Kung Ma's departure meant the end of the sisters' house. For so many years, she had silently led the house, and now they grieved to see her go.

Kung Ma nodded her head, and hugged each one of her remaining sisters. "We'll see each other again, I'm sure of it," she said, climbing into the sedan chair. "When this is all over and life's once again gentle." Kung Ma turned around and took one long, last look at the sisters' house. "Take care of the old place for as long as you can."

As they watched the sedan chair move quickly down the road, Kung Ma turned around once and waved her hand, still carrying the small white box.

Eight days later, Pei and Lin closed the sisters' house and moved back to the girls' house for the remainder of the month. With the food and oil shortage, it made little sense to stay in the large, almost empty sisters' house. Chen Ling and Ming welcomed them back with great joy. Even Moi fussed over them, preparing a special meal in honor of their return, using ingredients no one dared ask how she procured.

A Northern Wind

It was on a rainy evening, with the winds blowing relentlessly, that Ji Shen found her way to the girls' house. In the blinding rain it looked like a place that might offer her some food and a dry place to rest, if just for a short time. She was cold beyond belief, and the sores on her feet had swelled to double their original size and filled with a yellowish pus. By the time she came upon the girls' house, Ji Shen could no longer feel anything below her ankles, and the hunger she felt burned a hole in her stomach.

In her feverish condition, Ji Shen crawled toward the back of the house with every last bit of her strength. To keep herself going, she dreamed that her family safely awaited her inside; she prayed that the rain would wash away the nightmare of the last month. She pulled herself toward the back door and tried to stand, but when she fell hard against it, Ji Shen had already fainted.

"Death to those devil cats!" Moi said, grabbing her broom and moving toward the back door. For weeks they had come to the back door, crying for food, and Moi no longer had patience for them. She held the broom high as she opened the door, promising to scare them away once and for all. But when Moi opened the door, it wasn't a parade of hungry cats she found, but the apparently lifeless body of a young girl.

"Aii-ya!" said Moi, dragging the soaking girl into the kitchen. "What will the gods bring to me next?"

Then Moi allowed Chen Ling and others into her kitchen to carry the girl out. They took her upstairs and placed her gently on one of the many empty beds. When they saw her swollen feet and feverish condition, Chen Ling told Moi to boil the bitter tea that brought fevers down, while Lin and Pei carefully cleaned her swollen feet and wrapped them in cloth.

For the first time in months, the conversation that evening centered not on the war, but on the young girl lying feverish in the bed upstairs. From the looks of her bone-thin body and high cheekbones, she came from far away, somewhere up north. Each of them took turns watching the girl through the next few nights; when it was Pei's turn, she eagerly took her place beside the sleeping girl, whose restless sleep seemed filled with nameless nightmares.

On her third morning at the girls' house, Ji Shen opened her eyes and tried to move. Every muscle in her body seemed to hurt, so she lay still, letting her eyes grow accustomed to the long room she was in. On the bed next to hers slept another woman, but the numerous other beds were empty. Ji Shen tried to lift herself up higher, accidentally knocking over a teacup that sat on the makeshift table next to her bed.

"What is it?" Pei said, sitting up quickly.

Ji Shen tried to say something, but her mouth felt so dry she didn't think the words would come out. By then Pei was already standing, looking down at Ji Shen with a smile.

"Ah, I see you have finally awakened," said Pei. "We have been very worried about you."

Then, seeing that the girl was thirsty, Pei poured her some tea from a thermos and leaned over to help her take a sip. When her thirst was satisfied the girl leaned back and seem to rest from the effort.

"Would you like more?" Pei asked.

The girl shook her head no.

"What is your name?"

"Ji Shen," the girl whispered, with a heavy northern accent.

"My name is Pei."

"Where am I?"

"You are in the village of Yung Kee, in the Kwangtung province. Where have you come from?"

"From Nanking, in the Chen-Chiang province."

"How old are you, Ji Shen?"

"Almost fourteen."

"And where are your parents?" asked Pei.

Ji Shen turned away and closed her eyes.

Three days later, Ji Shen had regained enough strength to sit up and receive the entire household, including Moi. They quickly adopted Ji Shen as their "Moi Moi," their younger sister. Ji Shen viewed all the women in wonderment. Never before had she seen an entire group of women dressed exactly alike. Yet it didn't take long before she grew to trust each one of them and know their differences. She especially liked Pei, the tall one who had first spoken kindly to her.

"What do you do here?" Ji Shen asked Pei.

"We were silk workers, and this is the house we all stayed in while we worked at the factory," Pei answered, taking Ji Shen's empty soup bowl from her.

"You no longer work at the factory?"

"I'm afraid there isn't any work left for us to do. We're the last of the workers."

Ji Shen looked puzzled. "What about your families?"

"They gave up on us a long time ago." Pei laughed. "I'm afraid we have to find our own way now."

"I don't understand," Ji Shen said.

Pei stroked her forehead and said, "It's nothing to concern yourself with now; there'll be plenty of time for you to find out everything. Now, I want you to rest."

Ji Shen lay back in the bed, feeling warm and safe. She watched Pei move across the room straightening up, then closed her eyes and fell into a deep sleep.

When the sores on her feet began to heal, Ji Shen walked slowly downstairs, supported by Ming and Lin. It was in the reading room, surrounded by her new family, that Ji Shen finally told them her story.

"My father was a shopkeeper in Nanking. He sold curios and dry goods. My mother sewed for others on the side. We didn't make much money, but we lived in the rooms behind the shop and my mother, my sister, and I were very happy with our lives. Many of our friends and neighbors had warned us about the Japanese, but my father never believed they would get much farther than Manchuria, so rather than move away from his life's work and the place in which his ancestors were buried, he made the decision to stay in Nanking. My older sister Juling and I were attending a local school, and my father didn't want to pull us out. Juling was so smart—she easily finished her lessons each day and helped me with mine every night. It was on one of these very ordinary nights that they came upon us without any warning, like the devil himself had descended upon us in the form of the Japanese soldiers. Just because they wore tan uniforms and came in the image of men, it made no difference. Nothing was sacred. When the Japanese first came to Nanking, they ravaged everything, taking what they wanted and burning what they felt like, including people. We did everything we could to become invisible and stay out of their way. Then that night, they came to my father's shop, pulling us out of bed and making all of us kneel outside in front of the shop before them. They called my father a traitor and beat him. When we tried to stop them, they beat us also. I screamed for help but nobody came. They continued to beat my father while others took my mother, my sister, and me back into the shop, where they lay us side by side and raped us over and over. To ease my fear, Juling turned to me and began singing a nursery rhyme we sang as children. When they were finished, they shot my mother through the head, while another took his bayonet . . . and . . . "

"You don't have to say any more," Lin said, stroking Ji Shen's back.

Ji Shen looked up with tears in her eyes and continued. "Maybe it was because of the song that he wanted Juling to suffer, but the devil took his bayonet and went inside her, the same way he himself had just been inside her. I will never forget her screaming. I grabbed whatever I could find and hit the head of the soldier watching me and ran. I kept running until I saw the light of day. I don't know why they didn't come after me, maybe because I wasn't worth their time. They already had what they wanted."

Ji Shen stopped and took a deep breath. Across the room she could see Pei standing by the window.

"I hid, and caught up with others moving south. They took me in for a while, until it became too much of a burden to have another mouth to feed. I don't know how I survived the rest of the journey on my own. I just kept moving, and each time I wanted to lay down and die, I saw Juling, who gave me the strength to continue. The rest is like a dream, something that I can only vaguely remember, until I woke up and saw Pei."

On hearing her name, Pei looked over and walked back to Ji Shen, taking hold of her hand. The room was perfectly still, since the rain and wind had subsided. The sun glared weakly through the delicate curtains, and in the distance they could hear the birds singing in the trees.

Gradually, Ji Shen was able to sleep through the night. Her nightmares still came, but slowly they began to take on a new aspect, one that no longer frightened her with the faces of the devil soldiers. One night she dreamed of her parents, and the next brought her sister, Juling. Their faces came back to her, and in them she found comfort. The days moved on, one after the other, and Ji Shen grew stronger.

Chapter Eighteen

1938

Pei

After Ji Shen stumbled upon the girls' house, Pei nursed her back to health, protecting her like the little sister she'd never known. Ji Shen had added a spark of life to the girls' house, dampened by the mass murders of over a hundred thousand Chinese and the ongoing news of city after city falling into the hands of the Japanese. They controlled many of the major seaports and railways, crippling most of China. Through the dark clouds that hovered over them, it was a miracle that Ji Shen had somehow managed to find her way to the house.

Even Moi was taken by Ji Shen. She made strengthening soups, and herbal teas that brewed all day, then had to be drunk quickly while still hot to insure their potency. Moi also nourished Ji Shen with an abundance of food, which came from her secret source. Moi never ceased to amaze Pei and Lin each evening with her plentiful bowls of rice or noodles. Where she got the rice when others scrambled for the smallest grains would remain her mystery. When Chen Ling questioned her, Moi shook her head and said nothing.

From the moment Ji Shen was well again, she did her share of work and never complained. She seemed to live only in the present, hiding from the pain of her past. She had not spoken of her parents and sister again, and there were no more tears. Yet even if she remained silent, Ji Shen's flight from the north repeated itself over and over again in Pei's head. Sometimes, Pei looked at Ji Shen and searched her face for a trace of the fear she must have felt. After the horrible scene of seeing her family murdered, she had survived the horrendous journey from Nanking to Yung Kee with little food or water, and with a burning emptiness in her heart. It was an unbelievable feat, of which Ji Shen still had no memory. Pei wondered if Ji Shen carried these fears in the earliest hours of the morning, when she might wake and find herself in the strangeness of her new room, lost and alone. But what Pei saw every morning on Ji Shen's face was an eagerness to be accepted. And every time Pei mentioned her past, something distant glazed her eyes.

In body, Ji Shen was well again, though she still limped. She had adapted to the girls' house with an urgency that kept her busy with any chore Moi granted her. And when the chores ran out, Ji Shen kept Pei company during the day while Lin was away at the factory with Chen Ling. Sometimes, they would walk to the marketplace with Moi and watch the women bargain for what little fruit and vegetables lined the empty stalls, or go down to the river and, half-hiding, watch Chiang's soldiers gamble away the time.

The days moved swiftly in Ji Shen's company. Pei continued to write her father, praying for a response before they left Yung Kee, only to be disappointed when there was none. By the end of the week, Lin and Chen Ling would finally be finished at the silk factory. Pei kept telling herself there were only a few more days until they would be safely on their way to Canton. But as much as she looked forward to their new life, Pei worried about the fates of her remaining sisters, especially her newest one, Ji Shen.

Pei had wanted to speak to Lin about Ji Shen, but each night slipped by with nothing said. Pei was afraid there would be no room for Ji Shen on the boat, and she was afraid to hear it from

Lin. She knew there was no sense in her fear. Lin liked Ji Shen as much as she did, and it was clear Ji Shen couldn't stay in Yung Kee with Moi, where it wasn't safe, or hide in a vegetarian hall in the countryside with Chen Ling and Ming.

So one evening, after their meal, Pei simply asked, "Would you mind if Ji Shen came with us when we leave?"

Lin looked up, and smiled. "Of course not."

"Yes, well, she really doesn't have anyone anymore, and since she gets on so well with us, I thought it might be better for her to come with us."

"I know," Lin said. "I've already written to Ho Yung to find a place on the boat for Ji Shen. We should hear from him any day now."

From the kitchen, Pei could hear Moi's voice mumbling something inaudible.

"Why didn't you say anything?" she asked.

"I took it for granted you knew she would be coming with us. Where else would she go?"

Pei laughed. She then walked over and gave Lin a quick hug.

Pei went immediately to ask Ji Shen if she'd like to go to Canton and Hong Kong with them. At first, Ji-Shen was tongue-tied, then she nodded her head. "Yes," she finally said aloud, "I want to go."

Pei knew Ji Shen had just found a new rhythm to her life at the girls' house, and it would be hard to start over again. But she also knew the girl's feeling of safety would be short-lived. The Japanese devils were approaching the south with great speed.

Pei laughed and hugged Ji Shen. "Everything's going to be wonderful in Hong Kong. We'll find work there, and see all the new things we've only dreamed about!"

"What kinds of things?" Ji Shen asked.

"Everything! Buildings taller than you can imagine, and people who have come from all over the world to do business."

"What kind of work would we do?" she asked, fearful.

"We'll do whatever we can, and learn what we have to—it will be like having a new life!"

"And what about Chen Ling and Ming?" Ji Shen suddenly asked. "And what about Moi?"

Pei turned serious. "They prefer to stay here. Chen Ling and Ming will most likely go to live at a vegetarian hall in the countryside."

"And Moi?"

Pei hesitated. "Moi's stubborn," she finally said with a sigh. "She thinks nothing will touch her as long as she remains at the girls' house. We've all tried to persuade her to leave."

Ji Shen said, with genuine concern, "She can't stay here alone."

"Moi will do as she pleases, no matter what anyone tells her. Her life is at the girls' house; without it, she might as well not live."

Ji Shen sat a moment in thought. Her lip quivered before she raised her head and asked, "Will we be safe in Hong Kong?"

Pei answered, "I promise."

Pei woke up sweating, her cotton gown soaked. She didn't know why, since the heat was nothing compared to that a few months ago. It might have been a bad dream, or the anticipation of their leaving. But as she watched the sunlight slowly grow into their room, everything else seemed far away. She turned toward Lin, who was sleeping soundly. For the first time in weeks, Lin had slept well and seemed happy. There was only one more day before Lin would be finished at the factory and they would leave for Canton.

For a day and a night, Moi had been preparing a special meal for them before their departure, humming and talking to herself all day as she moved in and out of the kitchen. Whatever Moi's secret was, it remained tucked away in the confines of her kitchen and Auntie Yee's room. Chen Ling no longer cared, and declared those rooms Moi's own domain, to do as she wished. But even if the others didn't dare to bother Moi as she sneaked from one room to the other, Pei hoped to solve the mystery once and for all before they left.

That morning, after their meal, Lin and Chen Ling left for their last day at the silk factory. Moi suddenly dashed out the door after them. "You must not be late," she yelled out to them. "Moi has a surprise for you. You must not be late!"

Moi walked back in, mumbling to herself and taking no notice of Pei and Ji Shen as she went back into her kitchen. Pei decided then that this would be her last chance to find out what Moi was hiding in the two rooms. With Ji Shen suppressing her laughter, they waited out of sight for Moi to come out of her kitchen and gingerly make her way upstairs to Auntie Yee's room, which she always kept locked.

Pei had almost given up hope of Moi's ever coming back out from her kitchen when the door opened and, without a sound, Moi emerged. She looked around to make sure no one was nearby before stepping out of the safety of her kitchen. In her arms, she cradled two large jars with great care. Quickly Moi made her way up the stairs. When they were sure she was safely out of sight, Pei and Ji Shen quietly followed. They waited around the corner so Moi would not see them when she came out again. Usually Moi made several trips up and down the stairs before she relocked the door to Auntie Yee's room. When Moi emerged, they waited until she was back downstairs and they heard the creaking of the kitchen door closing before daring to come out. Then, while Ji Shen watched for Moi's return, Pei quickly stole through the door into Auntie Yee's room.

The heavy aroma of Moi's cooking seemed to linger in the darkness. The thick, dark curtains Moi used to shield the room from the outside made it difficult to see anything at first. Pei waited a moment before her eyes adjusted to the darkness. An eerie feeling moved through her, but she'd come too far now to turn back. Besides, Ji Shen was watching and would warn her if Moi returned.

Nothing looked out of place. Slowly Pei made her way around the room, noting the familiar and recording anything that might have made Moi want to keep the room off limits to the rest of them for the past year. Pei moved toward Auntie Yee's bed, which seemed the only large and concrete thing in the shadowy light. Then her foot kicked something solid that clinked across the bare floor. When she tried to turn around, her foot hit something else that crashed into still another object. Pei grew hot, and scared that Moi would be running upstairs wielding her knife. There was a small tapping sound from outside the door. She could hear Ji Shen asking in a whisper if everything was all right, but Pei's voice went dry when she looked down in the semidarkness to see that the floor was covered with jars. As she bent down to set them straight, Pei saw that their contents were rice and sugar and dried herbs. Pei straightened all the jars she had knocked over, only to see one jar had been broken, its contents spilled across the wooden floor. There was no time to clean up. Pei did what she could before quickly making her escape.

"What does Moi keep in the room?" Ji Shen asked when they were safely down the hall in Pei's room.

"Jars," Pei answered, keeping from Ji Shen that they were filled with dry food.

"But why?"

Pei shrugged her shoulders. "Who knows the habits of an old woman," she answered, keeping Moi's secret.

"Were they empty?" Ji Shen asked.

"As far as I could see," Pei lied, though she was certain all the jars were filled with rice and sugar.

"It's a good thing she didn't catch us, she would have skinned us alive!" Ji Shen said, laughing. "Why would Moi want to collect jars, anyway?"

"I don't know," Pei said.

But she did know. As Pei stood amid the sea of jars, she knew at that moment that Moi was showing her how much she cared for them. In the only way Moi could, she was trying to protect them. She would never let them go hungry, no matter how bad the war became. Moi was storing food for the hard times, readying herself for the long winter ahead.

Pei saw Moi in a different light after this discovery. When Moi went back downstairs, she said nothing about the jars or their scattered contents, though Pei felt she somehow knew. She wanted to talk to Moi about her jars of food upstairs, but kept silent. They shared the secret now, and Moi trusted her with it. Instead, Pei tried to help her in any way she could. Under Moi's watchful eyes, Pei set the table as if for a banquet, covering the table with a lace tablecloth and placing upon it Auntie Yee's best bowls and dishes. When there was no more to do, Pei sat and waited for Lin, the sharp aroma of cooking coming from Moi's kitchen, filling her up.

Moonfire

When Lin closed the books for the final time, she leaned back in her chair and took a deep breath. Already her mind had traveled outside to the warm evening air and the almost full moon that loomed brightly in the darkening sky. It had been months since she felt so good, relieved at the fact that her work at the factory was finally over. At long last they would be leaving for Canton. The uneasiness she'd been feeling about leaving also disappeared, with something closer to excitement taking its

place. She looked around her small bare office and was thankful
for not having to return to it ever again. Very carefully, Lin
placed Chung's account books in her desk drawer and locked it.
She'd have to hurry back to the girls' house, since Moi was
preparing a special meal for them that evening. Lin didn't want
Moi to be upset at her being late, but she was relieved to have
told Chen Ling to leave earlier, since there was no use in both
of them being delayed.

Lin stood up, her hand still resting on the rough surface of her
desk. With her other hand she touched her face; her skin felt wan
and dry from working under the harsh lights. As soon as they
arrived in Hong Kong, she would take care of herself. She and
Pei would spend some of their hard-earned money on luxury
items, like a set of silver brushes and combs and some newly
translated books. She had grown as eager as Pei to know more
about the outside world, with all its colors and languages. Pei
read voraciously, and sometimes peppered their conversations
with the strange-sounding names of places like New York and
the Taj Mahal. Lin couldn't help but smile at the thought.

Lin looked up when something foreign captured her attention.
There was a vague smell of something burning and a sound like
the clapping of hands. Lin moved quickly toward the door and
listened hard before opening it. The clapping continued, yet it
seemed muted and faraway. Slowly she opened the door and
stepped carefully out of her office, making her way toward the
machines. When she reached the outer room, the rising smoke
hit her squarely in the face, and just behind it a fire raged,
engulfing the reeling machines and everything in sight. A solid
wall of fire was making its way toward her, blowing out the lights
and blocking the only exit left unboarded when the factory was
shut down. Lin turned around, her mind and heart racing. She
looked up at the dirty skylights, barely visible in the moonlight.
They were the only windows in the building and were impossi-

ble to reach. Quickly she ran back toward the drying room, where the reeled silk once hung in long blond strands. The back door leading to the alley was her only hope out. Lin pushed against the door, but it wouldn't budge, tightly secured from the outside. Frantic, Lin grabbed a wooden hanging bar and began hitting the door with all her strength, only chipping away at the thick wood. She turned back to see the spreading fire and the billows of smoke making their way toward her. The intense heat shattered the skylight windows as one of the two main wooden beams that held up the roof collapsed. With one last furious effort she struck the door again and again, until she began to struggle for breath and her eyes stung. Moving along the wall, Lin covered her face and felt her way back to her office, closing the door and falling weakly against it.

At that moment Lin knew she had come to the end of her life. There was no way out of the burning factory. Even as the thought filled her head, she could feel the intense heat against the door. In minutes the choking smoke would envelop the small room and suck the life out of it. "Not now," Lin said aloud. "It isn't fair!" Then, in the darkness, she found her way back to her chair and crouched close to the floor, waiting. Lin closed her eyes. She could hear the fire exploding and feel the suffocating smoke slowly overtake her. Over and over again she whispered; "Pei, Pei! Oh, dear Pei, I have to leave you now."

When Lin had not returned as expected, Pei began to worry. With every little sound she looked toward the door, expecting it to open and to see Lin looking radiant, apologetic for being late. Everything was ready and Moi paced in and out of the kitchen, each time bringing with her the alluring aromas of the dishes waiting to be served.

"Lin said she would only be a short while," Pei said, looking toward Chen Ling as they sat around the table.

Chen Ling looked up and said reassuringly, "There were only

the final figures to copy down; then we were supposed to be finished. Don't worry, though—you know Lin, she may have found out we made some mistakes and it's taking longer than expected."

Pei tried to smile, but she couldn't help feeling something unsettling in the pit of her stomach.

"Come look!" cried Ji Shen, who stood by the window watching for Lin.

Above the trees and buildings of Yung Kee loomed a large dark cloud, its borders growing and spreading a deep black against the twilit sky.

"Come on!" Chen Ling reacted first, running out the door and into the street. She stopped and looked toward what she knew could only be a very big fire coming from the direction of the factory.

Halfway there, Pei came to the realization that it was the silk factory that was on fire. The smoke billowed from its direction as the air they breathed thickened. Their eyes began to water and ash clung to their hair and clothes. By the time they arrived at the factory, most of the main building was in flames. A group of Chiang Kai-shek's soldiers gave orders as men, women, and children brought bucket after bucket of water to quench the flames, and were just beginning to gain some momentum against the inferno. Pei frantically searched the crowd gathered, asking those she recognized if they had seen Lin.

When no one had, Pei turned to Ji Shen and screamed above the noise: "Lin could have left earlier; maybe she stopped to buy something—she could have, couldn't she?"

Ji Shen nodded her head and took hold of Pei's arm, trying to get her to sit down, but Pei jerked away from her.

"Tell me! Tell me Lin is alive!" screamed Pei, in a voice not her own.

"Yes, yes she is," said Ji Shen.

Pei turned toward the fire, which now seemed a smoldering black cloud that filled the entire sky, and then back to Ji Shen and Ming, who had come to comfort her. Chen Ling had gone to find out whatever she could about how the fire started and whether anyone was hurt. The minutes seemed like hours as they waited, not knowing if Lin was dead or alive. Pei watched the flames and could feel the burning emptiness moving through her even before Chen Ling came walking toward them, her face dark and grave.

"No one has seen Lin, and no one seems to know how the fire began. It will take some time before they can even know if anyone was still inside or not. We might as well return to the girls' house now," said Chen Ling, her eyes focused on the burning remains of the factory.

"No!" said Pei frantically. "I can't leave. What if Lin needs me?"

"It may be hours before they know anything," pleaded Chen Ling.

"I have to stay," Pei said in a whisper.

There was no more struggle in her as she sat down, and very quietly the tears came. Pei turned and felt Ji Shen close beside her as they began the long, torturous wait.

By dawn the fire had burned itself out; the smoking remains had just begun to be sifted through when a cry from one of the soldiers rang out in dim light. "Over here! Over here! It's a body!"

Pei and Ji Shen, who were moving slowly through the ruin of the factory, ran toward the voice. Pei's heart was racing with the fear that it was Lin, but even before she reached the spot she knew the answer. Lin was dead. Miraculously, the small office and back section of the building had remained, blackened yet intact. And there beside the crouching soldier was the slender, charred body of Lin.

Pei stopped at the first sight of her. A small choking sound came up and out of her, but it was the cries of Ji Shen that filled the air. Then calmly Pei walked toward Lin and knelt beside her. Very carefully she lifted Lin into her arms and cradled her against the hard, still smoldering ground.

Pei sat in the room she had shared with Lin and could not sleep or eat. Sometimes the tears came in choking heaves and sometimes not at all. The others took turns watching her. Even Moi volunteered, and tried in vain to feed her turnip soup. Every sound startled her. Pei gazed at the door for hours in hopes that Lin would walk in. She closed her eyes and willed herself the strength not to let the barren feeling overtake her. It was as if Pei were trapped in her own body, immobile against all the motions of life. She had no desire to live without Lin, to never again hear her calming voice or feel Lin's warmth beside her. Pei sat remembering in the stillness of their room, a dark numbing pain moving through her mind.

It was Chen Ling who finally came to her, laying her hand gently on Pei's shoulder. "Lin has been washed and lies waiting downstairs."

Pei nodded, but didn't look at Chen Ling.

"I have wired Lin's family in Canton," Chen Ling said, as she knelt down beside Pei and took hold of her hand. She then said quietly, "I've known Lin such a very long time, I'm so sorry."

When Chen Ling didn't let go of her hand, Pei turned toward her. Chen Ling was crying, the tears softening her stern face. Pei had never seen tears from her in all the years they'd known each other, not even when Auntie Yee died. Her quiet sorrow filled the room. Then, very slowly, Pei raised her arms and put them around Chen Ling.

Chapter Nineteen

1938

Pei

Pei lost her voice after Lin died. Words felt useless and flat against the great dark wall that surrounded her. Ji Shen stayed with her, afraid she might harm herself. The soothing words Ji Shen tried to say fell lifeless around her. There was no way Ji Shen could know that the pain moving through Pei had taken away all her strength. Lin was dead. Pei was paralyzed with something she had not felt since her childhood: loneliness.

When Pei finally slept, it was a sleep filled with nightmares. She would rather have died herself than thought of Lin's agonizing death from the heat and smoke, but her sleep gave her no peace. Pei found herself choking on the thick, black smoke, gasping for breath, always just out of reach of Lin as she tried desperately to pull her to safety. "Lin! Lin!" she cried, but Lin didn't answer. Then there was nothing, blackness.

Pei woke with a scream.

"Pei, it's all right, it was just a dream," she heard Ji Shen telling her, holding her shoulders and shaking her awake.

Pei sat completely still for a moment; then, with a deep cry of pain, she said, "I could have done something, I could have saved Lin!"

"No, you couldn't have saved her; no one could have."

"You can't know. How could you know?"

"You couldn't have saved Lin, just like I couldn't have saved my sister! I was right there, don't you remember, right next to my sister, and there was nothing I could do!" Ji Shen stopped, her face flushed. When she spoke again, her voice was tight, yet calm. "When I first came here, you told me I had to go on living, because that's what my parents and sister would have wanted. Well, I know it's what Lin would want."

Pei stared at Ji Shen for a long time. She no longer seemed like a young girl as she spoke the words of an adult. Pei loosened her grip on Ji Shen and fell slowly back down onto her bed. She couldn't move or say a word. Over and over she asked herself how Lin could have left her. Why had the gods turned against her? It couldn't really be true. Pei bit her lip until it bled, and then she wept.

Ho Yung came immediately from Canton after receiving the news of his sister's death. He arrived at the girls' house just after evening meal the next day. When Pei was told that he was waiting in the reading room, she dressed quickly, not caring about her appearance, and hurried downstairs to see Lin's favorite brother. When Pei entered the room, Ho Yung had his back to her, and when he heard her and turned around, Pei felt a pain so sharp in her stomach, she thought she might faint. The physical likeness between them, caught at that moment, was so striking. Even though Ho Yung was dressed in his Western clothing, it was as if some part of Lin had returned to her. The same intense, dark eyes watched Pei as she crossed the room toward him.

Ho Yung looked tired and anxious. "I came as soon as I received the cable," he said, without formalities. He carried a hat, which he turned over and over in his hands. "Do you know how the fire began?"

Pei swallowed hard. "A thousand different ways," she answered, her voice soft and halting at first, then gathering strength. "Some say it was Chung, others say it had to do with bad wiring. There's no one answer."

Ho Yung bowed his head. He seemed much older than the carefree young man she'd met in Canton. "I told Lin to come home to Canton immediately. There was no reason for her to stay here."

"She felt we needed the extra money."

"I could have provided her with some," said Ho Yung in anger. "There was no need for her senseless death! Where is this Chung? I want to talk with him!"

Pei said nothing, feeling the sting of his words. She could feel the heat rising behind her eyes as she turned away. When he saw Pei's reaction to his anger, Ho Yung instantly softened. "I'm sorry, I know how close you and Lin were. She often wrote to me of you. Lin was very happy here with you."

Pei bowed her head. The tears came slowly at first, and before she knew it, Ho Yung was beside Pei, wrapping his arms around her and helping her to sit down. There was a long silence between them until Pei slowly pulled away, realizing with embarrassment that she'd never been held by a man before. His hands felt strong and sure of themselves.

Ho Yung pulled back and cleared his throat. "I've received word from my mother in Hong Kong. She wants me to bring Lin back to Canton, so she can be buried next to my father."

Pei nodded her head. She couldn't begin to think of Wong Tai.

"I would be honored if you would accompany us back to Canton. Afterward, it'll be easier for you to leave from there for Hong Kong."

Pei looked up at Ho Yung, surprised. "Hong Kong?"

"It has all been arranged. There's no reason for you not to go. You can't stay here—the Japanese are moving closer each day. It would be wise if we leave here as soon as possible."

"Ji Shen?" Pei suddenly remembered.

"Don't worry, Lin wrote to me about Ji Shen. There's room enough for both of you."

Pei choked back her tears. Lin had taken care of everything. She hesitated, her hand smoothing back her disheveled hair, then said, "I don't know about Hong Kong now."

"I'm afraid I must insist that you leave for Hong Kong. The Japanese are one step behind us. They've killed for nothing more than a malicious look," said Ho Yung. Then he said softly, "It's what Lin wanted for you."

Pei nodded, unable to speak. She couldn't look at Ho Yung, who reminded her too much of Lin.

Ho Yung rose slowly. "Would it be all right if I see Lin again?"

Lin's body lay in the small, dark room next to the reading room. Pei led Ho Yung to it and closed the door quietly behind him. She still hadn't had the courage to see Lin's body since it had been returned to the girls' house.

Pei went back into the reading room and waited. She quietly began to cry again. Could she really leave Yung Kee without Lin? The thought left Pei so empty, she felt as if she'd disappear. Pei looked around the reading room, trying to memorize every small detail of it. The last light of the day set everything aglow, as if it might vanish when the sun fell to shadows. At that moment, Pei knew that no matter how far away she might be from Yung Kee, she could never forget its years of kindness. Lin and the sisterhood had been her life for so long. They were burned into her heart.

The Journey

Ho Yung immediately left to make arrangements for Lin's body to be brought back to Canton. He would then return for Pei and

Ji Shen early in the morning. When Pei closed the door behind him, she felt a cold fear move through her.

Pei went to tell Chen Ling first. Chen Ling didn't flinch at the news. As always, she was serious and businesslike even in accepting the news of their leaving so quickly. She cocked her head sideways, listening, then asked Pei to follow her upstairs to her room. Pei had been in Chen Ling's room only a few times before. It always seemed to be a part of the house as restricted as Moi's kitchen, yet as she stood in the midst of it Pei felt comfortable, its clean spareness a strong reminder of Auntie Yee. From the top drawer of her desk, Chen Ling took out a yellow envelope and handed it to Pei.

"This is yours," she said.

"What is it?"

"Lin's money from the last few months of work. I wanted to wait for the right time to give it to you."

Pei held the envelope. The smooth outer paper felt cool and deceptive as to what it held. Lin might be alive if it weren't for this money. Her death made so little sense Pei wanted to scream out loud. And in the end, the money was useless, she thought: It couldn't buy back Lin's life. Pei turned the envelope over in her hands and folded it in half. She looked up to see Chen Ling's eyes following her every move.

"Thank you," Pei said.

Chen Ling shifted and looked away. "It belongs to you."

Pei cleared her throat. "Will you and Ming be leaving soon for the countryside?"

"Very soon."

"And Moi?"

"She refuses to leave the house. She told me she would rather die at the girls' house than leave it."

"What should we do?"

Chen Ling turned slightly, her body solid and heavy against

the desk. "Nothing," she answered. "We'll let Moi fight her own battles, just as she always has."

"But what if she loses?"

Chen Ling smiled. "She hasn't lost one yet."

Pei and Ji Shen nervously gathered their few belongings together. Only two possessions really mattered to Pei. They had come to her early in life and retained their value. With great care, she first placed the painting her mother had given her, and then Lin's set of brush and combs, in her bag. There was little need for much else. In time, it would be as simple as Ji Shen said: Pei knew she would have to go on living, even if Lin wouldn't be there to accompany her on the rest of her journey.

Downstairs, Pei could hear voices. First Moi's, and then Chen Ling's caught her ear, then the low rumblings of strangers. She left her room and was at the top of the stairs when she heard Chen Ling calling her name. Her first thought was that Ho Yung had returned, but as she descended the stairs, she saw two coolies and another man waiting at the door.

"What is it?" Pei asked.

"These men have come to take Lin's body," said Chen Ling. "They were sent by her brother."

Pei swallowed hard. She had hoped to spend one more night with Lin at the girls' house.

The small, bespectacled man with the coolies stepped forward and said, "Please excuse us, but Mr. Wong has arranged for his sister's body to be taken to the ferry tonight."

It was all happening with such swiftness that Pei was taken by surprise. In her head she made a list of things she had to do before she could leave the girls' house in the morning. Since Lin's death, sleep did little to comfort her. She wanted to use the dark quiet of night to say her last good-byes.

"Yes," Pei said hesitantly. "But could I have a moment first?"

"Of course," the man said, bowing slightly.

Pei walked toward the little room and slipped in quietly. Her heart was beating so fast, she thought she might not make it. The room was dimly lit by candles, and the overpowering smell of incense thickly filled the air. Lin lay wrapped in a white sheet, just as Mei-li had been. When Pei moved closer and saw the smooth, sharp features of Lin's ashen face, she began to cry softly, like a small child waking from sleep. She stroked Lin's hair and felt the coldness of her skin, but it didn't frighten her. Pei moved closer to her face and whispered, "Lin," just once. It filled the room and seemed to comfort her. There was so little time left, and so much she still had to say. So Pei said nothing more. She simply leaned over and pressed her lips gently against Lin's.

The next morning, while they were waiting for Ho Yung to return, Ji Shen fidgeted with their belongings and asked over and over again, "Are we really going to Hong Kong?"

Pei felt the dull and sickening ache of leaving, and tried to smile. "Yes, we're really going," she said.

Chen Ling and Ming waited awkwardly with them, pacing and checking the road for any sign of Ho Yung. Moi stayed hidden in her kitchen, despite the news that Pei and Ji Shen would soon be leaving. Every once in a while they could hear the soft murmuring of her voice from behind the kitchen door, but that was nothing unusual.

When Ho Yung finally arrived, it was with two sedan chairs, which would take them down to the ferry. He had arranged everything for them, and appeared drawn and tired. Pei wondered if he had slept at all the night before. He smiled wearily and waited patiently at the gate for Pei and Ji Shen to say their good-byes. For Pei, there were no more tears. She hugged Chen Ling and Ming, feeling the immediate loss of the two closest friends she had left. "We will meet again," Chen Ling whispered, "when all this is over."

Then, just beyond them, Pei caught the smallest glimmer of movement at the top of the steps. Without a word she returned to the house and found Moi lingering about the front door.

"I knew you would return," Moi said, stepping back from the door.

"I wanted to say good-bye," Pei said. "We'll miss you. I'll miss all your wonderful meals."

Moi looked away and smiled shyly. From the floor beside her, she lifted up a cloth bag and handed it to Pei. It was heavy and dense, like glass bricks hitting against each other. "For you and Ji Shen," she said.

"Thank you," said Pei. She looked down at Moi, and was filled with emotion for the crippled, stubborn woman who had kept them so well fed for so many years. Then, something almost desperate and pleading filled Pei's voice. "Won't you go with Chen Ling and Ming to the countryside? It'll be better for you there. You can return to the girls' house when it's safe again."

Moi shook her head from side to side in small, jerking movements. "No, no, I will stay here with Yee."

"But . . ."

Moi pointed out the door. "You take care of the young one; she will keep you good company."

Pei wanted to say something more, but she knew it would be fruitless. She wanted to make any small gesture to let Moi know how she felt. For a moment, they stood swaying slightly in their uncertainty. When Pei held out her hand, Moi hesitated, then grasped it tightly in both of hers.

The trip to Canton aboard the ferry was crowded and troublesome. The air was thick and salty. Soldiers were everywhere, asking to see their papers and detaining them longer than necessary. Pei felt sick to her stomach. Only Ji Shen felt any excitement. When they finally found some seats, Pei and Ho Yung seemed lost in their own thoughts. Only when they approached Canton harbor did Ho Yung come alive, leading them to the front of the crowded ferry and pointing out places of interest. Pei listened with little regard for what he was saying, his words falling like stones. Lin had said them all to her the first time she had seen Canton. Now there was only a heaviness that filled her, that made her think the ferry couldn't possibly float under her weight.

The same dread flowed through Pei as they made their way through the streets of Canton. While Ho Yung arranged for Lin's body to be brought back to the family house, she and Ji Shen waited to the side. A few large, monstrous cars sounded their horns to clear the street. Soldiers in scattered groups of muted greens and grays eyed them suspiciously, their hands caressing their loaded weapons. What once seemed so big and magical to Pei now appeared dark and dirty. Anxiousness and unrest filled the air. Filthy beggars in tattered clothing lined the streets, from old men to mothers with young children. Many of them had come from up north, struggling to stay alive among those who had yet to see the terrors the Japanese had inflicted upon them. Pei took Ji Shen's arm and held on tightly.

Suddenly, a beggar stood before them, maimed and blinded by the horrors of the war. "Please, Missy, a little something for food!" he begged, thrusting his fingerless stump out in front of them, and following as they boarded a sedan chair. His stench was fishy and nauseating. Before entering the sedan chair in front of theirs, Ho Yung finally turned and threw out a handful of coins, which clinked and scattered across the ground. Pei watched as the beggar fell to his knees, his arms sweeping the ground. He was quickly joined by others, who pushed and fought for the coins.

Only when Pei turned back did she realize Ji Shen was shaking, pressed against the back corner of the sedan chair. Very gently, Pei reached over and took hold of Ji Shen's hand to calm her fears. "It's all right, they're gone now," she said soothingly. In silence, they moved slowly forward, gradually picking up speed and leaving behind the voracious crowd.

"Right here," she heard Ho Yung tell the carriers as they rounded the corner.

The same large, dark houses came into view. When their sedan chair came to a stop, Pei paused a moment before stepping out into the heavy aroma of eucalyptus. It filled her head and made her dizzy for Lin. She felt then that nothing would ever be the same, that fate had always taken away everyone she loved. First her parents and Li, then Mei-li and Auntie Yee, and now finally Lin, her beloved Lin. Pei struggled to stay calm, but when Lin's old servant, Mui, opened the gate, Pei saw a sorrow equal to hers, and fell like a child into her arms.

Early the next morning Pei went out with Mui to buy flowers, returning with as many blossoms as they could carry. These they draped on the plain coffin that housed Lin's body until they could no longer see the wood. In the gray morning light, they buried Lin next to her father. It was a simple ceremony, with Ho Yung saying a few brief words. Pei stood between Ji Shen and Mui, clutching a yellow blossom. When Lin's flower-draped coffin was lowered into the ground, Pei stood before the open grave and bowed three times. Then, with a small, painful release of breath, she let go of the blossom.

That evening, Mui made a light meal, of which they all ate very little. Pei and Ji Shen were to leave for Hong Kong early the next morning. Pei spent half the night lying awake, unable to sleep, even though she and Ji Shen shared not Lin's room, but Ho Chee's. Pei couldn't bring herself to go into Lin's room, yet something in the darkness called out to her. She made sure Ji Shen was asleep, then very quietly got up and made her way down the hall to Lin's room.

Pei stood in the moonlit darkness among Lin's childhood possessions. The closed, stagnant air of confinement surrounded her, holding her. The room had remained the same, with nothing out of place. Pei walked to the center of the room and waited. In the darkness, she began to see vague outlines, which grew sharper and clearer as her eyes grew accustomed. Directly in front of her were Lin's dolls. Their white faces seemed to be watching her. Pei spoke silently to them, asking for direction. She stood waiting for the longest time. Then beyond the room came the sudden creaking of the old house, which distracted her. When Pei turned back to the frozen faces, she saw that the dolls were only relics of a past Lin had left behind. Pei knew that she would also have to leave them, just as Lin once had. The memories fell upon her, like small whispered secrets. And what she found in the darkness was a new strength.

"Is everything all right?" A voice startled Pei as she stepped out into the hall. In the approaching light she saw that it was Ho Yung.

"Yes. I couldn't sleep. I hope you don't mind, but I wanted to see Lin's room one more time."

"It might have been easier in the daylight," Ho Yung said kindly.

"Answers seem to come to me in the dark."

"Did they?"

"I think so."

Ho Yung smiled. "Are you hungry?"

For the first time in days Pei realized she *was* hungry. "Yes, I am," she said.

"Come, then."

She followed Ho Yung downstairs. He left her in the dining room and went to the kitchen to find something for them to eat. As Pei waited, she remembered how uncomfortable she felt the last time she'd eaten in this room. When Ho Yung returned, he carried a tray of sweet buns and coconut tarts.

"The tea is coming," he said, setting the tray down.

They ate in a silence Pei felt very comfortable with. When they had finished eating, Ho Yung sat back and asked, "What will you do in Hong Kong?"

"I'm not certain yet," Pei said, though she knew many of her sisters had gone into domestic work. "I have some money saved."

"If you should ever need anything, I'll be happy to assist you in any way I can," Ho Yung said, looking away from her.

"Thank you," said Pei shyly. "But we can take care of ourselves."

Ho Yung remained silent, watching her. Thinking she might have offended him by her response, Pei then asked, "When will you leave for Hong Kong?"

"In a few days, after everything here has been settled and I can close the house."

She simply nodded, feeling awkward under his gaze.

Then, before Ho Yung could say anything else, Pei stood up, thanked him for the food, and quickly made her way back upstairs.

The next morning, as they waited for the ferry, Pei saw crowds of people negotiating for the few seats left on the boat. Cars inched their way toward the dock, loaded down with household possessions. Soldiers patrolled the area, and watched as those who were turned away vowed that they would be back the following morning. Each day it became more difficult to leave Canton. Rumors of the Japanese moving in brought fear and hysteria to those trying to leave.

Ho Yung looked on anxiously and gave Pei a card with his Hong Kong address on it. "If you ever need anything..." he said.

Pei tried to smile. "I will call," she said.

"Take care of yourself," he said awkwardly. Then, without any warning, he leaned forward and kissed Pei quickly on the forehead.

Pei stepped back, hot and flushed. Ji Shen was pulling on her arm to leave. "Thank you" was all she could say before she began moving away from him.

As they boarded the ferry, Pei knew she was leaving a large part of her life behind. The sisterhood had scattered, but she would remember it always. She prayed that Chen Ling and Ming would make it safely to the countryside, where her father still lingered alone with his ponds. And somewhere out there was her sister, Li. Pei vowed never to give up until she found Li again, no matter how long it took. She knew the Japanese would waste no time before descending upon Canton and Yung Kee. Like locusts, they would sweep down and leave nothing. She hoped that all those she loved would be safe. Yet she knew her own most frightening days lay before her in Hong Kong. She could only look forward.

As the ferry slowly moved away from the dock, Ji Shen moved quickly ahead of Pei, finding two seats near the front of the boat. Pei stopped once and looked over the railing to see Ho Yung still waiting on the dock. He was looking up, his hand shading his eyes against the sun, but he couldn't possibly see her in the crowd of people surrounding her. In him, she once again saw a glimmer of Lin, which warmed her. Pei missed Lin more than she would have thought possible. She stood watching, gathering strength to carry this last image of Lin with her on the journey. Then, reluctantly, against the rocking of the ferry beneath her feet, Pei turned around and headed toward the front of the boat, where Ji Shen was waiting.

Hong Kong harbor came into view after a long, uncomfortable journey. For hours the ferry moved along the calm waters, eerily empty of other boats. Only then did Pei remember the cloth bag

Moi had given to her when she left Yung Kee. Without knowing, she had carried it faithfully all this way, only to have it rolling back and forth under her seat with each rise and fall of the boat. She reached down and pulled the cloth bag up. Ji Shen had scampered up to see the approaching harbor. When Pei untied the string and looked into the bag, she saw several jars filled with herbs and dried fruit. Pei couldn't help but smile.

"Come look!" Ji Shen yelled to her.

Pei closed the bag and placed it back under her seat before joining Ji Shen at the railing. There was Hong Kong, rising before them in all her splendor. Pei had never seen anything so beautiful before, in the warm spray. Tall buildings loomed in the shadows as hundreds of sampans moved to and fro. The sky was open and clear as the peaks rose up toward it like dark gods, and an excitement punctuated the salty air. "It's so big!" cried Ji Shen. For the moment they were safe. Pei took a deep breath and could feel Lin's presence there beside her, watching and smiling as the boat danced upon the water toward Hong Kong.